Praise for *The Pirate Bride*

"I've always enjoyed Kathleen's vivid... romance. No matter the time period... bring the story alive through her characters and...

–Tracie Peterson, bestselling author of over 100 novels
Heart of the Frontier and Song of Alaska series

"In a captivating tale of the seas, Y'Barbo gives readers a unique story of history and romance. Not just your everyday pirate tale, readers will fall in love with the troubled soul of a ship captain, and an unclaimed waif destined to take ownership of his heart. A story of loss, of love, and of the budding foundations of a nation still in infant form. This is a don't-miss on my list!"

–Jaime Jo Wright, author for Bethany House Publishers

"I love pirate books, and *The Pirate Bride* is a delightful read that has a totally unique story line. Most of the characters don't fit the mold of other pirate books, so this story was a fresh and interesting read. I loved the twists and turns in the plot. A lot surprised me. It kept me turning pages as fast as I could read them. I highly recommend this novel for all readers of historical fiction."

–Lena Nelson Dooley, author of *A Heart's Gift*, winner of the 2017 Faith, Hope, and Love Reader's Choice Award for Long Historicals

"It is not often that I venture beyond the realm of my Kansas prairie, but for several days now, Kathleen Y'Barbo's *The Pirate Bride* has transported me to a whole new world of magnificent sailing vessels amid privateers and pirates, a beautiful little island inhabited by nuns and orphans, opulent mansions of New Orleans, and newfound love—all through the eyes of the precocious, wise-beyond-her-years Maribel Cordoba. Rich in history, it's a story I didn't want to end and will revisit again soon."

–Julane Hiebert, author of Brides of a Feather series
and I Plight Thee My Troth series

"Kathleen Y'Barbo's brilliant storytelling skills shine through in *The Pirate Bride*, taking her reader on a swashbuckling adventure onboard a privateer ship through th... life on the pages of this book an... ely capture your heart as she di...

–An... ighthouse series

"A captivating heroine, rich historical detail, and a fascinating setting make for a lovely, satisfying story. Readers will root for Maribel Cordoba every step of the way."

–Dorothy Love author of *Mrs. Lee and Mrs. Gray*

"Once again Kathleen Y'Barbo has written a story that will pull the reader into an exciting world of adventure, mystery, and romance. *The Pirate Bride* kept me up late at night turning pages to find out what happens next. To my delight, surprises awaited me at every turn of the plot."

–Louise M. Gouge, award-winning author

"Kathleen Y'Barbo's *The Pirate Bride* is a unique tale filled with characters who defy stereotypes and the expectations of their contemporaries to find adventure on the high seas, a new and action-filled slant on the classic story of pirates and their ladies."

–Julianna Deering, author of The Drew Farthering Mysteries

"A gripping tale of adventure on the high seas, *The Pirate Bride* will sail straight into your heart. Readers are going to adore this fiery heroine, and the piratical hero's nobility will have you cheering. Couldn't put it down!"

–Roseanna M. White, bestselling author of the Ladies of the Manor series and Shadows Over England series

"A spunky, loveable heroine, who reminds me of Anne of Green Gables, and a patient, determined hero encounter danger and adventure on the high seas. This fabulous swashbuckling tale of friendship and love is my favorite Kathleen Y'Barbo story to date. I didn't want to see it end."

–Vickie McDonough, best-selling author of 45 books and novellas, with over 1.5 million copies sold

"*The Pirate Bride* is a swashbuckling adventure set during the time of pirates and privateers. Engaging and fast-paced, this story is like an epic movie with plenty of romance and intrigue. Of all the titles Kathleen Y'Barbo has put out, this is one of my all-time favorites!"

–Michelle Griep, award-winning author of the Once Upon a Dickens Christmas series

The *Pirate Bride*

The
Daughters
of the
Mayflower

KATHLEEN Y'BARBO

BARBOUR BOOKS
An Imprint of Barbour Publishing, Inc.

Cover Photograph: Lee Avison/ Trevillion Images

Published by Barbour Books, an imprint of Barbour Publishing, Inc., 1810 Barbour Drive, Uhrichsville, Ohio 44683, www.barbourbooks.com

Our mission is to inspire the world with the life-changing message of the Bible.

ecpa Member of the
Evangelical Christian
Publishers Association

Printed in the United States of America.

DEDICATION

To the survivors:

As I type this, my beloved Texas has been drenched by the
Historical flood waters of Hurricane Harvey.

May God richly bless those who waded through water,
Either away from a flooded home or toward one.
May He allow His blessings to shine upon the heroes
And His mercy on those who mourn.

From the tip of the coast at Port Aransas to
Galveston where my youngest son lives,
To Houston where two of my children and I call home,
And to Port Neches and the rest of Jefferson County,
The place where I was born and raised,
To any place on Texas soil where rain and tears have fallen this week,
We are Texas Strong.

God bless Texas!

For where your treasure is, there will your heart be also.
MATTHEW 6:21

Daughters of the Mayflower

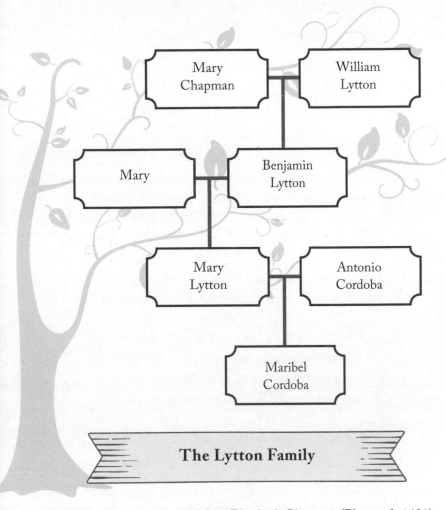

Mary Chapman

William Lytton

Mary

Benjamin Lytton

Mary Lytton

Antonio Cordoba

Maribel Cordoba

The Lytton Family

William Lytton married Mary Elizabeth Chapman (Plymouth 1621)
Parents of 13 children (one son is Benjamin)
Benjamin Lytton married Temperance (Massachusetts 1668)
widowed then married Mary (Massachusetts 1675)
Born to Benjamin and Mary
Mary Lytton who married Antonio Cordoba (Spain 1698)
Born to Mary and Antonio
Maribel Cordoba

"As the Testimony of your Conscience must convince you of the great and many evils you have committed, by which you have highly offended God, and provoked most justly his wrath and indignation against you, so I suppose I need not tell you that the only way of obtaining pardon and remission of your sins from God, is by a true and unfeigned repentance and faith in Christ, by whose meritorious death and passion, you can only hope for salvation."

From the Lord Chief Justice Judge Trot's speech
pronouncing sentence of death
upon the pirate Major Stede Bonnet,
November 10, 1711, at Charles Town

Maribel and the Privateer

Part I:

In the waters of the Caribbean Sea
April of 1724

He sent from above, he took me,
he drew me out of many waters.
PSALM 18:16

CHAPTER I

Aboard the Spanish vessel
Venganza near Havana

Mama may have been named for the great-grandmother who traveled from England on the *Mayflower*, but that fact certainly did not keep her in the land of her birth. Twelve-year-old Maribel Cordoba sometimes wondered why Mama refused to discuss anything regarding her relations in the colonies beyond the fact that she had disappointed them all by marrying a Spaniard without her papa's blessing.

The mystery seemed so silly now, what with Mama gone and the father she barely knew insisting she accompany him aboard the *Venganza* to his new posting in Havana. Maribel gathered the last reminder of Mary Lytton around her shoulders—a beautiful scarf shot through with threads of Spanish silver that matched the piles of coins in the hold of this magnificent sailing vessel—and clutched the book she'd already read through once since the journey began.

Though she was far too young at nearly thirteen to call herself a lady, Maribel loved to pretend she would someday wear this same scarf along with a gown in some lovely matching color at a beautiful ball. Oh she would dance, her toes barely touching the floor in her dancing shoes. And her handsome escort would, no doubt, fall madly in love with her just as Papa had fallen in love with Mama.

Her fingers clutched the soft fabric as her heart lurched. Mama.

Oh how she missed her. She looked toward the horizon, where a lone vessel's sails punctuated the divide between sea and sky, and then shrugged deeper into the scarf.

Nothing but adventure was ahead. This her papa had promised when he announced that, as newly named Consul General, he was moving her from their home in Spain to the faraway Caribbean.

She had read about the Caribbean in the books she hid beneath her pillows. The islands were exotic and warm, populated with friendly natives and not-so-friendly pirates.

Maribel clutched her copy of *The Notorious Seafaring Pyrates and Their Exploits* by Captain Ulysses Jones. The small leather book that held the true stories of Blackbeard, Anne Bonny, and others had been a treasure purchased in a Barcelona bookseller's shop when Papa hadn't been looking.

Of course, Papa never looked at her, so she could have purchased the entire shop and he wouldn't have noticed.

But then, until the day her papa arrived with the news that Mama and Abuelo were now with the angels, she'd only seen this man Antonio Cordoba three times in her life. Once at her grandmother's funeral and twice when he and Mama had quarreled on the doorstep of their home in Madrid.

On none of these occasions had Señor Cordoba, apparently a very busy and very important man, deigned to speak to his only daughter. Thus his speech about Mama had been expectedly brief, as had the response to Maribel's request to attend her funeral or at least see her grave.

Both had been answered with a resolute no. Two days later, she was packed aboard the *Venganza*.

She watched the sails grow closer and held tight to Mama's scarf. Just as Mama had taught her, she turned her fear of this unknown place that would become her new home into prayer. Unlike Mama—who would have been horrified at the stories of Captain Bartholomew Roberts and others—Maribel's hopes surged.

Perhaps this dull journey was about to become exciting. Perhaps the vessel on the horizon held a band of pirates bent on chasing them down and relieving them of their silver.

By habit, Maribel looked up into the riggings where her only friend on this voyage spent much of his day. William Spencer, a gangly orphan a full year older and many years wiser than she, was employed as lookout. This, he explained to her, was a step up from the cabin boy he'd been for nigh on seven years and a step toward the ship's captain he someday hoped to be.

Their passing annoyance, which began when she nearly pitched herself overboard by accident while reading and strolling on deck, had become something akin to an alliance during their weeks at sea. To be sure, William still felt she was hopeless as a sailor, but his teasing at Maribel's noble Spanish lineage and habit of keeping her nose in a book had ceased when she discovered the source.

William Spencer could not read. Or at least he couldn't when they set sail from Barcelona.

He'd been a quick study, first listening as she read from *Robinson Crusoe* and *The Iliad* and then learning to sound out words and phrases as they worked their way through Shakespeare's *Julius Caesar*. By the time she offered him her copy of Captain Jones's pirate book, William was able to read the entire book without any assistance.

She spied him halfway up the mainmast. "Sails," she called, though he appeared not to hear her. "Over there," Maribel added a bit louder as she used her book to point toward the ship.

The watch bell startled her with its clang, and the book tumbled to the deck. A moment later, crewmen who'd previously strolled about idly now ran to their posts shouting in Spanish words such as "*pirata*" and "*barco fantasma.*"

"Pirates and a ghost ship?" she said under her breath as she grabbed for the book and then dodged two crewmen racing past with weapons drawn. "How exciting!"

"Don't be an idiot, Red." William darted past two men rolling a cannon toward the *Venganza's* bow then hurried to join her, a scowl on his face. "This isn't like those books of yours. If that's the *Ghost Ship*, then you'd best wish for anything other than excitement."

Shielding her eyes from the sun's glare, Maribel looked up at William. "What do you mean?"

"I mean they're bearing down on us and haven't yet shown a flag. I wager when they do, we won't be liking what flag they're flying."

"So pirates," she said, her heart lurching. "Real pirates."

"Or Frenchmen," he said. "A privateer ship is my guess if they're not yet showing the skull and crossbones."

She continued to watch the sails grow larger. "Tell me about the *Ghost Ship*, William."

"Legend says the ship appears out of thin air, then, after it's sunk you and taken your treasure, all twenty-two guns and more than one hundred crewmen go back the same way they came."

"Back into thin air?" she asked.

"Exactly. Although I have always thought they might be calling Santa Cruz their home as it's near enough to Puerto Rico for provisioning and belongs to the French settlements." He paused to draw himself up to his full height. "And care to guess who the enemy of the men aboard the *Ghost Ship* is?"

Maribel leaned closer, her heart pounding as she imagined these fearless men who chased their prey then disappeared to some mysterious island only to do it all over again. "Who?"

"Spaniards, Red. They hold license from the French crown to take what anyone flying under the Spanish flag has got and split it with the royals. And they don't take prisoners."

She looked up at the flag of Spain flying on the tallest of the masts and then back at William. "No?"

William shook his head. "No. They leave no witnesses. Do you understand now why you do not want that ship out there to be the *Barco Fantasma* as these sons of Madrid call it?"

She squared her shoulders. "Well, I care not," she exclaimed.

"There are no such things as ghosts. My mama said to pray away the fear when it occurred, so perhaps you ought to consider that."

Of course, if she allowed herself to admit it, Maribel should be taking her own advice. Much as Mama reminded her of her status as a woman not born in Spain, her father's lineage and the fact a Spanish flag waved in the warm breeze above her head would seal her fate.

"I'm not scared," William said. "If those fellows catch us, I'd rather join up with them than stay here. Wasn't asked if I wanted to sail on this vessel, so I figure I might as well invite myself to sail on theirs."

"You wouldn't dare. You're not the pirate sort."

"Privateer," he corrected. "And who says I'm not? I read those books of yours. Sure, I'm not one for breaking the law, but if Captain Beaumont offers honest work for my share of the pay, then I'd be better off than I am here. Besides, I can always jump off at the nearest island and stay there like Mr. Robinson Crusoe did. If I tried that now, the Spaniards would come after me and beat me senseless."

She recalled the bruises she'd seen on the boy's arms and nodded. "If you go, I'm going with you. I'll join up with this Captain Beaumont and climb the riggings just like you do."

"You're just a girl," he protested. "Don't you know girls are bad luck on privateers' ships? It was right there in the book."

"It was indeed," she said as she cradled the book against her chest. "But I don't believe in luck. If the Lord allows, then it happens. If He doesn't, then it doesn't. That's what my mama says, and I believe it is true. So I'm going to pray that Captain Beaumont is a good man."

"That's ridiculous, Red."

"The praying?" she said in a huff. "Prayer is never ridiculous."

"No, of course not," he hurried to say. "But to suggest that Captain Beaumont might be a good man—"

"You there, boy," a sailor called as he jostled past William.

"Back to your post and look smart about it."

William fixed her with an impatient look. "While you're doing all this praying, go down to your cabin and hide," he told her. "Bar the door and, no matter what, do not let anyone inside except me or your papa, you understand?"

"Papa," she said as she looked around the deck. "I need to find him."

"Likely he's helping prepare for the attack and won't want a child bothering him," William said. "Do as I said and make quick work of it. Oh, and Red, can you swim?"

"I can," she said even as his description of her as a child stung. "My mama taught me but said we couldn't tell my papa because he thought swimming was undignified and beneath our station. Why?"

"Then if all else fails and you're faced with being captured or the threat of death, jump overboard. It's a known fact that most pirates cannot swim, so you'd be safer afloat in the ocean than aboard a sinking ship." He nudged her shoulder with his, a gesture that reminded her once again of their friendship. "Now off with you, Red. I've got work to do."

"But what about privateers and Frenchmen?" she called to his retreating back. "Can they swim?"

"You better hope you don't find out," was the last thing William said before he disappeared into a crowd of crewmen.

Maribel stood there for a full minute, maybe longer, surveying the chaos unfolding around her. Though she was loath to take William's advice—he was always such a bossy fellow—she did see the wisdom in making herself scarce until the fuss was over.

Oh but she'd not run to her cabin where she would miss all the excitement. There must be a place where she could stay out of the way and still watch what was happening on deck.

Pray away the fear.

She raised up on her tiptoes to look over the men gathered around the cannon. The sails of the approaching vessel were much closer now, their pristine white matching the clouds on the horizon.

A roar went up among the men of the *Venganza*, and then the cannon fired. Covering her ears, Maribel ran in search of the nearest shelter and found it behind thick coils of rope and stacked barrels. Only when she had successfully hidden herself inside the coil did she realize she had dropped her prized book. She had to retrieve it; nothing else would do.

She rose slowly, clutching the ends of Mama's scarf just as the vessel made a turn to the right. With the tilt of the deck, the book slid out of her reach. Braving the throng of people, she headed toward the book, now lodged against the mainmast.

Pray away the fear.

She removed the scarf from her neck and tied it around her head like the pirates whose likenesses filled her books. The ends fluttered in the breeze, and if she thought hard, she could remember Mama wearing this scarf.

She did that now, thought about Mama. About how she loved to tie the scarf around her waist when she wore her pretty dresses. Someday she would tie this scarf around her waist like Mama did.

Someday when she was a grown-up lady.

A cannon sounded from somewhere off in the distance, and then the vessel shuddered. Stifling a scream, Maribel took a deep breath and said a prayer as she grasped the edges of the scarf.

Smoke rolled toward her as Maribel struggled to remain upright on the sloping boards beneath her feet. She reached the book and then slid one arm around the mainmast to steady herself against the pitching motion.

Pray away the fear. Pray away the fear. Pray away. . .

The cannon roared again. A crack sounded overhead and splinters of wood and fire rained down around her.

Then the world went dark.

CHAPTER 2

Captain Jean Beaumont took ownership of the *Venganza* before any man aboard had given it up. He did so simply by claiming it for the crown and glory of France. From that moment, according to the rights granted him in the Letters of Marque, the issue was not whether but how the Spanish vessel would be turned over to its new owner.

Predictably, the Spaniards had resisted all efforts to be peacefully overtaken. A pity, for it was obvious these men stood no chance against his well-trained crew. Now they were paying the price.

All around him his men worked as a team to corral the ship's crew and passengers and prevent any brave souls from seeking retribution. Those assigned to document and remove all valuable items from the vessel had begun their work as well.

Of these men, Jean was most proud. It was a badge of honor to be known and feared by reputation but also to be considered fair in his execution of the privileges extended to him as a privateer.

Each item taken from the vessel would be accounted for, with a list being sent back to the king along with the crown's portion of the spoils. The remainder would be divided among the crew with Jean forgoing his own share.

If the crew thought it odd that their captain took no profit from their voyages, none had been brave enough to say so. This voyage, however, was different. He would take his share, but not in the supplies and silver coin that were now being carried across the deck.

With command of the ship now his to claim, Jean stepped over a fallen Spaniard and kept walking. He sought only one man: Antonio Cordoba.

His second-in-command, a mountain of a man who had escaped slavery to pledge his allegiance to Jean, stepped in front of him holding a man by the back of his neck. It was Israel Bennett's job to go straight to the man in control of the vessel and subdue him.

He did that job well.

The gentle giant offered no expression as he held his quarry still with seemingly little effort. "Claims he's the captain, sir."

Jean looked down at the pitiful captain, taking note of the terror in his eyes and the spotless uniform. Revulsion rose. There was only one reason a man's clothing would be spotless on an occasion such as this. The coward had hidden himself and allowed his men to do the fighting for him.

"See that he understands we have boarded under Letters of Marque on behalf of France and King Louis XV. We wish him and his crew no harm, but we must confiscate what now lawfully is ours."

Israel Bennett dutifully repeated the words in flawless Spanish, saying exactly what Jean would have had he wanted the captain to know he spoke the language fluently. Jean nodded when the message had been delivered.

"I thought he would be older," was the Spaniard's muttered response. "It appears the ghost captain has ceased to age. I claim sorcery."

Israel chuckled, his laughter deep and resonant. "He is of sufficient age to best you and your ship, and I assure you no sorcery was used."

This captain's response was a common one. Though Jean would soon see his twenty-fifth birthday, he was often mistaken for one of his crew rather than the man in charge.

Perhaps this was due to the legend that had grown up alongside the reputation of the vessel that had been dubbed the *Ghost Ship*, not by him but by those who hadn't seen the ship coming until they were close enough for the cannons to reach them. Or perhaps it was because he felt twice his age most days.

"One more thing," Jean added as he looked up at Israel. "Tell him I wish him and his crew no further harm. However, I demand he produce Consul General Antonio Cordoba immediately so that he and I might have a private discussion."

The captain's eyes cut sharply to the left at the sound of the nobleman's name. Jean recognized this as a telling sign of acknowledgment without the man having spoken a word.

While Israel repeated the demand in Spanish and clutched tighter with his massive fists, Jean looked over in the direction where the captain had glanced. Under the watchful eye of one of Jean's crewmen, a dark-haired man in fine clothing knelt at the base of the mainmast. The man's attention was focused on what appeared to be a puddle of cloth.

Then he looked up.

When his eyes met Jean's, he slowly rose. Every muscle in Jean's body went on alert, and his eyes never moved from the man across the deck.

Jean was vaguely aware of a spirited conversation between Israel and the captain, but he kept his attention on the stranger. His last memory of Antonio Cordoba was etched in his mind, although it had been two decades since he had seen the man.

Two decades since the Spaniard pirate and his murdering crew had accosted an innocent French passenger ship. Two decades since they sent every passenger aboard except for a five-year-old boy to the bottom of the sea.

Why he had been saved, Jean had long ago stopped asking the Lord. Every day he awoke alive and healthy, he did so with the realization that he had a debt of gratitude to repay.

What he would do when he found Antonio Cordoba, however, he had long ago decided. Two decades, and now the time had come.

Everything around him ceased to exist in that moment, leaving only Jean and Cordoba. Jean rested his hand on the grip of the jeweled cutlass he'd chosen for the occasion, the same weapon left behind on the deck of that French ship twenty years ago.

The cutlass that had been used to cut down his mother and baby brother.

Jean walked toward the Spanish murderer, stepping over fallen men and stepping around debris that tilted with the list of the ship. All the while, the man Jean knew must be Cordoba merely stood his ground and stared.

"Antonio Cordoba?" Jean called when he was close enough to make his move.

"Who is asking?" the Spaniard responded.

Jean's heart thudded against his chest, every muscle in his body taut and his nerves on alert. "The only survivor of the sinking of the passenger ship *Roi-Soleil.*"

Cordoba's expression never changed as he lifted one shoulder in an almost disdainful shrug. "The *Sun King*, eh? No, the name means nothing. Perhaps I have forgotten," he finally said with a dismissive sweep of his hand.

Forgotten.

The murder of his mother and brother.

Forgotten.

Jean's own brush with death and the long journey to be reunited with his father and brother. All of it as meaningless as a sweep of a Spaniard's jeweled hand.

Something inside Jean snapped. His tight rein on control slipped even as his fingers held tight to the cold metal of the grip. Something akin to a fog blocked out everything except the motions he wished to take.

He lifted the cutlass and held it up. The next blood that stained this weapon would belong to Antonio Cordoba.

Forgotten no more.

A fist grasped his shoulder and held him in place. Jean

attempted to break free but failed.

"This is not how you want to do this, sir," Israel said evenly, his deep baritone cutting through to gain Jean's attention. "Let the Lord handle that man His way. Revenge is His, not yours."

This from a man whose entire family had been separated and sold at the whim of others. Who had been beaten and chained and sold into slavery in Africa by kinsmen bent on revenge.

And yet his words had no effect on Jean. He'd been waiting for this day too long to be dissuaded.

"It is exactly how I want to do this," Jean managed as he kept his attention focused on the arrogant expression on the Spaniard's face.

"Fair enough. But it is not how this should be done." Israel released him and then moved to stand between Jean and Cordoba. "If you proceed, then you'll have to get past me first."

Not since the day Israel Bennett walked out of the hold of a slave ship that had just been taken by Jean and his men and announced he was joining the crew had he seen such resolve on the big man's face. Then, in an instant, his expression contorted and Israel crumpled to the deck.

Jean crumpled with him, dropping the cutlass as he ripped away the rough cloth of Israel's shirt to see blood pouring from a wound on his shoulder. Israel had been shot.

He removed his own shirt to use it as a bandage. "Connor," he shouted above the din. "Someone find Evan Connor. This man needs a doctor's attention."

Israel turned his head to look up at Jean, his face etched with pain. "And you, Jean Beaumont, need the Lord's attention. Do not do this thing you have planned, whatever it is. It will not bring you the relief you seek."

He looked up past Israel's prone body to where Cordoba now lay on the deck. One of Jean's men had wrestled a flintlock pistol from the Spaniard and held him in place with a foot to his back.

Connor arrived in the company of several other men and

pushed Jean aside. As he rose, he felt Israel's hand on his leg.

"Revenge will not be as sweet as you think," the big man said. "It is the Lord's alone and not yours or mine."

Several responses occurred to him. Jean said none of them.

Instead, he rose to cross the deck and removed the flintlock pistol from the sailor's hand. Giving the order for his men to leave them and not intervene, Jean stared down at the man who had haunted his nightmares.

"Stand and face me, Cordoba," he said through clenched jaw. "It is time to look reckoning in the eyes."

Antonio Cordoba climbed to his feet with what appeared to be some measure of difficulty. Jean watched dispassionately as the older man stumbled and required the use of the rail behind him to finally stand upright.

Standing in insolent silence, the defeated enemy dared to smile. *Forgotten.*

Jean advanced on the man, reaching for his cutlass only to realize he'd left it on the deck beside Israel. No matter, he decided, as his fist landed the first punch. Cordoba responded with a blow that glanced off Jean's shoulder.

Immediately his crewmen surrounded them to pull the Spaniard away. "Release him and leave us," Jean called. "No matter what happens, do not intervene."

The last man to leave released the nobleman. Cordoba made a show of straightening his coat and adjusting his sleeves. Still that infernal smile remained.

When they were alone—or at least left alone with wary crewmen grudgingly watching from a distance while they pretended to work—Jean moved closer. Though Cordoba's smile wavered slightly, it did not disappear.

"Something you wish to say?" the Spaniard asked.

"Much," he managed through clenched jaw. "But I would have you speak first in hopes you'll say something that will convince me not to dispatch you to the place you belong."

"Ah," he said slowly. "I see your dilemma. You wish revenge for something so inconsequential to me that I no longer recall it. That must upset you greatly."

Forgotten.

Jean managed a ragged breath. His fingers clutched air and wished for his weapon.

"Oh," Cordoba continued. "It does. I see it. I also see you've left your weapon with your unfortunate friend. A pity I missed when I was aiming for you."

Jean hit him again, and this time the Spaniard went down hard. As he lay on the sloping deck, Antonio Cordoba had the audacity to laugh.

"Feel any better?" he taunted as he lay there. "Go find a weapon and come back. I will wait. Then you can finish me off and be done with whatever revenge you've been seeking."

Everything in him wanted to do as the older man said. And yet Jean remained in place.

"Vengeance is mine; I will repay, saith the Lord."

"No?" Cordoba said with a lift of his brows as he sat up to rest on his elbows. "Ah, well, fine then. You're one who wishes to exact pain before vengeance. You wish me to hurt as you have hurt. Go ahead." He stood and held out his arms. "I'll not fight back. I no longer have it in me. Just be done with it."

Again Jean found he could not move. Could not do the one thing he'd plotted and planned for all these many years.

"Oh, I see," Cordoba continued. "You wish to make me remember those I've killed. I did kill someone you loved, yes?" He shrugged. "Well then, let me relieve you of that burden. I choose not to remember any of them because they were of no consequence."

Something inside Jean broke open, and all the hate he had held in check was released. What happened next was a blur of motion wrapped in blind anger. Despite his claim, the Spaniard fought back like a man half his age.

A burning pain seared across Jean's bare chest. He looked down to find a slash of blood and then at the dagger in Cordoba's hand.

Dodging a sweep of the blade, Jean landed a swift but sure kick to the center of the Spaniard's chest, sending him tumbling backward. Cordoba dropped the dagger, and Jean reached for it.

The deck tilted and Jean missed his chance to steal the knife. Instead, he toppled overboard with Cordoba right behind him.

Debris littered the water around them and the salt water stung, but the battle continued.

"Let him go."

Jean froze, his hands on the Spaniard's throat. He looked at the man in his grasp and saw nothing. No fear. No anger. No recollection of his sins against the family Jean had lost. Against Jean himself.

Just nothing.

"Let him go."

His feet treading water to keep himself and the Spaniard from slipping beneath the waves, Jean looked around to find the source of the words he'd once again heard so clearly.

"Who is there?" he called.

"No one." Cordoba sneered even as he gasped for breath. "You've called off your men. No one is there."

"Who is there?" he called again.

"I AM."

"Let him go."

So he did.

CHAPTER 3

Mary Lytton Cordoba stood in the foyer of her home in the most fashionable part of Madrid and willed herself to remain upright. Two words echoed in her head: *they're gone.* She gripped the stair rail, its newel post covered in pure gold, and tried to understand.

How could Antonio just take her? And more important, why? He'd rarely spared their daughter a moment since her birth.

"And where is my granddaughter?" Don Pablo Cordoba called from the front steps.

Antonio's father, a man closer to Mary than her own father had been, stepped inside and handed his hat to the cowering maid. The girl skittered away from the elegantly dressed nobleman, her head ducked as if he might strike her.

Don Pablo turned his attention to Mary, his ever-present smile in place. "In all the times I have paid visits to this home of yours, Mary, my sweet Maribel has never failed to greet me at the door."

"Oh, Papa," she finally managed when she could speak. "Our Maribel is gone."

"Gone?" Horror etched his features. "Impossible. I saw her only last month and her health was outstanding."

"No," she said as she moved toward Don Pablo to reach for his hand. "She has gone away. With Antonio." Despite her best efforts to calm herself, Mary's voice rose along with her fears. "He has taken her from me. He sent me off on an errand, and when I returned, he had her things packed up and she was gone."

The nobleman reached for Mary's hands and cradled them in his. He inhaled deeply and then let out a long breath before looking down into her eyes.

"I thought by securing this assignment for him in Cuba that he might be safely away from you and my granddaughter."

"As did I," she said. "You know I married for love, Don Pablo, but sadly I was the only one who felt that love. I was a fool."

"Do not believe that of yourself. My son, he is many things, but a man who would marry without thought of love? No, I do believe Antonio loved you, at least as much as he could."

He looked away as if attempting to collect his thoughts. Mary swiped at her wet cheek and gave thanks that the Lord had provided such a kind and loving man in the absence of her family.

A family she should never have left.

"My darling," the older man said gently as tears shimmered in his eyes. "If my son has taken our Maribel, then the duty and responsibility falls to me to go and get her."

Her hope soared for the first time since she returned home to find her daughter, her world, gone. Don Pablo held much power, both here in Spain and elsewhere. If anyone could find her Maribel, it would be him.

"Would you do that?" she asked, her voice soft as a whisper.

The old man looked into her eyes, his expression somber. "You have my promise, Mary, that I will not rest until our Maribel is found."

<hr>

"Nothing but a scratch, Connor." Jean stepped back aboard his ship with victory achieved and a stream of crewmen behind him carrying the spoils of the battle. "How is Israel?"

Stepping aside to allow his well-trained men to do their jobs, Jean turned his attention to his father's dear friend, a physician of great wisdom and advanced age. Though his hands were steady, he had to concentrate to keep the sword's grip from falling through his fingers.

"Our second-in-command is a hardy fellow, and the wound was not deep. He'll be fine soon with just a scar and a story to tell." The doctor fell into step beside him. "You're bleeding. I will have a look."

Not a question but a statement. Only Evan Connor would dare speak to the feared privateer in this manner.

Jean glanced up. The sails caught in the afternoon breeze as Jean's men carried the last of the cache of silver coins into the hold. The Spanish frigate *Venganza* had been cut loose and was drifting away, its smoking hull too badly damaged to claim as a prize but still seaworthy enough to limp to port somewhere before those who chose to remain aboard starved.

By far the most precious possession taken among the spoils of battle was the cutlass found among Antonio Cordoba's belongings. The heavy silver weapon bore a scabbard encrusted with precious stones and had obviously been made by a craftsman with great skill.

He secured the cutlass to his waist and felt the weight of the weapon against his side. Yes, this would do nicely. The men could divide his portion among themselves and he would keep this in return.

A heated argument caught Jean's attention, and he quickly headed in that direction. On a vessel of this size, any disagreement could quickly become more than a small inconvenience, especially one that began after a prize had been taken. He'd learned this the hard way and would allow nothing of the sort on his ship.

In the center of the circle of men were two children of barely more than a decade, one male and the other decidedly female. The prisoners were bound together with a thick rope, each of them wearing a gag and struggling to free themselves. The girl wore an absurd scarf tied around her head, with a bloodstain the size of a doubloon decorating the part that covered her forehead.

"What's this?" he demanded of those under his command. In

an instant, the braying crowd fell silent.

"The men found them," the doctor said as he easily caught up to Jean. "Because you were otherwise occupied, I made the decision to have them brought aboard."

"Did you now?"

When Jean took over this ship some three years past, he instituted a policy that any man who stepped aboard was free to join and free to go as he pleased. Jean cared not for the man's nationality or past but rather determined his worth by the work he was willing to perform.

However, he also refused to harbor fools. Thus, there had been many a man set adrift with provision enough to reach shore in relatively good health.

Unlike the man he had sought, he refused to harm innocents. Without exception, should he overtake a vessel carrying women or children, they were not to be accosted. Nor were slaves or the aged. The policy served him well and allowed his conscience to remain clear.

Until now, however, he had never had to decide what to do with children aboard his ship. Worse, his vessel now harbored a female.

The ship's carpenter was a bald fellow missing most of his teeth, and yet Sebastio Rao's smile was broad as he nudged Connor. "The boy there says he's ready to join up with us."

A smattering of chuckles followed this statement. "The young lady was found in the Consul General's cabin. She also wishes to join us." Evan Connor leaned closer to Jean. "Apparently the gag was deemed necessary due to the girl's insistence on telling anyone who might listen about the books she's read on pirating and how she knows their jobs well enough to do all of them." Humor rose on the old man's face. "She's a spitfire, that one. Watch yourself near her."

Jean regarded the girl sharply as the men burst into hearty laughter. She couldn't be more than eleven or twelve, not much older than his little sister. Even so, the child showed signs of one day becoming a great beauty. Her copper-colored hair fell in thick waves over her shoulders and spilled onto her once lovely but now bloodstained blue dress.

"What is the cause of this blood?" he demanded.

Evan Connor leaned toward him. "She sustained a crescent-shaped cut on her forehead during the battle, likely before we boarded given the look of the wound. Nothing of any consequence, though she may bear a scar."

Oh, but those eyes. Deepest emerald green, they were, and staring at the assembly of misfit sailors with a loathing that was palpable. Even as she seemed to express her opinion about her current situation, the girl stood tall and showed no fear. Indeed, she seemed willing to run him through should someone give her a weapon.

Jean couldn't help but be impressed.

"Consul General Cordoba's daughter as a privateer," Jean said as he stepped into the circle and allowed his gaze to sweep the length of the contemptuous young lady. "Now this is interesting. And we have a young man also wishing to gain our company, do we?"

The fellow tied to her offered a nod of deference. Jean nodded to the nearest sailor. "Remove his gag."

He looked over the lad, a gangly fellow who'd already reached the height of an average grown man despite not appearing much older than the Cordoba girl. Though his hair was dirty and his clothing stained and mended, there was something about the boy that seemed almost aristocratic.

"Name is William, sir, William Spencer," the boy said when he could speak. "I meant what I said. I'll join ye happily."

"And slit my throat soon as you're trusted with something sharp," Jean said with a laugh that held no humor.

"Not hardly," the boy insisted. "I know who you are. And I know this is the great *Ghost Ship* what scares the life out of the Spaniards."

Had he held an interest in doing so, Jean might have corrected the lad on his statement that the boy knew who he was. Only two men aboard this vessel could claim this, and William Spencer was not one of them.

"So you know all this, do you now?" Jean paused to allow another cursory glance at the lad. "Tell me why you believe you belong on this ship, and I'll have nothing but the truth or I'll send you overboard."

He would do no such thing, but the boy did not yet need to know this. Rather, a healthy fear of the captain was always a good thing in a new recruit. If, indeed, the lad could convince him of his sincerity and usefulness.

"The truth is, me pappy and brother, they died at the hands of the Spanish. Rest of my family's dead and buried too. That's how I got where I was on that ship what's thankfully sinking. Straight to the bottom with it, if you ask me."

"We are privateers, not pirates," he said, as much to inform the lad as to remind his crew. "We operate legally under Letters of Marque, and we conduct ourselves with honor and in accordance with the laws of France. This ship accosts only those vessels we are allowed to capture based on these letters, and each man aboard gets his share. More if he's earned it and less if he's new and only just joined up. I am in charge here, and no other man controls this vessel. So, if you're looking for a pirate ship, you'll not find one here."

"No, sir," he said. "I'm looking to join up with you and your men and no other. You can ask Red here. I told her exactly that when we spied your sails on the horizon. I told her I'd join you if you'd let me." He glanced down at the girl. "Didn't I now, Red?"

Jean nodded to a deckhand. "Remove her gag so she can speak for William Spencer here, if she so chooses."

The deckhand did as he was told and then jumped back when the girl aimed the point of her boot in his direction. Several crew members shouted jibes at the jittery deckhand while the remainder laughed at his expense.

"Watch her, Captain," the hapless fellow said as Jean walked past him. "Almost took out my knee, she did. And worse, mayhap I hadn't been so swift in dodging her."

"Duly noted," Jean said as he stopped in front of the girl. "Go ahead, Red. Answer the lad."

For a moment Jean thought she might not say anything. Her face remained unreadable, a feat he could only admire. Faced with this group of misfits and fearsome louts, he might not have been so calm at her age.

His attention went to the scarf around her forehead and the stain of blood there. He would have Connor see to whatever injury was hidden beneath that cloth, but for now he had a defiant child to deal with.

"Speak, or have the gag returned to your mouth," Jean snapped, his patience growing thin.

She let out a long breath but kept her attention focused solely on Jean. "So I'm to vouch for this fellow when he did no such thing for me when these ruffians were making their decision to gag me?" she said with a shake of her head. "Just what sort of arrangement would that be? Not a good one for sure."

"All right, then. Sir, what Red here said about the books she's read is completely and positively true. Why, she taught me to read, she did. I can't help it if I told the truth when those men over there asked me if I thought she might ever tire of speaking about it. Because in truth, the answer is she will not. Or at least in my experience, she has not."

Jean stifled a chuckle. Apparently the girl was not the only one who had difficulty tiring of speaking.

"Too little, too late, William Spencer," the girl called Red said. "Next time respond in my favor when you're asked and perhaps you and I will stay on good terms."

William Spencer rolled his eyes, although the gesture was accompanied by a patient smile. It appeared he and the girl sparred frequently.

"Now that all of that's been cleared up," Jean said as he gave the girl a wide berth as he returned to standing in front of the lad, "I believe we were discussing whether you were fit to join us, lad."

"Where do I sign up?" he said. "I can climb sails, do carpenter work and whatever else needs doing on a ship. Oh, and thanks to Red, I can read too, so maybe there's a job that would require that. And most of all, I'd be grateful to be here. I'd say that's all the fitness I need."

"You're certain?" He gave the boy a sideways look. "It's not an easy life."

He squared his shoulders and drew himself up to his full height. "I told you I was."

"You might be called on to work alongside people not like you." He paused to watch the boy's face. "People who are from other places. People who care not to have their identities discovered. Perhaps men from Africa taken from their homes against their will."

"Slaves?" the lad asked.

"Former slaves," Jean corrected. "Or men who were bound in that direction but relieved of that burden before they were sold."

William Spencer seemed to give the matter a moment's thought, and then he nodded. "Long as they don't mind working alongside me, I'd say we'd get along just fine."

Jean met the boy's gaze and saw he told the truth. He saw, too, a determination in those youthful eyes that reminded him of himself at that age.

"You'll do, then," he said before stepping around to the girl.

She, too, offered a look of determination, although it was likely she'd determined to do him whatever harm she might manage. "And you, Red?" He met her even gaze. "What do you propose we do with you?"

"You'll allow me to join you. I'm just as useful as William."

"Ain't no woman going to join us, is she, Captain?" someone called.

"It's bad luck and ye know it," another said.

Jean waved his hand and the crowd fell silent. He had no intention of allowing this female child to join their ranks, though he had no belief in luck, either good or bad. However, it wouldn't do to let the girl or his crew know that just yet.

"I am the captain of this vessel," he said to her. "As such, I regret to inform you that a woman will never be fit to join my crew."

"And why not?"

A few of the sailors chuckled, while the rest seemed to be watching to see what would happen next.

"Because you'd be a burden, Red, and a danger to the men. Should we be called upon to engage in battle, having you aboard would be a distraction. Someone would have to be assigned to protect you, and that could cost valuable time and lives. And ultimately, as captain, I am the one responsible for protecting all of you."

She met his gaze. "That's ridiculous. I've done a fine job of fending for myself."

Jean shook his head. "I doubt that. Do show me what you would do should someone accost you." He shrugged. "Please wait. I'm terribly sorry. Someone already did and managed to tie you up. You being bound by ropes proves my point exactly."

Before Jean realized what was happening, the young lady kicked him solidly with the pointed toe of her shoe. Pain shot up his wounded leg as he stumbled backward. Peals of laughter were quickly replaced by stunned silence when their captain let out a blistering yell.

CHAPTER 4

A nd that, sir, proves mine," Maribel said. "Although I hope you'll forgive me. See, I have been praying you would be a nice man."

"Keep praying, then," Jean snapped. "Because that is not the case as of yet." He looked over at the doctor, who appeared to be having difficulty keeping a neutral expression. "Mr. Connor," he managed through clenched jaw. "Put the girl in the brig and set the young fellow free."

"The brig? You're certain of this?" the older man asked, concern now etching his features.

Ignoring the quiet stares of the men around him, Jean focused on the man who had known him practically since birth. "I am. If Red wants to be a privateer, then we will show her what happens when a crewman accosts his captain."

Connor shook his head. "But, lad, surely you do not mean to—"

"Surely I do." He then turned to address his crew. "William Spencer here is to be afforded the rights and share of a new crew member once he proves his worth, and as such he is not to be harmed. Anyone who does not comply with this will feel the full fury of my wrath and join the girl known as Red in the brig until a suitable punishment is carried out. Is that understood?"

A low murmur of agreement permeated the crowd. Jean nodded and then continued. "The girl is to be considered under my protection, even though she is to remain a guest in my brig. Should I hear of any maltreatment against her, I will take it as a personal affront to me and deal with the perpetrator accordingly as well. Is that clear?"

This time the murmur of agreement was much softer and appeared to be reluctantly given. Jean locked eyes with the girl called Red, who now stood as if ready to run despite being held in place by two of his largest men. The lad had wisely moved away into the crowd and now stood silently watching.

"It appears there is no solid agreement to this command," he said. "Perhaps someone wishes to challenge me?"

He allowed his attention to sweep the crowd, enjoying them shrinking back, before returning it to the girl. Jean had allowed his temper to best his good judgment and he knew it. Still, he refused to back down.

"No," Jean said. "I thought not. Take her to the brig, and the rest of you mind my warning. And, Connor, see to whatever is hidden beneath that wretched scarf she is wearing. I warrant she will need one of your vile potions."

With that, he turned and walked away, secure in the knowledge that his orders would be followed. No one aboard this ship would dare do otherwise.

Once in his cabin, Jean closed his eyes and settled onto his cot. He took a breath and let it out slowly as he tried in vain to get comfortable even as he also worked to tame his temper.

The wound he'd received two months ago in a skirmish with a slaving ship off the coast of Jamaica ached thanks to the girl's assault on him, but that was the least of his concerns. The thought of the lives saved during that battle—the men who were freed to go back to home and family—was not enough to erase the ones lost today.

Unbidden, Antonio Cordoba's face appeared before him as he had looked before he slipped beneath the waves for the last time. Jean shook his head to rid himself of the vision.

Cordoba was dead, an enemy vanquished, and justice had been served. Calling him back, even in his thoughts, served no purpose.

He should have felt relief. Cordoba was nothing but a cold-blooded murderer.

Jean pounded his fist against the wall. The deaths of Jean's mother and baby brother had been avenged, yet all he felt was a vast emptiness.

"There should be more," he whispered in the French language of his childhood. "Vengeance should feel much sweeter than this."

He sighed. Perhaps Israel was right. Jean managed the beginnings of a smile, though he felt no humor. Indeed, Israel almost always was.

The thought of Israel sent him in search of his friend. He found the man asleep in the doctor's cabin, his legs far too long for the bunk where he lay. Still, he appeared to be sleeping comfortably, so Jean left him there and returned to his cabin to attempt some rest of his own.

Sometime later, Connor opened the door without any pretense of knocking. "I've come to bind your wounds," the doctor said as he crossed the brightly colored Persian rug—bounty taken so long ago Jean couldn't name the vessel from which it came—and dropped his bag of ointments and bandages beside the cot then knelt with a heavy sigh.

Jean removed his boot and let it drop. Bright red streaked the bandages.

"You've gone and opened it again. I could blame the girl for this, but we both know you had it coming when you taunted her."

Refusing to admit what he knew to be true, Jean remained silent. Outside, the watch bell rang indicating that sufficient time had passed that he must have managed to sleep. Why then did he still feel so very tired?

Connor opened his bag and began searching through its contents before looking up at Jean. "Now that you've got your revenge, will you be taking my advice and laying low awhile? I wager you're needed back in New Orleans."

"A wager you would likely win," he said, as they both knew his life there put demands on him that never seemed to cease. "Yet there are details left to handle before I can return."

Connor looked up at him. "Such as?"

He met the old man's even gaze. "Such as what to do with Cordoba's child."

"Ah, yes. That." The doctor went back to work swabbing the wound with a clean piece of muslin then applied a foul-smelling poultice.

Though he wanted to cry out in pain, Jean remained stoic. Finally he'd had enough.

"Can you not treat this with something that smells less like the garbage heap? Truly I've smelled dead animals that were more pleasantly fragrant."

Connor leaned back on his heels and regarded Jean with a look that told nothing of his thoughts. He rose. "Do you know what would please your father greatly, lad?"

Jean forced himself to smile. "There are many things that would please him, chief among them things I have no interest in doing."

"Therein lies the problem," Connor said as he settled onto a chair nearby.

"I know that look." Jean grimaced as he shifted positions. "You're about to tell me what to do, and then I'll ignore it."

"That is generally how it goes with us, isn't it? You avoid the difficult questions I ask."

"As do you," Jean reminded him. "Else I'd know why you don't leave this leaky tub of a ship and make your living doctoring a better lot of people than are found aboard."

Connor chuckled as he leaned down to hand Jean his boot. "Why would I leave? With all the trouble we manage to find, I keep up with my doctoring skills. Now get that boot on, and then I'll look at that scratch of yours."

"That scratch" was the slash across the muscles of his chest made by the murderer Cordoba just before Jean sent him tumbling into the sea. Jean eased his boot on. The long gash had ceased bleeding, but Connor insisted on treating it with more of his vile potion.

"A few inches deeper and you'd not be with us, lad. You won't need stitching up, but do try to stay out of trouble until you can heal proper." He shook his head as he returned his doctoring supplies to their case. "What am I saying? Trouble finds you."

Ignoring the comment, Jean climbed to his feet to retrieve a clean shirt. "I paid a visit to Israel. He appeared to be sleeping in comfort. Will he recover?"

"Completely and swiftly, I do believe. Had he not been standing between you and the flintlock, you would not be alive, my friend. However, his constitution and the fact he carries much more muscle than any of us has saved him yet again. It's been all I could do to keep him immobile and allow some measure of healing."

"So you gave him a sleeping draught."

Connor chuckled. "Not that he is aware of, no. But, yes, it was all I could think of to keep him from returning to the deck and seeing to your safety."

Jean smiled. Indeed Israel had appointed himself to that task. A pity it was proving so difficult. Another thought occurred. "How does our prisoner fare?"

"She's holding her own down in the brig. Other than a cut on her forehead, she bears no marks from her ordeal." He paused. "Don't you think it's a bit harsh to lock up someone so young and innocent, especially so soon after the loss of her father?"

"Innocent? Did you see what she did to my leg?" he said as he donned his shirt. "I wager she can hold her own anywhere."

"Perhaps you're right. Seems she can certainly stand up to you, lad. 'Tis a brave thing to kick a ship's captain when you're bound and gagged." Connor paused. "She puts me in mind of a younger version of you, Jean Beaumont."

"Perhaps," he said slowly, "but my accommodations in the brig can only be temporary. Women are not allowed about my vessel, and there's certainly no friend or relative of mine who would accept her. Not that I'd risk the exchange, mind you."

"I understand your dilemma," the doctor said. "And yet despite her parentage, she's innocent in all of this. We cannot exactly put her off somewhere without friend or family to look after her."

"Then we contact Cordoba's family and settle on a price for her return." He let out a long breath, his body aching. "Surely there's someone willing to ransom her."

"The girl says she's not Cordoba's daughter," Connor said. "She won't tell me who she is, only who she isn't."

"Of course she's his daughter. Why else would she be on a Spanish merchantman with a king's ransom in silver in its hold, all of it belonging to the new Consul General?"

"A worthy question," Connor said. "I do not disagree. Perhaps the lad should be questioned. He appears to know her well enough."

"Agreed. Would you have that handled, Connor? I do not wish to intimidate the lad into answering in a way that isn't truthful out of fear."

"You do have that effect," the doctor said. "I'll see if perhaps we can get to the truth without terrifying the lad."

"Thank you." He paused to think a moment. "Connor, no one with any sense would bring a child on such a risky voyage except for a fool like Cordoba. Have you seen what the Spaniard had hidden away in the belly of that ship? A fool's errand it was to bring such wealth on the same vessel with his own child. He mistakenly believed he was invincible."

The doctor nodded. "Apparently his daughter has inherited the same attitude, although she does execute the behavior with a much more charming demeanor."

"Has she caused more trouble already?"

Jean steadied himself as he carefully put more weight on his injured leg. The wound already felt better, a testament to the doctor's medical skills. Still it did plague him.

"Doctor?" he said when he realized Connor had not yet responded to his question. "What is our prisoner up to down in the brig?"

The older man shrugged. "I did check on the young lady before coming up here to dress your wounds and found a perplexing situation afoot in the brig."

"Perplexing?" He shook his head. "Elaborate, please."

Connor nodded toward the door. "Perhaps you'd best see for yourself," he said. "If you're fit for the walk, that is."

"I am easily fit for the walk." Jean straightened his spine and marched past the doctor without limping, a feat that took concentration.

Stepping out into the starry night, he nodded to the young man posted to the watch and then headed down the sharply descending stairway that led below the deck. Navigating the dark-as-night passageways with skill learned through years of experience, he turned a corner and heard, of all things, laughter.

Several of his fiercest sailors, men whose penchant toward ill temper was well known, were standing outside the open door of the brig while a circle of men gathered inside on the straw-covered floor. It appeared the men inside the brig were wagering on something. Laughter filled the close space and spilled out into the passageway where Jean stood.

The ship lurched, parting the men and allowing him to see what was causing all the uproar. Situated cross-legged in the center of the men was the Cordoba girl, a blanket spread out beneath her as if she were at a picnic instead of being held prisoner in his brig. Her copper-colored hair and fashionable dress set her apart from the attentive crew, as did the sound of her childish laughter.

Though she still wore the stained scarf, the ends of a length of muslin showed. Apparently Connor had been able to doctor the girl's wound without sustaining bodily harm.

Seated directly across from her was the burly carpenter, Rao. As he stepped closer, Jean realized Rao and the girl were playing a board game that looked deceptively like draughts.

Jean frowned. Surely not.

And yet that is exactly what he saw. Grown men, brutal men of war, encircling a child's board game while the toothless carpenter entertained their prisoner. To make matters worse, Swenson, chief rigger, seemed to be leading the cheers in favor of the girl.

The girl moved her game piece over the carpenter's last two black pieces and then looked up at him and grinned. "I win, Mr. Rao."

"Best three out of four?" Rao inquired.

A small roar erupted. Jean let out a long breath, his temper at its peak.

"Gentlemen," he said with as much sarcasm as he could manage. "Am I interrupting something?"

A hush fell over the crowd. Slowly those nearest to Jean pressed past him to slink away, their eyes downcast.

"Not at all." The Cordoba girl looked up at him with a smile and no appearance of fear. "Would you like to play? We don't wager, although it's awfully fun to win anyway."

"This is a privateer's ship and not a gaming vessel."

"I've only heard the *Ghost Ship* called a ship for pirates," she said, her face a mask of innocence.

At the word *pirate*, any man still remaining nearby turned to disappear down the passageway. The distinction between piracy and privateering was what allowed Jean to keep his conscience clear and the coffers of his vessel full, all under the protection of the French crown. Any man who used the word in his presence swiftly felt his wrath.

But this was a child, and a female child at that. Still, his blood boiled. "Privateer," he said.

She shrugged. "Same thing."

Jean took a deep breath and let it out slowly. "Your ignorance is understandable," he said as gently as he could manage. "Given the fact you know nothing of the subject of which you speak. But one is most definitely not the same as the other."

"I am not ignorant on the subject of pirates," she protested. "As William Spencer attested, I have read *The Notorious Seafaring Pyrates and Their Exploits*."

Jean met her stare with an impassive look that defied his temper. "And this book, of which I am well aware, makes you an authority?"

"I read that book two full times, going on three except that I dropped the book on the deck when the pirates shot at us, and then I retrieved it but lost it again when I—"

"Silence!"

CHAPTER 5

To Jean's surprise, the girl actually ceased her chatter. He decided to take the opportunity to change the subject rather than dwell on her persistent need to argue this one.

In order to achieve his goal of having her confirm what he felt he already knew, Jean took a gentler approach. "What is your name, child?"

She climbed to her feet and crossed her arms over her chest. The girl he'd heard called Red was a skinny thing, barely a wisp of a girl with innocent eyes big as saucers, and yet he wouldn't dare trust her given the result of their last encounter.

"Your name?" he repeated.

"I see no need to tell you unless you plan to allow me to join your crew. And then, I would most likely prefer to change it to a pirate name," she responded matter-of-factly. "However, I suppose I could admit that my mother named me Maribel."

"Maribel Cordoba." Her eyes narrowed, but Maribel said nothing, so Jean continued. "You were found in the cabin belonging to Consul General Antonio Cordoba, so do not bother to try and convince me otherwise."

"As you wish," she said with a shrug. "But I am still trying to decide on a pirate name, so I cannot comment as to what I will eventually be called."

"Privateer," he corrected.

"Yes," she said sweetly. "My privateer name. I welcome your

advice, of course, since you will be my captain."

"I will be no such thing," he snapped. "Stop this. You are Maribel Cordoba, and you belong with your family. My dilemma is how to best reunite you."

"You cannot," she said softly. "My mama is gone."

Jean paused. Until now, he hadn't thought about the child's mother.

"I see," was the only response he could manage. "Is there another family member somewhere who would take you in?"

"I have a grandfather," she told him. "He is an important man, so I only see him sometimes. Although I've seen him more than my papa, and Grandfather Cordoba is certainly more important."

"Cordoba, is it?"

She shrugged. "Yes, you've caught me. But I still plan to change it once a proper *privateer* name is chosen for me."

The bravado she attempted with these words seemed brittle and nothing like her previous attitude. His heart lurched, but Jean held his feelings—and his words—in check.

"You are the ward of your grandfather now," he said. "Any change of name for you will be his choice, not yours or mine. How do I find your Grandfather Cordoba?"

"He is dead too." For the first time, the girl's lip quivered. "Papa told me they're both dead, Mama and my grandfather. I pretend they're not, but. . ."

"What else?" he encouraged, even as his heart broke for this motherless child. "Surely there are others with whom you can stay."

Maribel plopped back down on her blanket, her face a mask of defiance. "There is not," she said. "My mama had no one else, and when any member of my father's family wishes to appear, they appear. I cannot call on any of them, nor can I tell you a place where I am welcome because my mama's home in Spain is being sold so I had to go and live with my father, only. . ."

"Only?" he asked.

She paused only a moment then began again. "That is truly

all I know, and all the torture in the world will not get anything further out of me."

"Torture?" Jean laughed despite his heartbreak at the tears shimmering in the girl's eyes. "What kind of man do you think I am? You're perfectly safe here."

"Am I?"

A smile rose, and so did the girl. She wrapped her arms around Jean to envelop him in a hug. "I knew you would turn out to be a nice man. I prayed for that, you know. William told me I shouldn't bother because privateers are not supposed to be nice men, but I told him I was going to pray anyway, and he said—"

"Maribel. Stop. Talking."

She closed her mouth and took a step back to look up at him. He waited for a word or two to come tumbling out, but the girl remained silent.

Then slowly a smile tried to wobble into place as she reached out to grasp his hand. "You're alone too, aren't you?"

Jean looked down at the girl with the eyes of a man who had seen too much for the amount of years he had lived. He tried to form an answer to her question, but no words would come.

Her coppery hair flamed around her dirt-smudged face as she waited for him to speak. Though the wound on her forehead was small enough, as Connor had said, for the rest of her life she would bear a reminder of the day her father died.

For a brief moment, he felt a bond growing between them.

A bond he could not allow, for the girl could never be subject to a privateer's life. He would find another solution.

He must.

Jean slipped his hand from her grip and took two steps backward. "Are you hungry?"

"I prefer to work for my food," was her response.

Stubborn girl. "That is not possible at the moment. Are you in need of anything else?" he continued, still grasping for words that would release him from the obligation of remaining here with her.

"To join your company and be put to work on your crew just as you allowed William Spencer," she said. "Beyond that, nothing more."

"And you know my answer to that," he said evenly.

"It is the wrong answer," she quickly responded.

"Miss Cordoba, I will remind you that I am the captain of this vessel. As such, any answer I give—should I determine a question is worthy of answering—is not only the correct answer, it is the only answer."

"I understand," she said. "But I also disagree."

"The first rule for a crew member in my employ is that he never disagree with anything I say. Thus, you have just proven yourself unfit to join us."

He turned then to walk away, his verbal victory temporarily won. She would continue to argue the point, of this he had no doubt, but for now he could claim a small victory.

Jean left the girl in her cell but did not bother to lock the door. Should she try to escape, there was truly nowhere she could go. Besides, unless he missed his guess, there were several of his crewmen hidden in advantageous places along the corridor listening to their exchange.

"Rao," he said as he spied his crewman lurking just around the corner. Likely he was eavesdropping and not just lurking, but Jean gave him the benefit of the doubt. "See that Miss Cordoba is moved into a cabin of her own. Also, see that she is fed properly and looked after so that she is not bothered by the crew."

"Aye, Captain. Will you be giving her a job too?" he asked, his toothless grin broad.

The humor Rao offered grated on what little good temperament Jean had gained. "I suppose I could give her yours," he snapped and then continued walking.

Even reaching the deck and finding a nice breeze in the ship's sails did not repair his mood. Several more of his crewmen appeared to be waiting for him to leave the brig, as witnessed by the group gathered near the mainmast.

"Whoever was next on the list of opponents at draughts should be advised that Miss Cordoba will be available to best you as soon as she is installed in a proper cabin and fed a meal."

Though no one nodded or even acknowledged his statement, they all scattered to their posts with smiles on their faces.

Maribel watched the captain go, taking note that he was limping. Whether the cause was the shot Papa fired at him or something else that happened while aboard the *Venganza*, the result had been that the pirate captain had been harmed.

"Privateer," she said under her breath.

Captain Beaumont was mighty proud of his distinction as a privateer, and her stating otherwise was something she would need to remedy. Apparently there was some sort of honor among men who acted like pirates but followed the rules of the Letters of Marque.

If she had her favorite book, she might be able to read up on the subject. However, with nothing but quiet this deep into the belly of this ship, she had plenty of time to try and remember what Captain Jones said on the matter.

She leaned back against the wall, the straw making for a soft spot to do her thinking. Back on the Spanish ship, she had shared a cabin with her father but had never felt as comfortable there as she did here.

Papa.

His face came to her, and she banished it just as she had done when she was a young girl. Missing Papa had become so much a part of her life that the word *missing* ceased to have meaning.

He was the man who married Mama, and he gave Maribel her name. Beyond that, Papa was the man in the painting over the fireplace and the man who caused Mama's tears when she thought Maribel wasn't listening.

She had seen him take aim at the captain. Heard him curse when she kicked his leg to ruin his aim as he fired and the African went down in the captain's place.

Maribel closed her eyes. She would have to beg the African's forgiveness for causing him to be shot. That hadn't been her intention. At the same time, she gave thanks that the Lord had spared Captain Beaumont.

For she truly knew in her heart that someday he would be a good man. He had to be, for God always answered prayers.

That's what Mama told her, and that's what she knew to be true.

Mama.

Oh, Mama.

A wave of sorrow so deep and dark that she had no name for it or control over it rolled up from some bottomless place inside her.

Mama. "What will I do without you, Mama?"

Pray away the fear.

She tried, really she did. But every word that rose in her heart died before it reached her throat. Though she knew prayers were not useless, at this moment they just seemed impossible.

Mama would tell her to pray anyway, so she did. When she opened her eyes, the big African man who she'd been certain her papa had killed was standing before her.

"Are you an angel?" she said softly as she climbed to her feet. "Because you sure do look real, and I see you've got a bandage on your shoulder where my papa shot you, and my mama told me that God heals every wound, so if you're an angel and you've still got need of that bandage, then either my mama was wrong or you need to go back and remind God He forgot to take that wound away."

Out of words, Maribel stood very still waiting for the African angel to speak. In the Bible, Mary was visited by an angel and she ended up with the baby Jesus in the manger after she rode on a donkey a long way then had to sleep in a barn on straw just like this. Surely the Lord would be sending a different message to her through this angel.

One that didn't involve donkeys, a husband, or sleeping on straw.

Slowly the corners of his mouth lifted into a smile. Then, without saying a word in regard to her question, he began to laugh.

Whether or not the man with the bandage was indeed an angel, Maribel decided this is exactly how an angel's laughter ought to sound. When the laughter stopped, silence filled the small room.

"Mr. Angel?" she finally said. "I want to ask you to forgive me for what my papa did. He shouldn't have shot you like he did, although to be fair he wasn't aiming at you. Though he was aiming at Captain Beaumont, and that was also wrong. But I did try and stop him, and when I couldn't, I hit his leg and he got mad at me so I ran and hid in his cabin, but I saw he still shot you anyway, so I'm very, very sorry."

"Little one," he said gently, his voice so deep and beautiful, "I am no angel. I am just a man, and a flawed one at that. But you need to learn right now that the sins of your father are his alone. Do you understand?"

She studied his brown skin and eyes the color of the dark coffee her grandfather loved, and then smiled. "I suppose, but if I had been able to stop him, then you wouldn't have that bandage."

He nodded and seemed to consider her statement. "That is true, but if you had been able to stop him from taking that shot, who is to say that the next one might not have killed someone? You and I will never know the answer to that question. Only God knows, and we cannot possibly know everything He knows."

"That's what my mama says too." She pushed back a thought of her mother and the big Bible that filled her lap as they read it together. "So if you're not an angel, then who are you and why are you here?"

"Israel Bennett is the name I am called on this ship."

Her eyes widened. "You got to pick your own name? Captain

Beaumont told me that wasn't allowed." She paused to think about her conversation with the captain. "But he also told me I couldn't be on his crew because I disagreed with him, and I guess he's right because when I read the book about pirates that is my favorite, all the captains insisted that everyone do what they said. So since I told him he was wrong about something and didn't do what he said, I think I understand why he told me I couldn't be on the crew."

Israel Bennett nodded. "It is important to follow whoever God has put in charge of you."

"Unless what he is doing isn't right?" she said.

The big man's expression softened. "You're a very wise person, Miss Maribel. If you ask me, you've got a fine name and ought to be proud of it. What purpose would it serve to change your name just to become a member of this crew?"

She thought about the question then offered one of her own instead. "What purpose did it serve you?"

"Ah well," Mr. Bennett said as he nodded. "My new name kept me and the captain out of trouble."

Maribel shifted positions and looked past him to where Mr. Rao seemed to be trying to hide from them. "I don't understand."

"No," he said gently, "and I hope you never do." His face brightened. "But right now I need to get you out of here. Did you bring anything with you?"

She shook her head. "I had a book with me, but I dropped it on the deck of the *Venganza*. It was my favorite. The pirate book. But maybe the captain would be happier if I didn't have a copy of that book, what with the fact he seems particularly sensitive to the use of the word *pirate* on this ship."

"Would that happen to be *The Notorious Seafaring Pyrates and Their Exploits* by Captain Ulysses Jones?"

Again her eyes widened. "Yes. How did you know?"

Mr. Bennett chuckled. "Because I've read it. Twice. Now come with me and let's get you out of here."

CHAPTER 6

I've read it twice too," Maribel said as she followed Mr. Bennett out of the cell. "And part of a third time until I lost it on the deck. I might have finished reading it more times than two, but I loaned it to William Spencer so he could practice his reading." She stopped short. "How is William? Is he faring well as a crewman?"

"Hasn't been long enough to say for certain, but I do believe he's going to make a fine ship's doctor." He nodded toward his shoulder. "The lad helped our Mr. Connor to patch me up, so I'm told."

"A doctor?" she said softly. "I had no idea he possessed doctoring skills. Although, there was quite a good chapter on medical attention at sea in the pirate book. I suppose he may have taken an interest in the study of medicine by reading that chapter."

Mr. Bennett took her hand and started her progress down the corridor once again. "Or, he was assigned the job of doing what Mr. Connor told him and he did it."

"Yes," she said thoughtfully. "I would guess that's the correct answer. It pains me to say this since I have been the one teaching him, but I suppose I could learn something from William Spencer."

"Considering what I've heard, I'd agree, Miss Maribel." He nodded toward the corridor ahead. "Now follow me or you'll get lost. And remember you just decided you'd follow orders from now on."

"Yes I did, Mr. Bennett, but I feel like I ought to warn you about me. See, what I decide to do and what I turn out to do is not always the same thing. So if I don't follow orders very well right now, I would like you to know I will only get better at it the longer I keep trying. I'm working on it, but I've got a long way to go."

Again he chuckled. "Miss Maribel, you and me both. You and me both."

Rocking at anchor in the warm turquoise waters of Havana, Jean's ship was taking on supplies for the trip back to New Orleans. The time had come to lay low for a while.

Jean walked down the sandy street in the direction of the town square. If anyone could help him with the problem of what to do with Maribel Cordoba, it was Rose McDonald.

She spotted him before he saw her, and hurried to greet him with a warm embrace. "Welcome back, love. Have you changed your mind about sweeping me off my feet and marrying me?"

He laughed at the joke, an old one but one that never ceased to bring a chuckle. Though Rose was a beauty, she was twice his age and the widow of a former crewman.

"You'd not have me and you know it," Jean said. "However, I do have a favor to ask. It concerns a situation I find myself in that is in need of your assistance."

Rose gave him a serious look and then nodded toward her home, a cottage perched on the edge of the hill overlooking the harbor. "Come in and let's talk about this, shall we?"

Jean followed her inside and then produced a heavy bag of coins from his coat. "I have a business proposition, Rose, but I want you to think carefully before you accept it."

"What is it you want me to do?" she said as she studied him carefully.

An hour later, the talking was done and it was time to introduce Maribel Cordoba to her new home. Rather than tell her what he intended to do, Jean coerced Israel into bringing the girl to Mrs.

McDonald's cottage for what she believed was a tea party.

"Just us girls," Mrs. McDonald said as she shooed the men out the door.

"You will take good care of her," Israel said. A statement, not a question.

"Yes, of course," Mrs. McDonald said softly. "I shall treat her like my own daughter." She turned her attention to Jean. "You have my word she will be treated well."

Those words were little comfort when he and Israel returned to the ship without Maribel. Ignoring the silence of his crew, Jean stalked to his cabin and slammed the door with a resounding thud. A short time later, a timid knock sounded at the door.

"Enter," he said and then looked up to see Israel standing in the door. "The ship is fully loaded up and ready to sail, sir."

He took note of Israel's woeful expression and decided to ignore it. "Weigh anchor and head for New Orleans then."

Israel did not move from the doorway. Rather, he appeared to be considering what to say or perhaps whether to say anything at all.

"Will there be anything else?"

"There would be, yes," he said slowly. "Are you sure this is best, leaving the girl here? I know you can vouch for Mrs. McDonald, but is it the best thing for the girl to be raised here in Havana? And should we not have said good-bye to her? Seems wrong to just walk out the door as if we were coming back then sail away."

He felt the same way, but his position as captain would not allow him to admit it to Israel. Or perhaps it was his fear that if he did admit such a thing, he would be forced to go fetch the girl and haul her back on board.

"Wrong?" he said instead.

"Nothing, sir," he said. "I'll give the order."

"Thank you, Israel."

It did not escape Jean's notice that his second-in-command slammed the door a little harder than necessary. Nor did he miss the four solid days of silence his crew offered him on their sail back to New Orleans.

Finally, Jean could condone the silent protest no longer. He called a gathering of the entire crew and then climbed the quarterdeck to speak to them when they had assembled on the deck below.

"Let any man who would challenge my decision to leave the girl in a safe home in Havana rather than subject her to the rigors and dangers of sailing with us step forward and speak up."

The startled crew gaped and a few even laughed as one lone sailor broke through the line of men and presented himself to the captain. "I offer my challenge, sir."

The youth was small in stature and wore a pair of trousers that had been made for a much larger man. A thick leather belt appeared to be the only thing that kept the threadbare garment in place. The lad's dirty muslin shirt was knotted at his waist, and a length of blue muslin covered his head.

"Draw your weapon, sir," the small voice squeaked as he held a stick of wood aloft.

Jean stared down at the angry young man and tried not to laugh. "Do I know you, lad? Perhaps you were misinformed as to how we conduct business on this ship, so I will take your obvious youth and inexperience into account." He allowed his gaze to travel across the men assembled on the deck, and then he returned his attention to the boy. "Whomever vouched for this cabin boy and is responsible for bringing him aboard, please silence him now."

Jean waited, but no one came forward. "All right, then. What do you wish, boy? Shall we duel to the death with pistols, or would you prefer to feel the bite of my cutlass?"

Before the impudent youth could respond, William Spencer stepped in front of him. "This is none of your concern, young man," he told the new recruit.

With a swift move of his hand, Spencer pulled the length of muslin off the youth's head, revealing fiery curls that could only belong to one person. The crew began to applaud.

Maribel Cordoba faced him with a broad smile on her face and then bowed deeply. "Now can I be a pirate, sir? If I swear to follow your orders from now on, that is?"

"How did you get here?" he demanded, ignoring her questions and the cheering crew.

Her pale face held the innocent expression of a child at play. He noticed the crescent-shaped wound was on its way to healing.

"I told you I wanted to join this crew," she said as the men crowded around her. "Mrs. McDonald was a nice lady, but I am much happier here. This is where I belong, not in Havana."

If esteemed Widow McDonald had taken his money knowing she had no plans to keep her end of the bargain, he would be very disappointed. He was usually a decent judge of character, and he'd truly thought she would raise the girl as her own and not let her slip away like this.

"Does Mrs. McDonald know you're here? And I'll have the truth."

"Oh no," she said. "Miss Rose thought I was waiting for her at the mercantile. We had gone there after tea, and she let me pick out sweets while she ordered new dresses for me. I slipped out while she was looking at unmentionables for herself." She paused and shrugged. "She told me to make myself busy, so I did."

Peals of laughter erupted among the men. Jean grabbed the girl by the elbow and relieved her of her weapon.

"Back to work, all of you," he shouted at the crew. Immediately the men scattered.

Dragging her back to his cabin, he seated her on a chair and glared at her. "How did you get aboard? I will have the name of the man or men who brought you back aboard my ship, and I will have those names now."

"It was none of them," she said. "I did it myself."

"Your friend William Spencer helped you, didn't he?"

"He most certainly did not."

Jean paced the room, sorting through possible scenarios for how the girl got past his men. Then he stopped in front of her, his arms crossed over his chest. "No, he's a rule follower. I don't see him amenable to breaking the rules for you."

"Nor would I ask that of him."

"So," he said as he gave the matter more thought, "was it Rao? He has a certain fondness for you. I warrant he would gladly do your bidding if you asked him to bring you aboard without my knowledge."

"I told you, I did it myself. I climbed into a barrel of silk cloth that bore a label with your name on it and hid myself inside. It was quite comfortable, and I did fall asleep for a short time, but that is how I ended up back aboard this vessel."

Jean let out a long breath. He knew the barrel to which she referred, for it was meant to be a gift for his stepmother, long considered his mother, and sister. To think the girl rode onto his vessel in that barrel was almost funny.

Almost, but not quite, because someone allowed her to climb into that barrel. Someone else missed finding her when he inspected the barrel's contents. He had an idea of who that someone was.

"You don't believe me, do you?"

He paused. "I'm not sure if I do or if I do not. Where did you get the clothes you are wearing?"

"I found them myself," she answered proudly. "I just looked around the hold until I found something appropriate to my new life. A privateer cannot be seen parading around in a dress."

Jean tried to keep a serious expression, but his laughter got the better of him. "Yes, I do see the dilemma. And I am willing to strike a compromise, at least for the remainder of this voyage."

"And what would that be?" she asked.

"You are welcome to remain with us until we reach New Orleans. Once there, proper arrangements will be made for you."

She shook her head. "I want to remain on the ship. I'm not

interested in whatever arrangements you think you'll be making for me in New Orleans."

"You've no choice in the matter," he told her. "The vessel will be dry-docked for repairs and the crew released from their duties until such time as the vessel is ready to sail again."

Her haughty expression fell. "Yes," she finally said. "I do see the dilemma."

He wouldn't dare tell her yet that his plans involved turning the troublemaking girl over to his mother for her assessment. Either Maribel would end up spending the remainder of her childhood under a New Orleans roof or Abigail would find a more suitable solution such as taking her to the Ursuline convent.

Of course, there were serious complications in allowing the girl to be privy to a side of his life that Jean shared with very few people. He would have to give this plan serious consideration before he decided a course of action. In the meantime, it appeared he was now the captain to his first female crew member.

"I'm sure a solution can be found," he told her. "But for now, do I have your word that you will abide by the rules of my ship and cease your infernal arguing with me?"

She grinned and offered a smart salute. "I promise."

"Then there is one more requirement." He ignored her exasperated expression to continue. "You will write a letter of apology to Mrs. McDonald asking her forgiveness for running away from her. Likely she has the constables searching for you. I'm sure you've given her a terrible fright."

Maribel looked contrite. "I didn't think of that," she admitted. "I will write a very nice letter and be sure to tell her how wonderful her tea and cookies were and how very much I enjoyed getting to know her for the hour we spent together. How's that?"

"That is a good beginning." Jean could stifle his amusement no longer. His laughter filled the room as he looked down at the newest member of his crew. "Welcome then, Maribel."

The loud boom of a cannon and the sudden pitch of the ship

punctuated his words. The vessel momentarily righted itself before another blast tore through its hull.

"Get under that bunk, and do not come out until someone comes for you," he snapped. "That is an order."

He waited just long enough to be sure Maribel complied and then strode out toward the deck. Israel met him in the passageway. "What is going on?" he bellowed over the noise and chaos unfolding on deck.

"Over there." Israel pointed toward a low, fast schooner heading toward them. "Her French flag claimed her for a friend. Until she started firing on us."

The gunners had already begun to return fire, but the ship listed heavily to port and its torn sails hung uselessly in the breeze. The schooner continued to approach, its hull cutting swiftly through the waves.

"I will have the necks of the cowards who refuse to strike a proper flag," Jean shouted as he took his place behind one of the port cannons. Because of the dangerous incline of the deck, he had to hold on tight to avoid slipping into the water.

"Hold our fire," he shouted above the din. "Wait for my signal."

The acrid smell of smoke burned his lungs as Jean watched the schooner's swift approach. Waiting until the last possible moment to adjust for the sharp angle of the listing ship, he finally shouted the order.

"Fire away."

The schooner was hit broadside by eleven cannonballs at once. The vessel burst into flames and immediately began to founder. A rousing cheer went up on the deck as the schooner began to disappear below the water.

"Good work, Captain," Israel said when he caught up to him.

"Too early for celebrating," he said as he rubbed his sore leg. "Get the carpenter and our sailmaker up here."

Jean squinted his eyes against the setting sun. The holes in the deck were large but reparable, and the mainmast still stood sound. He would not celebrate until his hunch was confirmed, but it appeared that the damage below would be minimal.

"Send a party to search for survivors," he told Israel. "I want to know who is behind this unprovoked attack."

"Aye, sir," Israel said, though he lingered just a moment longer than expected. "Regarding Miss Maribel. . ."

"If you're about to confess some transgression regarding how the girl was able to slip aboard my ship and remain here for several days, I advise you to wait until we've reached land and I have had sufficient time to decide if whatever decisions were made were the correct ones."

Israel studied him a moment and then nodded. "Agreed," he said.

Jean paused to give him an assessing look. "Go and carry out my orders. I'll be in my cabin. I left our newest crew member there."

To his surprise, Maribel had not only followed his orders but remained under the bunk exactly where he told her to go.

CHAPTER 7

Using the blankets she found on the bunk, Maribel had snuggled herself into a cozy spot.

She watched the boots walking toward her. Thankful as she was that the captain had survived whatever happened, she made no move to leave her hiding place. In fact, she liked where she was hiding just fine.

The boots stopped inches from her. "You are unharmed?" the captain said.

"Yes," she managed.

Later she would add that somewhere between the cannon fire and the fear that William Spencer and the captain might die she had decided to give up on the life of a privateer. To lose her father was awful. To lose people who treated her as if they cared. . .

She bit her trembling lip and turned her face away. The last thing she wished to do was allow Captain Beaumont to see his newest crew member shedding tears.

"So you wish to sleep, then?" he said. "I'll not keep you from it, although I can report that your companion Mr. Spencer showed himself admirably during the battle. You were correct in vouching for his abilities as a sailor."

Maribel let out a long breath. She hadn't dared think of William, because to think of him would mean to worry about him while the cannons were firing and the noises of battle were sounding. She hadn't managed the same ability regarding the captain. Instead, she'd kept up a prayer that he would survive.

The boots stepped away to stop at the desk where the captain's log was kept. She knew this because she might have peeked at what was in this cabin while the captain was away taking care of whatever disturbance was unfolding outside.

But she only peeked for a moment and only long enough to see that Captain Beaumont was much more than just captain of this vessel. Not that she would ever tell.

The cabin door opened and another pair of boots stepped inside. These she recognized as belonging to the kind doctor who reminded her a little of her grandfather.

Her heart lurched just a little at the recollection of the man she called Abuelo. Only knowing that he and Mama had been together when their lives were lost kept her from being completely devastated.

Now that she was an orphan and unfit for service as a privateer, what would she do?

"She is sleeping," Captain Beaumont said. "What news have you brought me?"

"Rao reports the repairs to our ship are minimal and will be completed before sunset. Piper sends a similar message in regard to the sails."

"Then we lift anchor as soon as we are able." He paused. "And what of the vessel that attacked us?"

"We fished a man out of the water, but the rest of the fools aboard were not so lucky. The crew voted to burn it rather than surrender. Israel is with him in the brig. I've been to see to him, and he's told quite a tale."

Maribel's ears perked up at that statement. She'd read something similar in *The Notorious Seafaring Pyrates and Their Exploits*. Though she hadn't understood why men would rather go down on a burning ship than submit to their captors, she did admit it was an effective way to keep a vessel from being used in illegal trade.

"What is his condition?"

"Burns are nasty injuries to treat, and as extensive as his were, it is unlikely he will live beyond a day or two."

She clenched her eyes shut against the image of a man on fire. Still she could not stop thinking of what that must be like. More proof she was not suited for life aboard a privateer's ship.

The doctor spoke for a moment in a voice too soft for Maribel to hear clearly. From the few words she could make out, the discussion had turned to pirates.

The captain shifted positions as Maribel opened her eyes. While the nice doctor was still standing by the door, the captain seemed poised to jump from his chair at any moment.

"Is he talking?" Captain Beaumont asked.

"Indeed he is. I suggest you hear the story directly from him."

The boots moved again, and this time the captain rose. "I will have the abbreviated version first, please," he said with the tone of a man most unhappy with whatever he'd been hearing from the doctor. "Then I will decide if I wish to pay him a visit."

"The abbreviated version is there is a bounty on us all, but more specifically, there is a bounty on your head."

Captain Beaumont took a step to the side and laughed. "Connor, you had me worried. Of course there's a bounty on us. We've made quite a few Spanish ships' captains unhappy when we've relieved them of their cargo in the name of France." He sat back down. "I thought this would be of interest to me."

"It should very well be," the doctor snapped. "That ship was just the warning. They've got a much bigger and well-provisioned vessel coming along behind her, and the man in the brig believes that's the one that will take us down."

"A strategy that does not surprise me," the captain said far too lightly, in Maribel's opinion. "We will be long gone before the companion ship can find us. Have Rao and Piper double their efforts. Take every man off his duty to assist them if necessary."

"I will pass on your order," he said. "However, there's more, and I'd like you to hear it from me first."

"As you know, last year the regent died and Louis XV has ascended to the throne. With that change of events comes a change in the leadership on many levels, albeit a slow change."

"Get to the point," Captain Beaumont snapped.

There was a moment of silence, and Maribel wondered if the doctor would continue. Finally he cleared his throat.

"Yes, well, the result of all that tumult is that after the passage of a year's time, those who were friendly to us in the higher levels of government have been replaced with others who do not take lightly the death of a Spanish nobleman at your hands. We are technically at peace with Spain, you know, and perhaps this particular nobleman had French friends in high places."

"More likely French friends to whom he owed vast sums of money. As to your statement regarding Spain, I agree we are technically at peace," the captain echoed, his sarcasm thick. "But still charged with carrying out the duties our Letters of Marque allow."

"I will call upon your own use of the word *technically* to respond. Yes, we technically are still charged with carrying out these duties."

The captain pounded his fist on his desk, resulting in a small glass object falling to the floor. The crystal shattered into a thousand pieces of sparkling debris.

"And has anyone accused me of being derelict in these duties or holding out profits that rightly belonged to the crown?" the captain asked.

"To my knowledge, they have not."

"I wager those same men would not take it lightly if I were to surrender my letters and walk away from the enterprise that has lined their pockets these past few years."

"I doubt you'll be given the chance," Mr. Connor said. "That ship was sent to kill you by men who hold the purse strings of the king's coffers and are capable of ordering any vessel in the Royal Navy to fire against us. Likely the next attempt will not be such an abysmal failure."

"So I am now a pariah and my friend is now my enemy?"

"You are a wanted man, yes." The doctor moved toward the captain. "But this is not completely unexpected. That is why we made the plans to. . ."

The rest of the doctor's words were lost as Maribel's heart thumped hard against her chest. How she hated the privateering life.

Please, Lord, just put me on solid ground somewhere and leave me there. Anywhere.

"Then we sail for New Orleans," Captain Beaumont said.

"We cannot do that, lad," the doctor countered. "Where do you think these French vessels call their home port here? If you were to attempt to sail into the city, you would be immediately arrested as a traitor to the crown."

"Which crown?" the captain quipped.

"Truly, lad, it could be either, if you really think on it. Though the French are after you, I warrant the Spaniards would like to see you strung up as a pirate."

"And the rest of you along with me," he said thoughtfully. "Yes, I see the dilemma. Then we sail for another port, and along the way we make plans to find another vessel. Would that solve the issue?"

"It would solve one of the issues," he said. "The other, you and I have discussed at length on more than one occasion."

"I will not consider it."

The room fell silent for a moment. "You may not be given the option."

Seven weeks later

Don Pablo Cordoba paced the confines of the vessel and paused only occasionally to look outside at the stars that shone above them. Word traveled fast in his world, and knowledge of a nobleman's death at the hands of a man who held French Letters of Marque could spell disaster for those in power in France.

Thus Don Pablo had stepped in to mediate what could quickly have become more than just an unfortunate situation. He had done so, not letting any of the parties know he had motives other than keeping peace between the country of his birth and the country where his roots went deep.

While he had never held much love for the place where his grandmother was born, he did have numerous relatives scattered across the positions of power in the French capital. Relatives who were happy to prove loyalty to him by seeing that the death of his son was avenged.

Not that he had any particular interest in avenging Antonio's regrettable demise. Like as not, the son he hardly knew deserved whatever had happened. At least his Isabel was not here to see what had become of her only son. A mother's love transcended the truth of her child's true personality. Don Pablo, however, had a very clear idea of just what Antonio had become.

Sadly, his attempt to remove Antonio from the lives of Maribel and her mother had turned into a disaster that he must remedy. Of course, he would not tell Mary about Antonio's death until he could also tell her what happened to her daughter. To his granddaughter.

At least he could count on the silence of his friends on that matter. And for those who were not friends, he could count on allegiance. To cross him was something few dared to do.

None now that the regent was no longer in charge.

He took up his pacing again, this time walking out a solution to how best to retrieve a girl he prayed with each step would be found alive. Testimony freely given by men who he believed were truly witnesses to his son's murder led him to believe the girl was spirited away aboard a vessel known to sailors as the *Ghost Ship*.

All agreed the girl was very much alive and unharmed when she was taken. Thus, he would continue to believe this until the moment he held her in his arms once more.

So as to keep her from learning she was a widow, Mary was installed in the cabin next door and would be traveling with him to

New Orleans. The appointment he had secured would provide for him a home and a salary that would hardly compensate for all he left behind in Spain.

However, it would provide a base of operations that would allow him closer access to the ruffians who saw fit to steal his precious Maribel. And as he had promised Mary, he would stop at nothing until she was returned.

What he did not tell Mary was what he planned to do with the men when they were found. That was certainly not a fit conversation for a woman of her delicate disposition.

One room past the door to Don Pablo's cabin, Mary Cordoba leaned against the wall and stared up at the stars overhead. The night was clear, eerily so since their passage had met with such terrible weather until they reached the warm waters of the Gulf of Mexico, or *Seno Mexicano* as the crewmen had been calling it since they reached this latitude just before sunset.

Somewhere her Maribel was looking at the same stars. She had to be. The alternative was unthinkable.

Mary turned her back and closed her eyes. It was her fault. Had she not defied her mother and father and fled to Spain to marry Antonio, life would not have taken her to this place of desperation.

She let out a long breath and opened her eyes once more. If she had not married him, there would be no Maribel.

That was also unthinkable.

CHAPTER 8

From her place in the lookout post high up in the rigging, Maribel studied the stars overhead. Though to most of the sailors on this vessel, duty in the lookout post was considered the worst assignment, it was her favorite.

Not only could she see for miles in all directions during the day, but she could also dream beneath the stars at night. Dream with her eyes wide open and her senses finely tuned to detect any approaching vessels, of course.

Seven weeks ago, the captain had sailed their other ship—the one people called the *Ghost Ship*—into a secluded bay somewhere off the coast of Mexico and burned her to the waterline. Waiting for them was this sloop, a fast ship with a low draft that allowed them to slip in and out of narrow channels and bays.

It also allowed for a much smaller crew, which displeased those who were not chosen to rejoin them. Those men were much happier when they discovered the amount they would be paid for remaining behind.

Several storms had kept them from sailing out into open waters, but Maribel did not mind. With the vessel rocking at anchor in the shallow green waters of the Caribbean Sea, life aboard the ship that had been christened the *Escape* was idyllic.

Though they were all under orders not to leave the ship, the captain did allow for plenty of time for Maribel to read when she was not otherwise assigned to a task. Thus, in the past seven weeks, she had begun the task of reading every book in the captain's library.

Maribel had also convinced the captain to allow her to bring whatever book she might be reading up to the post with her, although she had to prove to him after many weeks of work that she could read and remain alert at the same time. Oh, but prove it she did.

However, that was the only negative to the night watch. No matter how hard she tried to convince him, the captain refused to allow her a lamp or even a candle up in the watch post, so her reading was limited to nights when the moon shone at its brightest. She understood the reason behind it, of course, but the night watches seemed so much longer this way.

"Are you trying to read up there?"

She peered down in the direction the voice had come from. "No sir, Captain," she said.

"Good," came his good-humored reply. "Reading in the dark will damage your eyes, you know."

The same thing the captain said almost every night when he came to check on her. "Yes, sir," she responded as usual.

The ship rocked and swayed over seas that were only slightly more choppy than usual. The moon was a mere fingernail in the southern sky, so she would not be reading tonight.

In the east, lightning skittered across the clouds from east to west, as it often did on warm nights like tonight. She had learned to tell the difference between what the men called heat lightning and the other type, which indicated a squall was present.

William Spencer told her he'd once seen a book with pictures in it that showed different types of clouds and gatherings of stars called constellations. Someday she would find that book and read it from cover to cover, memorizing all the patterns of stars so she could recognize them up in her watch post.

Likely she would have plenty of time to search and even more time to read and remember what was in the book. No one aboard the ship wanted this job, likely because she was the only one who did not get sick from the rocking motions.

What Maribel would never admit is that the first time she was assigned to this task, she nearly lost her breakfast of porridge on the heads of the men working on the deck below. Pride alone kept her from embarrassment, and pride taught her how to remain that way.

Lightning flashed again, this time zigzagging west to east. Something on the horizon caught her eye. Was that a sail?

Her heart lurched. In all the nights she spent on watch, she could count on one hand the times she thought she had seen something out on the water. Only once had there actually been another vessel, and it had turned out to be a stranded merchantman flying the English flag.

She lifted the spyglass to her eye with trembling hands. The sky remained dark with only tiny pinpoints of light to remind her there were stars overhead.

"Calm down," she whispered. "It's probably nothing. Probably not sails at all."

Maribel lowered the spyglass and waited with more patience than she thought she could possess. As each second ticked by, she wanted to scream. Wanted to have an answer to the question that was causing her heart to race and her hands to shake.

There! Lightning once again showed in the clouds, winding its way parallel to the horizon. A horizon where three sails had gained on them.

She opened her mouth to shout a warning and found her breath frozen in her lungs. *Pray away the fear. Pray away the fear. Pray away. . .*

Trying again, she managed to cough out a cry. Nothing like words but a noise all the same.

"What's that?" William Spencer, who always seemed to be assigned to a watch below her post, called from below.

"There is a ship," she managed with more strength. "I see sails! Due east."

William sounded the alarm as Maribel gripped the edge of the watch post with one hand and lifted the spyglass up to her eye with the other. This time she held it still, and after what seemed like endless moments of blackness, she saw the sails again.

Having learned all the vessels by name, she called out what she saw. She counted the masts and made sure there were two and that they were square-rigged. The next time the lightning illuminated the vessel, she confirmed there were two sails on the mainmast. Yes, there was the topsail and the gaff sail.

"Brigantine," she called. "No flags showing."

Probably British in origin, she decided after considering the drawings of vessels she had seen in the captain's books. Rather than be wrong, however, Maribel kept her opinion to herself.

From what she knew of the brigantines, they were swift and easily maneuvered in all types of seas. They were a favorite of pirates and as a naval vessel.

She took a deep breath and let it out slowly to calm her racing heart. Whoever was at the helm, this was no stranded merchantman.

She remained still, watching and waiting until the sails were once again illuminated. Or should have been.

Maribel lowered the spyglass and swiped at the glass on the end to see if perhaps it was smudged. There was nothing on the eastern horizon.

Swinging her attention across the horizon, she spied the sails now tacking to the west. After taking a moment to calculate, she called out the new coordinates. She continued to repeat this process, forgetting her fear. Down below on deck, the crew was going about the business of preparing to engage in battle, all the while remaining silent and working under cover of darkness.

Finally she became aware that someone was climbing up to join her. "William Spencer?" she called as she trained her spyglass on the horizon. "What are you doing up here?"

"Captain sent me to fetch you. Said he doesn't want you up

here in harm's way."

"You know you cannot spend five minutes up here without getting ill. How in the world will you manage to continue to call out coordinates if your supper is on the men below?"

"That is not. . ."

She turned around to spare her friend a glance. Even in the dim light, she could see from his expression that the motion of the vessel was already causing him discomfort.

"I told you I can manage this. I know the captain won't like what you have to tell him, but I will take the blame once this kerfuffle is finished, all right?"

Maribel waited for William to speak or even nod, but he said nothing. Instead, he stood very still and gripped the edge of the lookout post.

"For goodness' sake," she told him. "Get out of here before you keep me from doing my job. If I am worrying about you, I cannot be tracking that brig."

At that, William complied. She imagined he carried a mixture of relief and dread with him as he shimmied back down the mast, but at least he did not carry the remains of his supper on the front of his shirt.

She returned to her task, lifting the spyglass to her eye. What was it about some men, especially the ones aboard the *Escape*, who held the opinion that in times of danger they ought to protect her? There was nothing she couldn't do just as well as they could.

Maribel let out a long breath as she waited for the next lightning to dance along the clouds. Indeed, there were some tasks she could do better than any of them, chief among them the job she was doing tonight. William had just proved her point.

Lowering the spyglass, she glanced over the edge to make sure William hadn't fallen due to his impending illness. Behind her something cracked with a noise so loud it deafened her.

Something white tangled around her. Her ears rang as she fought to find fresh air again.

Another crack, something she felt rather than heard.

Then came the sensation of flying.

Or falling.

And then the world went black.

⚜

"I can't find her, Captain," Israel said. "We've all looked, and she just isn't anywhere."

Jean looked up at his second-in-command, exhaustion tugging at the corners of his understanding. They'd outrun the French ship, but only after they disabled their opponent by taking out the vessel's mainmast.

"That cannot be," he said as he let out a long breath and scrubbed at his face. The smell of blood, gunpowder, and smoke clung to him, and he wanted nothing more than to fall into his bunk and sleep. "She would not leave her duty. Go look in the top of the mainmast. And if she's fallen asleep, wake her and tell her she'll spend time in the brig the next time she is derelict in her duties."

Israel's face wore a stricken look. "That's just it, sir. The lookout post is gone. Shot through by a cannonball, I'd guess. Missed the mainmast but got. . ." He shook his head. "I can't say it, sir."

Jean stumbled to his feet, his exhaustion gone. "Turn the ship around and go back to where the first shot from the French brigantine was fired."

"Consider it done," Israel said, moving much faster than a man of his size should have been able to move.

The sloop had been a wise choice, for this vessel was easily able to maneuver around and head back toward the scene of the battle at a fast clip. With all its sails unfurled, the *Escape* practically flew toward their destination.

At some point during the voyage, Connor came to stand beside him at the wheel. They remained in silence, watching the waves with Jean preferring not to speak. Apparently the doctor felt the same, for he remained stoic with his attention focused straight ahead.

"Lad," he finally said. "I would be remiss if I did not remind you that we are taking this vessel back into waters where a French Navy vessel may be nursing her wounds." He paused. "And not only nursing a grudge against us but also likely aware of the bounty on your head."

"I am aware of that," Jean said through clenched jaw. "And if there was a way for me to search for Maribel without the rest of you, I would certainly exercise that option."

"You are once again taking on a responsibility that is not yours alone to bear," he said.

"I'll not have another of your lectures, Connor. Not tonight, and certainly not on this topic."

"So you do not wish to hear that I believe you are a fool for risking your life to go back and try to find that girl?"

"I do not," Jean said evenly as he concentrated on the horizon.

"Good," he said. "Because I do not believe that at all."

"No?" Jean spared him a glance. Slowly a smile dawned. Connor answered the smile with a nod.

No more words were necessary. As he always had, and as he had done for Jean's father before him, Evan Connor would follow him into battle and remain at his side.

When Israel called out that they had reached their destination, there was no sign of the French vessel. Jean ordered the anchor dropped. Though the danger was there, so was the opportunity to retrieve the child.

A loud splash announced that the skiff had been lowered down into the inky water. Evan held the lamp as Jean slid down the rope to land in the craft.

"Send down the lamp, then release the ropes," Jean told him.

"Not yet," came the booming voice of Israel Bennett.

His second-in-command tucked the rope into the crook of his

arm and slid down with his free hand. The skiff rocked as Israel landed.

"I'll row," Israel announced. "You hold the lamp." He paused, obviously realizing he had overstepped his position. "Unless you prefer it the other way around, sir."

"No," Jean said as Connor released the rope. "Head us off in that direction. I will let you know if I see any sign of her."

"You worried about those Frenchmen coming back after us?" Israel asked.

"Not my concern right now," Jean said.

"Mine either, sir," was his swift response. "I figure I do my part and the Lord'll do His. That generally works best for me."

Jean gave the statement some thought and then discarded his responses. No need to comment on something he struggled to understand. Israel was generous in sharing his faith, although Jean understood that even less.

How was a man who was taken prisoner at the hands of his enemies and sold into slavery able not only to forgive those men but to rise above it all to still hold on to his faith in God? It made no sense.

"You got questions, then you go ahead and ask them, Captain," Israel said as he continued to row.

"Don't know what to ask," Jean said.

Israel gave a thoughtful nod. "Well then, when you do know, that'd be the time, sir."

Jean nodded. A comfortable silence fell between them as Israel rowed and Jean searched the waters for even a scrap of sail or piece of the lookout post.

Though they remained on the search well beyond the time when the sun rose, there was no evidence that Maribel had been lost here. Jean ordered the anchor lifted, and they moved to another location where the lookout thought he saw debris.

The process continued throughout the day and into the night. Still nothing was found that would offer any idea as to where the youngest member of the crew had gone.

The crew of the *Escape* was lifting anchor to move to yet another location when Connor intervened. "Israel, please call Mr. Rao up to take your place. I will stand in for our captain while the two of you get some rest."

Both men argued the point, but the doctor refused to back down. Finally Jean nodded. "We are of no use to Maribel if we can hardly hold up our heads or keep our eyes open." He turned his attention to the doctor. "I will have four hours' rest, and then we go out again. I've given the coordinates already. I trust you to find that location and drop anchor there."

"It will be done as you ask," Connor said as he handed Jean a dipper of water. "Although as your doctor I would suggest more sleep than just four hours."

Jean regarded his old friend with an icy stare and then took several grateful sips. Though he understood why Connor would make such a suggestion, the idea of any rest at all while Maribel might be floating in the ocean was appalling to him.

A stronger man would not need such a thing. And yet as he looked at Israel, he knew the thought was absurd. No man could live long without sleep.

"Argue with me," he finally said to Connor, "and I will make it three hours. Perhaps two."

"And what do I do to make it six, Jean? Or eight?" The doctor returned Jean's stare, his expression showing concern.

"Nothing," Jean said as he turned to walk away. "Connor, send someone to wake us in four hours' time."

"Aye, Captain," he said. "And I'll have Cook prepare a meal for you to take with you." He held up his hands as if to fend off any response from Jean. "When you find her, she will likely be hungry."

A point he could not argue, so he made no attempt to try. For as much as he held out hope that Maribel Cordoba was floating nearby and awaiting discovery, serious doubts had taken root. Given the time that had elapsed and the distance she would have had to fall, human logic and reason told him survival was unlikely.

Something else, though he was unwilling to call it faith, told him otherwise. So in four hours he would rise from his bunk and commence the search again. He would continue to search until whatever it was inside him that sent him out called him back in.

Jean allowed his eyes to fall shut, but still sleep eluded him. Never once had he allowed himself to reconsider any decision he made as captain of a vessel. To do so could cripple his ability to lead.

But tonight, in the darkness of his cabin, Jean let his mind sort through the steps on the path that led him here. The choices that sent an innocent if exasperating girl out into open water during the blackness of night.

He slammed his fist against the wall beside him and sat up. There was just no sense to any of it.

Then it came to him, the knowledge of his fault slamming against his chest with enough force to knock him backward. Jean Beaumont, the notorious privateer with a bounty on him, hung his head and cried.

The green water was pretty and warm, just like what Maribel had imagined in the books she read about the Caribbean Sea. Her head hurt and her eyes wanted to close, but every time she tried to sleep she fell off the piece of wood that kept her floating along.

If she tried hard, she could remember a disagreement she had with William Spencer. To be exact, she could remember that she and William exchanged words, although the particulars of the discussion were unclear. If only he were here to remind her. And maybe to continue the discussion.

Looking up at the stars, she had counted more constellations than she thought she knew. When she could find no more familiar star patterns, she began to create names for her own until the sun peeked over the horizon and ruined her game.

Maribel rolled over onto her stomach without sliding off the board, a skill she had developed with practice in the hours since she woke up from whatever nightmare landed her in the water. Until now she hadn't thought about how the water turned from inky black to deep purple and finally to red, gold, and then green as the sun rose, even though she must have seen it happen from the watch post.

The seas were calm now, with only a slight wind to propel her over the waves, putting her in mind of Robinson Crusoe. Maybe she would find her own island and live there.

Maribel gave that some thought even though her head hurt so much that it became hard to string ideas together. Yes, she could live on an island, but no, she would not like to live there without friends. And certainly she would miss reading her books.

Oh, but a nice island where she had friends and books? She smiled even though it hurt her lips. Now that sounded just right.

Sound.

She opened her eyes but closed them again because they were too heavy to control. Yes, there it was again, a sound that wasn't the waves or the wind or the occasional seabird squawking.

But what was it? People talking?

"Captain?" she called.

Still the talking continued, but she could say nothing more. Not right now. Just a little nap, and then she would call out so Captain Beaumont would find her.

Because he would find her. She knew it.

She absolutely and positively knew it.

CHAPTER 9

Evan Connor walked down the passageway toward the captain's cabin. Jean Beaumont may believe himself to have superhuman endurance, but as his doctor and longtime friend of his family, Evan knew otherwise. He'd patched up the man since he was a lad, and likely would continue doing so until the Lord took him home.

Thus, Jean might eventually forgive him for not following the specific command to awaken him after four hours of rest. He took a deep breath and let it out slowly. And because Jean would probably not forgive him for the sleeping draught Evan slipped into the dipper of water he'd offered the captain, that information would not be mentioned.

He opened the door slowly and was greeted by the sound of the captain's rhythmic snoring. Though he was sorely tempted to let the man sleep even longer, a full seven hours had elapsed since Jean laid his head on his bunk.

Israel and Rao had resumed the search two hours ago. A second boat had been made seaworthy and was heading off in the opposite direction with two more crew members.

The carpenter's assistants were working on a third boat, but it might be another hour or more before the craft was ready for use. That news would be delivered gently and only if the captain asked.

Evan closed the door and let out a long breath as he set his medical bag on the floor beside him and then lit the lamp he'd brought along for this task. Where had the time gone? Only yesterday the man in the bunk had been a lad on his papa's knee.

When he swore an oath to his best friend to protect this son of his, Evan had not expected where that oath would lead. Nor had he questioned it.

The snoring had ceased. "Who's there?" Jean demanded, his speech slurred.

"It is I, Evan Connor," he said. "You wished me to let you know when it was time to awaken."

Silence.

"Jean? Are you awake?" he said as he crept forward.

Loud snoring met his question. Perhaps he underestimated the amount of sleeping draught he had slipped into the water dipper.

A roar of noise went up on the deck overhead. Evan froze. The men's shouts echoed in the cabin, but their words were undecipherable.

Jean shifted on the bunk, but his snoring continued. As the noise persisted on deck, Evan debated whether to leave him there or to wake him up.

The warning bell rang, and his decision was made. "Wake up, Jean. Your crew needs you."

Whatever was happening above them, the situation was urgent. Shouts of the men competed with the sounds of the bell that foretold an emergency.

"Jean," he called as he walked toward the bunk.

The sound of something crashing and a flash of light sent him reeling backward. Smoke engulfed him as he choked to find his breath. Beneath him, the ship listed heavily to starboard.

When he could manage to climb to his feet, Evan looked around to survey the damage. What must have been a cannonball had burst through the wall next to Jean's bunk, splintering the wood planks.

The bunk where Jean had been sleeping only moments before was practically gone, its wood splintered and the mattress destroyed. Seeing the oil lamp dangling precariously on the edge of the table, he caught it just as it fell.

The force of the blast had thrown Jean away from the place where he had been sleeping. Upon closer inspection, he found the captain lying on the floor beneath the ruins of his desk. His ever-present cutlass glittered in the lamplight as it slid away from reach.

A moment of grief pierced his heart rendering Evan immobile as he viewed the tangled wreckage. Had he not given Jean the sleeping draught. . .

He quickly pushed the guilt aside to allow his medical training to take control. Though he had to move the lamp to haul away heavy boards and debris, he managed to free Jean and pull him to a place where he could more readily assess his injuries.

First he felt for a pulse. Yes, there it was. Faint but still a pulse.

Evan went back to the spot where he'd left his medical bag only to find it gone. After a lengthy search, he found the bag—its contents spilled—in the opposite corner of the room. He managed to collect his medicines and tools and return them to the bag despite the pitching of the ship.

Screams pierced the air as another round of cannonballs hit the foundering vessel. The French, for likely that was the source of the attack, obviously wanted the vessel dispatched to the bottom of the sea.

Those same Frenchmen would want the man laid out on the floor before him dispatched as well, first to a French prison so their bounty could be collected and then to the hangman's noose.

"Can you hear me, lad?" Connor shouted above the din.

No response.

"All right, then," he said, keeping the panic from his voice lest the lad hear him. "I'll make do. Probably best you're not awake to feel this. I warrant it will hurt."

Removing the captain's shirt, he saw injuries that were a threat to the lad's life. Evan reached for the brandy to cleanse the wounds and found the contents of the bottle empty and the glass shattered. He tore strips of linen and fashioned rudimentary bandages to stop the bleeding and splinted the arm he knew must be broken.

Evan swiped at the sweat on his brow and saw blood on his sleeve. He felt nothing, so either the cut was minor or shock had already set in.

In either case, it would not hinder his ability to care for his patient. He continued to bind wounds and assess Jean's condition despite the sounds of shouting and metal clanging that indicated the battle had moved from the sea to above him on the deck.

The bleeding was profuse, and it appeared Jean might not survive. All Evan could do was continue to pray as he dabbed at wounds and administered treatment that in all likelihood would be futile. He'd seen men in much better shape die of their injuries. Only the Lord could intervene and keep the lad with the living.

Footsteps sounded in the hallway, but there was no way to tell whether they were from friend or foe. When the door burst open, the question was answered.

"In here," a French sailor called.

Evan ignored the men to continue to administer more of the sleeping draught to the dying captain. If he could not save Jean, at least he could keep Jean from remembering his death.

Three French sailors stepped aside to allow a man of middle age and exceptional girth to enter the cabin. A lieutenant by the looks of him.

"What is this?" The lieutenant kicked debris out of the way to move closer in a manner that told Evan he must be their leader. "It appears your man is not doing well, sir. Who is he, and who are you?"

Evan ignored him. The head wound he thought he had closed was open again, and he would need more bandages. He reached into his medical bag for linen and continued the process of treating his patient.

"From what I see, it appears this is the captain's cabin," one of the sailors said. "See over there on the floor? That's the captain's log."

"Yes, I see that," their leader said as he nodded to one of

his men. "And somewhere in that desk would be the Letters of Marque, I would assume. You there." He nodded to one of the sailors. "Search the desk until the letters are found. If other items of value are there, take those as well." He offered Evan a smile that held no humor. "Confiscate them for the crown."

One sailor headed for the desk while the other fellow picked his way toward Evan and yanked him to his feet. Jean's head fell to the floor with a sickening thud.

The captain's eyes fluttered, but he remained unconscious and unaware of what was happening around him. Evan gave thanks for that mercy even as he prayed for a miracle. Prayed that somehow God would save them both or, failing this, that He would save his best friend's son.

There was more to this lad's life. More than this. Evan knew this with more certainty than any other living person other than the lad's father as he wrenched free of the Frenchman to once again cradle the man's head and apply pressure to the most troublesome of the wounds.

Please, Lord, give him another chance to go back to who he was.

"Which of you is the captain of this vessel? The man called Jean Beaumont?"

He stared into the eyes of the sailor who towered over him and said nothing. Blood flowed freely now and clouded his vision, but Evan held his ground and did not move.

Screams from somewhere above them tore through the silence. The ship heaved furiously as the smell of smoke once again filled the room. As the floor tilted, the sailor at the desk lost his footing and skidded into the wall.

In his hand, the sailor held up a document. "Got those letters, sir," he said. "Looks like we got our man."

"We're going down with this ship if we remain much longer," the lieutenant said as he nodded toward Evan. "Take the old man out and feed him to the fish. Those letters from this vessel will be enough to prove our victory and gain the bounty on Beaumont's head. And you," he said to the nearest sailor, "take the dead man on the floor and do the same."

Something inside Evan snapped. "Do not touch this man," he said.

The sailors pushed Evan aside to jerk Jean to his feet. His limp body hung between them, his eyes closed. The steep incline made for slow going as the men carried Jean toward the door. Behind Evan, the third sailor grasped his arms and held him in place.

"Wait! That man is innocent!"

As soon as the words escaped Evan's mouth, the men stopped. Their leader frowned. "What do you mean?"

"He is not part of our crew, sir," Evan said, affecting a deference he did not feel. "He is a hostage. A lawyer from New Orleans held against his will."

"Well now, that is interesting," he said. "Can you prove this?"

Evan squared his shoulders and stood straight despite the shifting floor beneath him. "His father will attest to what I say and likely provide a handsome reward for his return."

"How can you expect me to believe this?" their leader said.

With a shrug, Evan affected a casual expression. "I don't suppose a man of your intelligence could be fooled. I will give you the name of the man's father and you will tell me if you've heard of him. Perhaps that will convince you that you are better off delivering him to New Orleans and his family than dispatching him to his death."

"Go on," he said, and Evan knew he had him.

"Perhaps it is better I write a letter to his father. Give him an explanation of how he came to us so that he will not have you arrested on the spot when you bring his son home in this shape."

The Frenchman's thick brows rose. "Surely you cannot mean to threaten me with that sort of thing, sir. My reputation is impeccable."

"As is Monsieur Valmont's," he said as he looked down at Jean, his heart breaking but his face stoic. "Perhaps you have heard of his family? His father, Marcel, is well known in New Orleans as well as back home in France. And his uncle is Jean Baptiste Le Moyne."

Evan made this statement in French, all the more to impress the haughty sailor. Apparently his ploy worked, for the older man's thick eyebrows rose at the mention of the Valmont name.

"Valmont and Le Moyne, did you say?" The man's voice gave away that he was impressed by the names. Then abruptly his expression went serious.

"Perhaps you realize Le Moyne is once again the governor of Jeaniana? And no Frenchman could claim he did not know Marcel Valmont. He has the ear of the king, you know."

He shook his head. "Impossible. What would the son of Monsieur Valmont and the nephew of the *Sieur de Bienville* be doing here in the company of a wanted man? Take them both to the deck and throw them over. I have no more time for such foolishness."

"I doubt that is what his family would call this. They would deem it murder, of course."

"Murder? I call it service to the crown. Good riddance to bad men."

Mustering the last of his strength and every bit of his courage, he laughed. The ruse worked, as the Frenchmen stopped in their tracks to look at him as if he had lost his mind.

"You find this funny?" their leader said as he stormed toward him and slammed his fist into Evan's gut and sent him doubling over. The older man wrenched Evan's head up, forcing him to look into his eyes. "If he is a hostage, then who are you?"

"Captain Jean Beaumont at your service."

It was the leader's turn to laugh. "You expect me to believe an old man is the cause of all the trouble this ship's given our country? Not likely."

"Any trouble attributed to this crew is a lie told by those who wish to better themselves at our expense. This vessel has Letters of Marque from the king himself, and those letters have been followed exactly." He paused. "Perhaps you wish to dispute my statement?"

"Oh, so that is how it will be, then?" The man in charge laughed. "We are of a certain age, are we not? And men of our age, we are proud and brave until perhaps we are confronted with the shortness of the remainder of our days." He retrieved his flintlock pistol and made a show of loading it. "But what do we do when our days can either be lengthened or shortened by the mere response to a question? To tell the truth may be to lengthen your days, or perhaps a lie will save you. What to do?"

He refused to look away. His hands trembled, but as a physician Evan knew the response to be medical and not panic. In this moment, he felt absolutely no fear.

Evan returned his attention to Jean, who he hoped was still alive. He was broken and bloody but recognizable. Blood trickled down his forehead despite the bandages placed there. Still, his father would know him if he saw him, and Evan hoped he would also know that his old friend had tried his best to keep the lad safe.

"I am a man of honor, so I choose to tell the truth."

"Why should I believe you?"

"As I said, I tell the truth." He refused to blink as he stared down the barrel of the flintlock pistol. "That man is Jean-Luc Valmont. Take him to his father or his blood is on your hands. Either way, should he die before you reach New Orleans, the Valmont family will see that you all will hang for murder."

"We are protected by the French government," the lieutenant snapped.

He gave the older man a steely look. "Sir, I do hope you are extremely confident in that fact."

"Why wouldn't we be?" he asked, his tone haughty but his expression showing the slightest bit of discomfort.

"If you know the name Valmont, then you know the power Marcel Valmont wields in the higher levels of the French government and the power his brother-in-law has in the city of New

Orleans." Evan shrugged. "I am not certain the king or his men will stand behind a man of your rank should they be informed you chose to go through with this execution."

The lieutenant turned his attention to the sailor still rummaging through the desk. "Leave it and bring me those letters."

Obliging his commanding officer, the young man did as he was told. After reading the Letters of Marque, the lieutenant looked back over at Evan.

"So you say the young man is Jean-Luc Valmont?"

"He is indeed, and if you hope to get him to New Orleans without hanging for his murder, I will go with you to treat him. I am a physician. Make haste, though. He needs a soft bed and clean bandages."

"If he is Valmont, then that would make you a doctor, a ship's captain, and a fugitive with a bounty on his head." He gave Evan a sweeping look and then shook his head. "How do you manage it all?"

"We are wasting time, sir." Evan pressed past him, not caring that he'd pushed away a fully loaded flintlock. The only way off this sinking ship was to convince these men that they were more valuable alive than dead.

Before Evan could reach the door, one of the sailors had stepped up to block his exit. The young man grasped him by the arm and hauled him out of the way.

"Make way," the lieutenant said as he gave the order to remove Jean from the cabin. "See that he is given a bed and medical care," he added as two of the sailors carried the lad away.

A man came running down the passageway. "Sir," he called. "There are skiffs in the water. Our men saw two with men aboard heading this way. Shall we go after them?"

Evan schooled his expression so as not to give away his thoughts. "You have no time," he told them. "If you chase after small boats, you may be putting Mr. Valmont at risk of dying before he can reach the city. Do you want to explain your decision to his father?"

The lieutenant seemed to consider his statement a moment, and then he nodded. "Captain Beaumont is right," he said as he tucked the Letters of Marque under his arm and followed his men out into the corridor.

Gathering up his medical bag, Evan hurried to catch up to the sailors. He kept his attention straight ahead, knowing if he looked at any of the fallen crewmen, he would be unable to keep from stopping to help.

The walk across the deck seemed to take an eternity. It took everything he had not to be swayed by the cries of the men who needed him. But he had made a promise to his friend Marcel Valmont to deliver his son safely home, and he would stop at nothing, and for no one, until he kept that promise.

Evan watched while the lieutenant supervised his men as they hauled the lad over onto the French vessel, and then waited for his turn. Around him, French sailors were fleeing back to their ship, some of them with items they did not appear to own.

All the cannons on the *Escape* had either been moved to the other ship or tossed into the sea. Around them in the green waters, debris and bodies floated.

Finally the lieutenant gave one last sweeping glance around the vessel and then returned his attention to the last few members of his crew still aboard. "Burn this tub to the waterline and shoot anyone who tries to flee."

Then he lifted his flintlock and shot Evan through the heart.

CHAPTER 10

Jean Baptiste "Bienville" Le Moyne had been pacing the confines of his home near the river ever since news arrived that his sister's son had been found aboard the vessel of a notorious privateer. Captain Jean Beaumont was well known, both in France and here in New Orleans, and the news that there was now a French bounty on his head had come as a surprise to many.

A Spanish bounty, of course, but for the king of France to turn on a man who allegedly brought much in the way of coin and supplies into his royal coffers? There had to be more to the story than what he'd gleaned from those few Frenchmen willing to speak to him.

The door opened and his aide stepped inside. "They've got him down at the dock, Governor."

"Thank you," he said as he hurried to greet the man he hoped would someday follow in his footsteps.

Bienville had been reluctant to bless the marriage of his sister to a much older man, but theirs had been a love match. And though the Spanish pirates had taken her when their sons were but babes, she had not been forgotten in the Valmont household.

The crowd parted ways as his aides alerted them that their governor was en route to the docks. A blustering fool in the uniform of the French Navy came hurrying in his direction.

"What an honor it is for you to be visiting my ship, Monsieur Bienville. Please come with me and I will show you to where we have kept your nephew in comfort."

He gave the vessel a cursory glance, offering a brief nod toward the men assembled on the deck in his honor. "My nephew, please," he instructed the officer.

"Yes, of course. Please follow me."

Bienville attended the captain until they reached the room where Jean-Luc was being kept. Nodding to his aide, he pressed past the officer. There a man lay on a cot, a sheet covering him. Where there once had been a handsome and strong young man, a broken and bloody image of Jean-Luc Valmont stared back at him with unseeing eyes.

Bienville dropped to his knee beside the cot. "How long has he been like this?"

"Since the men brought him aboard," the captain said.

"Do not let this man leave," he told his aide as he nodded toward the man in charge. "His father will have questions, and I will have the answers."

"Yes, of course," the Frenchman said, his head nodding in obedience. "When the old man told us he was your nephew, of course it was my privilege to deliver him back to you in a suitable condition."

"If that is your definition of suitable, I am grateful he was no worse than this," he snapped. "What have you fools done to him?"

"I assure you, sir, we have given him the best of care," he protested. "Any injury to his person can be attributed to the pirate Beaumont. The old man claimed this Monsieur Valmont was his prisoner. I found nothing to dispute this."

The Frenchman wrung his hands as perspiration dotted his brow. This man knew more than he was saying.

"As soon as he has been given a cursory medical examination, I will authorize his transport to his father's home for further care." He looked to the captain. "Send a man you trust to arrange for a litter and men to carry it. And if you botch this job, it will go even worse for you."

"Even worse?" He tugged at his collar and then removed his handkerchief to dab at his damp brow. "I do not understand."

"Of course you do," he said evenly. "And I wager every man on this ship understands as well. You attacked the ship where my nephew was being held. During that attack, the fact he suffered serious injuries is obvious to—"

"Forgive me, sir, but I must protest. We were fired upon."

"You, sir, are a liar. Find a better story and tell it to someone who might be more easily deceived. There was a bounty on Beaumont's head, and you went after him without caring who else might be on his ship. Did you sink it? And tell me the truth, because I will read the report myself when you claim your reward."

"We did, I believe," he said, "although the vessel was still burning when we set off. At that point we were more interested in making haste to New Orleans to see to your nephew's restored health than we were in following some protocol regarding pirate vessels."

"Privateer, sir, and if you don't know the difference, I can certainly see that you are taught."

"I do know the difference," he said, looking quite displeased.

"Your physician has arrived, sir," his aide told him.

"Send him in."

Bienville stepped back so his nephew could be examined. Once the sheet was pulled away from Jean-Luc's body, the extent of his injuries was obvious. A jagged red scar traversed the muscles of his chest while another snaked down his leg, ending just above the ankle. One arm had been bound with a rudimentary bandage from his fist to his elbow. Thick strips of muslin covered his forehead, allowing only wisps of his black hair to show beneath the bloodstained fabric.

"What matter of heathen. . ."

Bienville shook his head. Giving way to his temper would serve no purpose. He moved back to allow the physician to complete his examination and then called for the litter to retrieve the lad and bring him to his father's home.

"Will he live?" he demanded of the physician.

From the man's expression, he had his answer. Still, he needed to hear the words.

"You may speak freely," he told him.

"Then if I speak freely, I would have to tell you that this lad is as near to death as I have seen a man with breath still in his body. Whether he lives or dies, it is in God's hands."

Bienville clasped his hand on the physician's shoulder. "Go with him and see if you can explain to God how very much his family wishes him to live." He offered a smile that held no humor. "And I shall do the same."

The task of moving him to the litter and removing him from the vessel had been completed, and the litter carrying Jean-Luc was on its way toward the docks when a young French soldier hurried toward him.

"Monsieur," he said as he glanced around and then returned his attention to Bienville. "What the captain said, well, it is not completely correct. You see, there was a threat to throw both men off the ship until the old man, Captain Beaumont, he convinced the lieutenant that he was the one who deserved to die that day."

"So the man your superior officer killed saved my nephew?"

He seemed thoughtful and then finally nodded. "That's about the size of it, sir, although there was more to it than that. Talking and arguing and such before the shooting. Not Monsieur Valmont, of course. He was in no shape to argue."

"I see."

"But your man there, he was indeed as you see him now, although I have no way of knowing if the injuries were sustained before we overtook the vessel. He was in a bad way when we got to the captain's cabin, although there was one thing odd."

"What was that?"

"The privateer, he was doctoring Monsieur Valmont when we found them. Said he was a physician. Now, I've wanted the reward much as the next man on our ship, so I've studied up on the *Ghost Ship* and its captain. That wasn't the *Ghost Ship*, and not once did I hear anything about Captain Beaumont being a physician."

"I appreciate your candor, son. One more question: How did you overtake the vessel?"

He looked sheepish. "The usual away. We used our cannons, and then, once we had control of the ship, we. . ." He looked away. "Suffice it to say, the privateer's vessel was under attack when our men arrived on its deck, and that attack continued until such time as Jean Beaumont's life came to an end. And as to that not being the *Ghost Ship*, our lieutenant had word from fellows he knew in the navy who pointed out that ship as belonging to Beaumont. Beyond that, I do not know any more."

"I see." He paused. "Thank you." Noting the man's expectant look, he added, "Is there something else?"

"There is," he said. "Would you come with me? It'll only take a minute, but it is important."

Bienville nodded to his aide, and the three of them walked with the sailor to a spot in the rear of the vessel. There the lad opened a barrel and pulled out a heavy silver cutlass with a jeweled scabbard and presented it to Bienville.

"For what purpose would I wish to take this weapon?" he asked.

"We took it off your nephew," he said. "I thought it only right that it be returned to his family."

"You're certain Jean-Luc was wearing this cutlass when he was found?"

"Absolutely certain," he said. "Took it off him myself before the men could get him out of the captain's cabin."

"So my nephew, a lawyer by trade, was wearing this cutlass when he was found in Beaumont's cabin?"

"That's the whole of it, sir."

He nodded to the aide. "Reward this man for his diligence." He moved closer. "And see that he understands we wish this story to go no further."

Bienville held the magnificent weapon up to the waning sunlight and watched the jewels sparkle. The craftsmanship appeared to be Spanish, the stones exquisite. It was a ferocious instrument that should belong to a man of war, not a man of the law.

"Lock this in my library," he told his aide. "Someday I will have a conversation with Jean-Luc about this."

As he said the words, he knew they would not speak of it. And not because he believed his nephew would not be around to have this talk.

Rather, he had long ago learned there were things men did not discuss. Things that would lead to information best not given.

This cutlass and its provenance was most certainly one of those things.

It was better the girl did not recall when they found her. Had she opened her eyes or given any indication she recognized them, neither of them would have been able to leave her with the Mother Superior.

She was safe there. Much safer than she would be with them.

Had he not held a deep belief in the Lord, Israel might have believed their spying the floating plank on the vast green sea as some accident of nature. As a coincidence.

But there were no coincidences. Not when God directed paths and sent boats floating in just the right direction and at just the right time to arrive in just the right place.

They were meant to find her, just as they were meant to set aside their selfish wishes and see that she had a proper raising on the island of the nuns and orphan children. The island where his old friend, the Mother Superior, would keep her safe.

As the island appeared on the horizon, Israel cradled the girl while Rao did the rowing. It was only right given his higher rank aboard the vessel they'd served upon together. Anyone who might think it odd that a slave outranked a man whose skin was pale would never dare say it to the captain.

At least not more than once.

He and Rao prayed over that child as the skiff slid along toward Isla de Santa Maria. Prayed that the Lord would spare her.

Prayed that He would see she grew into a fine young lady.

And selfishly, they prayed that they would both see Maribel Cordoba again, even if she was never to know who they were or their connection to her survival.

When wood slid against sand, Israel held tight to the girl so as not to jostle her. Had he thought walking barefoot might keep from waking her, he would have tossed his boots into the skiff and headed off toward the chapel, caring not for what brambles and rocks pierced his feet.

But Maribel seemed unable to wake, something that concerned Israel greatly. Though he was no expert on medical conditions, he knew sleeping through all that had happened could not be a good sign.

He would be certain to tell Mother Superior of this.

"Bring her to the chapel," a soft voice said.

Of course Mother Superior had seen their approach. Nothing and no one arrived on this island without first being noticed.

Israel spied the nun coming around the corner, her dark gown hiding her from all but the closest inspection. He followed her instructions—and her—until he arrived in a small building that had obviously been converted to a chapel.

"I had a bed put in for her," she said, indicating that Israel should leave her there.

He would have. Should have. But he just could not.

Not yet.

Instead he told her of the girl's condition when he found her. Then he answered the nun's questions, all the while holding the sleeping girl in his arms. Finally, they arrived at a depth of silence that told him he was expected to leave her.

"A moment first?" he said as he carried her back outside under the last purple minutes before daybreak.

Here the light was just sufficient to take in her features and memorize them. "I want to know you when I see you again even if you do not know me," he told her, though she made no response. "Rao and I, we will find you someday, although you'll likely not know us."

"The captain too," Rao added solemnly. "He will want to find her."

"No," Israel said. "That is impossible."

CHAPTER 11

"If the captain is alive—and I believe the Lord has spared him—he cannot know about her. And she cannot know about him," Israel said.

"Why not?" Rao asked.

"Can you not see? There are two of us who were saved from the hands of the French attackers. Possibly there are two more, if the other skiff was launched as planned and had not returned. Four people who recognize the face of Jean Beaumont, and all of us are loyal to him as if he was our own blood."

"That is true."

He nodded at the girl in his arms. "But she also can recognize the captain, and she is but a child. She will someday grow to be a woman. Who can say then?"

"Aw, come on, Bennett," Rao said. "Surely the girl wouldn't do or say anything to harm the captain. He didn't take to her at first, and I know her being there broke the rule for females aboard ship, but he and she were fast friends by the end of it all."

"Fast friends, yes, between a young captain and a girl with her nose in a book and her mind carrying silly ideas of wanting to sail the seas as a privateer." He paused to look down at the sleeping girl. "But time will pass and she will grow to be a woman. Then who will she be? What will her allegiance be then?"

"I reckon I see your point, but it's awfully sad to think those two will never meet. He did save her life when he let her stay aboard. Might be good for her to know this."

"I warrant she will remember it," he said. "She will know there was a brief period of time when she was held in high esteem within the company of a crew of privateers who no longer live. It is good to allow her to have that memory. Not so good to believe more than this, I think."

"Are you certain?"

"As certain as I am that there is a bounty on all our heads." He paused to look Rao in the eyes. "Do you wish that bounty to extend to this girl? Because it will if she is considered to be associated with us."

Rao seemed to be sorting the thought out in his mind. Finally he nodded. "Then we agree to leave her be and let these nuns raise her."

"We do," Israel said. "And we agree should we ever have the occasion to come to this island, we will not give up our identities to her."

Rao nodded. "Agreed."

Israel looked up to see Mother Superior in the doorway. "It is time," she told him. "You have overstayed your welcome."

He nodded but still made no move to release the girl to the nun or to bring her in and settle her on the cot in the corner of the chapel. "She will be safe. You give me your word?"

"Yes," the old nun told him. "You have my word."

"And the other matter," he said firmly. "I will not have the man who saved me from slavery lose his life over what this girl might remember. The two can never meet, and she cannot know who he is. Promise me you will not allow this."

"I heard your conversation with Mr. Rao and can see that she might offer evidence that could harm your captain," she said. "I will tell no lies to her or your captain, but I will do my best to guide the girl away from those memories that might put them both in danger. Perhaps I can convince her to stay with us once she's grown. Is Miss Cordoba an intelligent girl?"

"Very," he said with pride. "Before the attack on our ship, I was teaching her to read Homer in the original Greek. She was a quick study. I warn you, though. Her favorite spot to read was up in the masts in the lookout's perch. More than once I found that a man who was assigned there had been convinced to give up his duties to her so that she could be up there with her book. You may be searching the treetops looking for her."

Mother Superior smiled. "Then we will discourage climbing as not appropriate for a lady but continue encouraging her to read so that someday she might become a teacher, although I do not believe our little library has such an impressive volume."

He smiled. "Then it will when I can manage it. And every time I am able, I will send more."

"We would accept your gift with thankful hearts, but you do realize we cannot allow anyone to know from whom this gift comes. To do so would be to lose all protection of your identity. I cannot protect the girl if she has any connection to you or your captain. Are we in agreement?"

He nodded. "We are."

"And there is one other requirement of accepting the child. She is the child of the deceased Antonio Cordoba and his late wife?"

"Yes," he said.

"It is my solemn vow to the Lord and to these children that I do all in my power to reunite families and see them returned to the homes where they once belonged. Should Miss Cordoba's extended family—perhaps grandparents, uncles, or siblings—search for her and find her here, I will not keep her from them. If that goes against my promise to you, then that promise will be broken."

"I understand," he said. "And I will not hold you to the promise should those circumstances occur. However, the girl believed herself to be an orphan, having watched her father die and claiming her mother and grandfather already deceased. She mentioned no siblings. I believe St. Mary of the Island will be the only home she knows."

"Very well, then," she said and then nodded at the girl. "I believe it is time, Mr. Bennett. These partings are best done swiftly else they might not be done at all."

"I suppose."

"Or there is another option," she said with that half grin she affected when she was teasing. "You could stay with us. I am certain a place like St. Mary of the Island could use a man of your intelligence, and I do enjoy our spirited discussions of literature and the Bible. Have you considered taking up the profession of teaching? You would have to give up your other endeavors, of course."

"As you likely expect, I must decline your very generous offer."

She met his gaze with an understanding look and then nodded to Rao, who had been standing in the shadows. "And you, sir? What say you about remaining with us here on Isla de Santa Maria? We could always use a strong man like you to do carpenter work and other tasks around the orphanage. Have you an interest in remaining with us?"

His eyes widened. "Thank you, but no, Mother Superior. Although my mother would be most pleased if I were to give up the seafaring life for work in a more godly location."

Mother Superior's attention lingered on Rao and then returned to Israel. "Then the offer shall remain open for both of you as long as you shall live, and you two will get on your way." She touched Israel's hand. "But first we pray for the girl, and we pray that your captain has survived. Then you will go and allow us to care for her while you search for him."

With a heavy heart, Israel carried the girl to the place the nuns had prepared for her. Rao said his good-byes and hurried past, likely ashamed at the tears in his eyes.

But Israel cared not whether anyone spied his sorrow.

The last time this gut-wrenching pain had taken hold of him he'd been in chains and saying good-bye to his bride Nzuzi under the shade of the judgment tree in Mbanza Kongo. Just as he promised her, he now promised the girl.

"You may not remember me, but I will find you again."

The weeks that followed were a blur of sounds, pains, and deepest black nights of endless slumber. Faint snatches of memories would rise up only to fade before Jean-Luc could make sense of them.

Faces appeared before him, but they swam in the filmy seas of uncertainty between life and death. None meant anything to him, and yet each one meant something. Their images blurred; the sounds they made, both loving and insistent, were only an echo in his head.

His mother spoke to him often, as did Jean-Luc's baby brother. Even in the depths of his slumber, he knew they were no longer alive. And yet in his fevered state, they appeared no less real than the parade of persons who attended his bedside.

Jean-Luc longed to ask his mother if she knew that the man who killed her had been dispatched to his death, but his mouth would not form the words. Instead, he listened to his mother tell her stories of French Canada where she and her dozen Bienville siblings enjoyed an idyllic life.

He heard his name being called, but Jean-Luc ignored it to give in to the tug of his mother's voice. To hear more of the stories she told. To be a child again at his mother's knee.

"It is no use," he heard another voice—perhaps belonging to his father—say. "He is beyond our reach. We must give him to the Lord and pray the Lord gives him back to us again."

A figure peered into the fog, her red hair visible even in the swirling grayness that surrounded her. She called his name. No, she called him the captain. Yes. Captain.

Jean-Luc tried to follow, but the girl was gone. Still the girl was calling to him. Reaching out and then oddly, telling him to go home. To return to those he loved.

Once again there was nothing but darkness. The girl was gone.

He tried to follow, tried to call out to her so he could tell her how sorry he was that he had somehow lost her to the ocean. Sorry that she would never grow up and never get another chance to sail again or read another of her ridiculous books.

But hard as he tried, Jean-Luc could not divest himself of the invisible chains that kept him in place. Could not make his legs work to chase her or his voice work to call out to her.

"Where is she? Where did she go?"

At the sound of his own voice, Jean-Luc sat upright. The shadows were gone, and his eyes stung as he looked into a blazing fire.

It was different here.

No gray swirling fog.

No feeling of being wrapped in chains.

Jean-Luc blinked again, believing the fog would return and so would the girl. Instead, a commotion sounded around him. Someone moved between him and the fire. A face he knew. A name that was just beyond the realm of understanding.

"Welcome back, Jean-Luc," she said in a silky voice that was warmly familiar. "We have been waiting for you to return to your family."

Abigail. His father's beloved wife. Yes, he remembered now. A second mother to Father's two grateful motherless sons and the mother of. . .

Of whom? He didn't know. Exhausted from the effort of trying to sort it all out, he allowed her to return him to his pillows.

"It is true."

Father.

Jean-Luc wrested his eyes open and then lost the battle to keep them that way. Even behind his closed eyes, Jean-Luc was aware of his father's presence, of his tight grip on his hand, and of the sobs that came from deep inside.

Whether they were his sobs or Father's, he could not say.

Then came the sounds of voices in the distance. They were

arguing, or perhaps it was good-natured debate he heard. Twins, yes. A brother and a sister.

Then the voices were gone and only Abigail and Father remained, although neither of them appeared to be looking at him. Rather, their heads were together—his silver hair mixing with her midnight curls—and they seemed to be praying. Beside them, a fire flickered in the fireplace.

Jean-Luc blinked and saw them clearly now. Remembered the moment his father introduced Jean-Luc and his brother to the woman who would take their mother's place.

Though she was a full two decades younger than Father, theirs had been a love match. Life had become good again when Abigail came to them. And she loved Father as much as he loved her.

All of this he remembered, and yet he could not recall what happened to the girl who eluded him in the fog. "Where did she go?"

Father and Abigail jolted, both climbing to their feet at the same moment. "He's asking for someone," she told his father, although their images had begun to swim again. "Who are you looking for, son?"

"Red," he managed before his eyes closed again.

"She is here," Abigail said from somewhere far away. "If the woman with the red hair is who you're looking for, she is here with us."

"Girl," Jean-Luc corrected, though he could not be certain he had managed to speak the word aloud.

Later, when he could manage it, he opened his eyes once more. The flames had died down to glowing embers. Embers that matched the hair of the woman who now sat in the chair beside the fireplace.

CHAPTER 12

"Maribel?" Jean-Luc managed through lips that refused to cooperate. "You?" was all he could add.

But it was enough, for the woman with the red curls stumbled to her feet, tucking her hair beneath a scarf as she hurried to him. "Hello, Mr. Valmont," she said as she knelt beside the bed. "Can you hear me?"

He reached to grasp her hand and then struggled to sit up as the room spun around him. He was weak, so weak. "I thought you were lost."

"Hush now," she said. "I've been with you all the while. I will just go and fetch your father. He asked to be alerted if you were to awaken."

"No, don't go," he said, but his grip was too weak to make her stay. His legs refused all demands to follow, and his eyes continued to be unreliable when commanded to remain open.

Finally, he awakened and found the room flooded with sunshine. There was the red-haired girl again, back in the chair by the fireplace after chasing him through the fog of his dreams.

Abigail was there too, her hands deftly working knitting needles as she created some object of clothing that would be far too warm for the New Orleans winter. The itch of last year's Christmas gift, a sweater made from wool taken from her family home, had been a source of much jesting between Jean-Luc and his younger brother Quinton.

"I sincerely hope that sweater is not for me."

"You are teasing me, Jean-Luc," Abigail said. "I refuse to jump and run to your bidding."

With that one comment, Jean-Luc knew he was fine. Knew he would live.

For as fiercely protective as Abigail was of him and his family, she would not make light of his situation unless she knew him to be safe. Though he wished to allow tears at the knowledge he was not being taken to heaven just yet, instead, he matched her humor with teasing of his own.

He shook his head and instantly regretted the action, all the while keeping his attention on the woman holding the yarn for Abigail. "Have I been much trouble?"

His father's wife laughed, a pleasant sound that reminded him of good days and smiles shared with this family of his. "A bit," she said, "although as the months went by, we did despair of hearing your complaints ever again. I am very happy to be wrong about this."

The red-haired woman looked away as if she might be uncomfortable with him watching her. Clearly the situation had been reversed for some time, because he could see now that the woman was obviously in the employ of Abigail, possibly as a companion or nursemaid.

No, that could not be right. The twins, Michel and Gabrielle, were beyond the age of needing that sort of supervision.

"Who are you?" he finally asked the woman before turning his attention back to Abigail. "Why is she here?"

"Back to your charming self, I see. I wonder if you will remember this conversation. You and I have had many these past months, but you rarely seem to recall them."

"In fact, I recall none," he said. "Not because what you say isn't worth recollection. I think there might have been some other trouble that caused me to be less than attentive."

"Yes, quite." She folded her knitting into the basket at her feet and cast a sideways glance at the woman beside her. "This is Kitty. She has been invaluable to us during your inconvenience."

"Kitty," he said as his gaze went back to the woman who now returned his smile. "Then I must offer you my most sincere thanks and an apology that I have not been able to fully appreciate your beauty until now."

She looked at Abigail. "Is he always like this?"

"No, dear," she said with a laugh. "Sometimes he is worse."

Jean-Luc almost managed a chuckle, though the effort pained him through his chest. "I don't know if I ought to be offended or not."

"You ought to be thankful that this lovely young lady gave up a good portion of her time over these past months to see to you. She was trained at the Hospital St. Louis in Paris. You could get no better care than in her hands."

Red hair, green eyes, and a smile that lit her face. Despite his current situation, Jean-Luc was intrigued. "I was fortunate to be visiting when this need was made known to me."

"Months?" he said as he tried to remember the last time he had been on his own two feet. Though he failed miserably, he somehow knew that when he did remember, he would not like what he recalled.

Her voice was heavily accented with her native French tone, but the words were beautifully spoken. "Indeed I do thank you for your care," he said in French.

"*De rien,*" she responded easily as she looked away, a coquette in nurse's attire.

"Come," Abigail said abruptly, "and let's send up his butler to handle his needs. You and I are no longer needed here."

She sent Kitty out first and then lingered until the young woman was no longer nearby. "You've given us quite a start, Jean-Luc Valmont," she said, her mock scolding light but her meaning clear as she grasped his hand and held it tight. "First, know that I am more grateful to God than I knew was possible that He chose to spare you."

"As am I," he said.

She released his hand to kneel at his side. "Then I will have two promises from you."

He leaned back on his elbows and offered what he hoped was a charming smile despite cracked lips and who knew what else. "And what would those be?"

"First," she said as her eyes held his, "you will never put your father in this position again."

Not knowing exactly what had been discovered regarding his last weeks at sea, Jean-Luc decided to let Abigail tell him exactly what she referred to rather than offering anything of his own. "I'm afraid you'll need to be more specific."

Her eyes narrowed. "Held prisoner by a wanted man and then nearly dying aboard a French Navy vessel?" Abigail shook her head. "I fail to see how you managed any of that. You are a lawyer, for goodness' sake. You manage your father's business interests in the territory and see to the details of trade agreements. How in the world does that translate to putting yourself in such danger?"

"I wish I had an answer for you," he said. "I do not."

"You do not remember or you do not want to tell me?" She held up her hand. "No, do not respond. Just understand I will not have you upsetting your father needlessly in his condition. Should you ever come back to my home battered and bleeding again, you had best have a good reason for it."

"I promise."

"I am not finished, Jean-Luc. Your father adores you, and I love you like my own flesh and blood. It was pure torture to watch you move between life and death for months on end. Your fever broke and you will live, but I do not want your father to have to endure this again. Do you understand?"

He stifled a smile. Though Abigail was barely older than him by a decade, she had taken to mothering him quite well. She also knew how to get her point across so that he comprehended clearly. And then there were the tears shimmering in her eyes. Indeed he must have frightened them all greatly.

"I do understand," he said, "and I shall endeavor to keep this promise."

"Don't you endeavor me, Jean-Luc Valmont. I am not some woman you can fool. I know whatever you were doing that landed you in this fix is likely something you will do again."

He let out a long breath. Sadly, she was right.

"But I will not do it in the same way," he said. "On that you have my word."

She gave him an even look and then nodded as she swiped at her damp eyes. "I will accept that as a promise and move to my next point, but not before I give you this book. It was a gift left on our doorstep some months ago."

"Thank you," he said as he lowered himself back to his pillow to look at the thin volume of Homer's *Odyssey*. As expected, inside there was a message from Israel letting him know he survived and where he would be waiting.

"How long ago did this arrive?"

She shrugged. "Not long after you were brought to us," she said. "So several months ago."

Several months. He let out a long breath. Israel could be anywhere by now. But what of the others?

"This doctoring that was done," he said. "Do I have Evan Connor to thank?"

She looked away and then rose. Trouble etched her beautiful features. "No," she said gently.

"Then he..."

Jean-Luc could not complete the question. Stupid, for he already knew the answer. Any man who did not step aboard the French vessel alive went down with the ship. Grief compounded with guilt coursed through him.

"Though I cannot blame you for this, Abigail," he said, all good humor gone, "my head is beginning to hurt again."

"No doubt you'd like me to call for your nurse," she said. "And that brings me to my second point. Do not toy with that girl's affections."

He looked up sharply. "What do you mean?"

"A woman knows things, Jean-Luc, and she has been by

your side for months. You may not be aware of this time passing together with her; she has been acutely aware of it. You are all she has known for months, and because of this I believe she has formed a bond with you."

Jean-Luc shook his head. "Yes, of course. I will proceed with caution."

"You will proceed with the intention of marrying her or keeping your relationship on a completely platonic level. I have promised her mother and father I would look after her, and that is what I will do."

He looked down at his broken body and then back up at Abigail. "I doubt she wants a weak man with the scars I bear. So your nurse is safe from me, I promise."

This was a promise he should never have made.

Four months later, with all weakness gone, he had fallen hopelessly in love and married the red-haired nurse whose care had brought him back from the grave. Eleven months after that, Kitty and his unborn son were buried in the same grave.

He was beyond inconsolable. When he finally realized the Lord had not meant him to die alongside them, he retrieved the book from the shelf where it had been hidden all those months ago and found Israel again.

With that reunion came news that others had survived, which made him grateful but could do nothing for the guilt he bore.

If he could not find happiness of his own, then he would turn back to the life he led before. The promise he made to Abigail would be kept, for this time he planned to do the same thing in a different way.

It took Maribel the better part of three years to realize the secretive man who sometimes did work for Mother Superior was the same man who once sat in a cell and played draughts with her. The carpenter kept to himself and never allowed anyone near while he was working, and no one considered it odd.

Then came the day when she was reading in the guango tree and he passed beneath it in conversation with Mother Superior. "As always, we at the orphanage appreciate your help in this matter, Mr. Rao. We've despaired of how to repair the trouble with our window in the chapel, so you've arrived at just the right time."

Mr. Rao.

Maribel was a young lady of almost fifteen now, and running to hug a man of Mr. Rao's age was not considered appropriate. Neither was plopping down from the guango tree to chase Mother Superior and her guest.

So she waited until the pair had parted ways, and then she edged up to him as he was repairing the window in the chapel. "Excuse me," Maribel called from the other side of the chapel. "Might I have a minute of your time?"

"Sure, miss. Something else that needs fixing?" He looked up from his work as she approached, and then froze.

"Hello, Mr. Rao," she said. "Do you remember me? I'm Maribel."

The mallet fell from his hand and barely missed landing on his foot. Mr. Rao dipped down to retrieve the tool and then took his time straightening again.

"What is this?"

Maribel jumped at the familiar sound and knew from her tone of voice that Mother Superior was displeased. Children were expressly forbidden from interacting with any adults other than the nuns, so she knew she was in deep trouble.

Slowly she turned to face the nun. As expected, Mother Superior wore an expression of irritation. "You know you should not be here. I will insist you leave at once."

"But Mother Superior, you see, I have a very good reason for being here."

She shook her head. "I will not hear excuses made when rules are broken. Go directly to your classroom, and I will come and get you once I have decided what your punishment will be."

"But I was just..." She had no good explanation other than the truth. "I am not excusing my behavior, and I will accept any punishment I have been assigned. However, I believe I know this man."

"What man?"

Maribel turned back around to see that Mr. Rao and his tools were gone. All that remained to show he had been in the chapel was the fresh repair to the chapel window.

"But Mr. Rao was here." She ran to the window to look out onto the grounds of the orphanage but saw no one fitting his description. "I know he was just here."

Mother Superior came to stand beside her and then lightly wrapped her arm around her shoulder. "Miss Cordoba, it is obvious we've had a carpenter on the island working on the chapel, so of course he was here."

"But he just left." Tears began to swim in her eyes, but she refused to cry in front of Mother Superior. "He didn't answer me and he didn't even say good-bye. But I know it was him. It just had to be him because nobody else smiles like he does, and he was so nice to me when I was on the boat. Did you know he built my own room for me? And Mr. Piper used a sail and made a hammock."

Mother Superior led Maribel out of the chapel and into the courtyard. "Collect yourself and go back to your classroom. And please exercise more control next time."

"But he didn't remember me," she said, hating how her words came out sounding so pitiful. "I remembered him and he didn't remember me."

"Miss Cordoba," she said gently, "you are assuming the man you saw was the man you believe him to be. You do not know this for certain. If this man was your old friend, then he certainly would not have left without acknowledging you."

She shrugged. "I suppose. So you think it wasn't him?"

"I think he is not the man you wish him to be," she said. "And I think you are now late for your class and likely earning an extra punishment from your teacher in addition to whatever I decide to assign you."

Several protests arose, but she kept them to herself as Mother Superior walked away. Abruptly, the nun stopped and turned around once more. "Miss Cordoba?"

"Yes?"

"Have you been having those dreams again?"

Maribel was reluctant to reply. Indeed she had experienced recollections of her days on the ship and the time leading up to her arrival on the island many times over the past few years. However, she had stopped asking questions of Mother Superior regarding their authenticity because her answer was always the same: it was a dream.

"No, Reverend Mother," she told her, "I have not had any more dreams."

Because they aren't dreams. They're memories.

MARIBEL AND THE PIRATE

PART II:

Isla de Santa Maria
Near Port Royal, Jamaica
and New Orleans, Louisiana
May of 1735

When I consider thy heavens, the work of thy fingers, the moon and the stars, which thou hast ordained; what is man, that thou art mindful of him? and the son of man, that thou visitest him? For thou hast made him a little lower than the angels, and hast crowned him with glory and honour. Thou madest him to have dominion over the works of thy hands; thou hast put all things under his feet: all sheep and oxen, yea, and the beasts of the field; the fowl of the air, and the fish of the sea, and whatsoever passeth through the paths of the seas.

O LORD our Lord, how excellent is thy name in all the earth!

PSALM 8:3–9

CHAPTER 13

St. Mary of the Island Orphanage

Y ou have a visitor, Miss Maribel."

Maribel Cordoba looked up from her reading to offer a silent chastisement. All the children knew she was not to be disturbed during her hour of respite. Furthermore, the boys and girls should be resting and not gadding about the orphanage to pop up unannounced in her place of solitude.

"Miss Maribel?"

She debated offering a response. After the last time she was found reading in a guango tree, Mother Superior threatened to relieve her of her teaching duties. It wasn't seemly for a lady, apparently, or at least that is what Maribel was told after she had endured a scathing lecture on propriety.

Of course she agreed with Mother Superior. It was not seemly to be caught reading in that guango tree. So she moved to a different tree and determined not to be caught.

She also made sure the sticky seedpods did not adhere themselves to her in places where the students and faculty might spy them but she would not. Of course, that humiliation had only happened once, but it had been quite terrifying to sit down on something that she had not expected to be there.

The children did enjoy her reaction, however.

So yes, it was a bit sly to climb a tree to hide and read, but it was not meant to be rebellious. As much as she loved teaching these beautiful children, she also loved having time to herself to escape to those books that had become her favorite.

With the orphanage being run on a strict schedule, these stolen moments were precious. Those and the other rare occasions when she managed to slip off to the other side of the tiny island a few miles across the bay from Port Royal to enjoy a swim or the view from the mahogany trees.

Owing to the risks involved in such an activity—and the fact that Mother Superior would fire her and banish her from the orphanage on the spot—Maribel rarely attempted this anymore. Oh, but perhaps someday soon.

"Really, Miss Maribel," little Stephan said as he jumped from one bare foot to the other. "Mother Superior, she said I should find you and see that you get to her office with the upmost speed."

"Utmost," Maribel corrected as she closed her well-worn copy of *Robinson Crusoe*.

Stephan gave her a gap-toothed grin. "Yes, that's what I said."

"Thank you, Stephan," she told him. "I'm curious. How did you come to meet with Mother Superior when you should have been resting in the classroom with the others?"

He looked down at his feet then back up at her. "I might have seen her while I was out and about."

"I see." Maribel stifled a grin.

It was well known that Stephan loved to hurry down to the little tributary that ran through the orphanage grounds just beyond Mother Superior's office when he thought no one was watching. She saw no harm in it as the stream was shallow and slow moving, but the knowledge was useful. The fact the boy's dark hair was slick with water gave him away.

"Then if you do not mention to Mother Superior where you found me, I will conveniently forget that you have been swimming instead."

She tucked her book into her pocket and waited until the boy had scampered off. When the coast was clear, Maribel carefully climbed down and straightened her skirts then adjusted the scarf that she wore tied around her waist.

Woven through with threads of silver, the scarf was not part of the uniform Mother Superior prescribed for her teachers. Thankfully, Mother Superior did not require her to remove it once she learned the length of cloth was all Maribel had left of her mother.

Taking a deep breath, she let it out slowly as she made her way toward Mother Superior's office. Though the distance was short, it felt much farther as she walked toward the front of the orphanage.

The afternoon sun slanted across the avocado trees that marked the boundary between the orphanage and the path that led to the beach. Out of habit, she cast a glance at the sparkling green water and then let her attention rest on the horizon.

There she spied white sails off to the northeast. "Sloop," she whispered under her breath. Another set of sails fluttered some distance away to the west. "Brigantine."

Her fingers curled involuntarily as she felt the imagined grip of the watch post. The sensation of standing so close to heaven that she could almost touch the stars had never left her. Nor had her curiosity as to what had happened to the kindhearted men who she often prayed had survived the battle that plummeted her into the sea and deposited her at this place.

When she first came to St. Mary of the Island, she was very ill. This she had been told by others. How she got here was a mystery, however. Someone brought her, but she had asked Mother Superior who that someone might be so many times and received no answer that she had eventually given up. Though she owed her life to a person she may never be able to thank, she nevertheless offered up a prayer for him daily.

"Miss Cordoba, do join us."

The sharply enunciated tones of Mother Superior preceded her as she glided around the corner. How this tiny woman always seemed to know where her students and teachers were without actually standing in sight of them had unnerved Maribel when she first arrived at the orphanage. Only later did she discover the old nun was blind.

"Yes, Mother Superior."

She picked up her skirts and followed Mother Superior's brisk pace around the corner and into the low-roofed building that served as offices, classrooms, and the chapel. Hurrying behind the woman who finished raising her and then hired her to teach, Maribel once again attempted to affect the elegant gliding gait of the older woman and the other nuns.

It was useless, of course. Rumor had it that Mother Superior had been a great beauty in her youth, trained and educated in the highest levels of society. Though the country of her birth varied depending on who was doing the telling, all the stories agreed: the loss of her sight sent her here to this remote corner of the Caribbean where the children and teachers took the place of whatever social life she left behind.

"Do keep up," Mother Superior said as she turned sharply and disappeared into the office she had carved out of this corner of the building after it was rebuilt following the hurricane last year.

The room was small but not at all dark, owing to the floor-to-ceiling windows that spanned the length of one wall. If anyone thought it odd that a woman without sight would insist on putting in a wall full of windows, no one dared approach Mother Superior about it.

Rather than take her customary place behind the rather simple desk in the center of the room, Mother Superior held the door open for Maribel and indicated she should take a seat. There behind the desk was a rather stern-looking bespectacled gentleman wearing the formal attire that marked him as one who had not spent much time in this climate.

Before she could turn around to ask Mother Superior who this man might be, the door shut and the nun was gone. Maribel returned her attention to the desk and the stranger.

He indicated with a sweep of his hand that she should sit. In deference to the behavior she always exhibited when called to this room, Maribel obeyed.

Perched on the edge of the hard wooden chair, she rested her palms on her knees. Out of the corner of her eye, she saw Stephan float past in the creek.

"You are Maribel Cordoba?"

The question caused her to jump as she swiftly returned her attention to the stranger. Her fingers clutched handfuls of her scarf as she tried not to allow his stare to unnerve her.

"Yes," she finally said. "I am."

"Yes, of course you are." His expression softened. "Forgive me, but I expected you would be a nun."

Maribel laughed despite her nerves. "I assure you it was not for the lack of trying. Mother Superior had hopes that I might join the novitiate, but unfortunately I am apparently quite unsuitable. She despaired of me ever learning to be still and quiet, but beyond that I read the most unsuitable books."

One silver brow rose above his spectacles. "Is that so?"

Horrified, she shook her head. "That just sounds terrible. Please understand I do not read books that are bad, I promise. Rather, I prefer stories of pirates and such, and Mother Superior believes that tales of adventure on the high seas do not qualify me for the more sedate and cloistered life of a nun."

He looked away, and when he returned his attention to her, the beginnings of a smile rose. "Yes, I do see your point." The stranger's expression sobered. "I'm sorry. You are likely wondering who I am and why I am here."

"The thought did occur," she said. "I assume you aren't here to learn why I was not accepted as a nun in this fine establishment."

"No, that is true," he said. "I will get to the point, Miss Cordoba. My name is Rafael Lopez-Gonzales. I have been sent to find you and bring you back with me."

"I don't understand."

"Yes, well, the matter is of the utmost urgency, but since you have no family here on the island, I did speak to Mother Superior before I broached this topic with you. After much spirited discussion, we are in agreement that you should take leave of your position here and—"

"I'm sorry to interrupt, Mr. Lopez-Gonzales, but I must stop you right there," she said. "I have no idea who you are or why you believe I should leave my teaching work here and just go off with you. St. Mary of the Island Orphanage has been my home for some eleven years now. Perhaps we should call Mother Superior back in to explain this urgency to me because you have not done a decent job of it as of yet."

"You are correct." He removed his spectacles and regarded Maribel with a smile. "Forgive me. Miss Cordoba, you are exactly as you were described."

"Again, Mr. Lopez-Gonzales, you have me at a disadvantage. Please speak plainly. I assure you I will not faint. What is the urgency that sent you searching for me and that apparently requires me to leave everything I know and love to follow you to. . ." She shook her head. "Where was it?"

"New Orleans," he supplied.

"Yes, well, all right. To follow you to New Orleans." She gave him the look she generally reserved for her most unruly pupils. "Do please continue, sir. My time is limited, and my students will be wondering where their teacher has gone."

"Mother Superior has assured me she will assign another teacher to see to your students so that you might have the remainder of the afternoon free to make your arrangements."

"Sir, forgive me, but you truly are maddening." She rose. "Your reticence to provide me with pertinent information leads me to believe you have something to hide, which also leads me to believe you very likely have not been honest with Mother Superior. Thus, our conversation is at an end. Now if you will excuse me, I have preparations to make for my afternoon class."

"If I am reticent," he said as he also stood, "it is because the news I bring is not easily delivered. You grew up here, so you have been raised an orphan."

"I believe it is obvious, given that fact, that I have, sir."

She crossed her arms over her waist and determined to give him no more than a minute longer of her time. He had already interrupted her precious reading time. Soon he would be interrupting her class time.

Mr. Lopez-Gonzales removed his handkerchief and dabbed at his forehead. "That is unfortunate because, despite the fact your convent dowry and maintenance has been paid by a donor who Mother Superior assures me is not a family member of whom you are aware, you are not an orphan at all, Miss Cordoba."

She heard his words, but they made no sense. Maribel shook her head. "Excuse me?"

"Please be seated," he said. "There is more to tell, and you will likely want to sit down. This heat is rather unbearable."

"I will do nothing of the sort, and as I said, I will not faint. How is it possible that I am not an orphan when my mother died and then I saw my father drown in front of my eyes?"

"Your mother is very much alive," he said gently. "As is your grandfather."

The breath slammed from her chest, and spots danced before her eyes. Despite her protests to the contrary, she did feel as though she might faint at any moment.

"Impossible," she managed as she gripped the back of the chair with both hands in order to remain upright. "Completely impossible."

"I assure you it is not." He nodded toward the stack of documents in front of him. "Your mother is the former Mary Lytton whose late father Benjamin descended from William and Mary Abigail Lytton. Your late father Antonio Cordoba did indeed drown at sea, and your name, I believe, is a mixture of your mother's name and your maternal grandmother's name—both Mary—along with your paternal grandmother's name, which was Isabel. I am told Isabel descended from Spanish royalty, but there has been no time to make a determination of this."

"Anyone could know these things," she said as she gripped the chair tighter, achingly aware that she had not known most of these facts until now. If, indeed, what he said was true.

"Fair enough. Your grandfather has anticipated your reluctance and has provided this as proof."

He shuffled through the documents until he retrieved a letter that bore a red seal adorned with what appeared to be her grandfather's coat of arms. His expression solemn, Mr. Lopez-Gonzales handed it to her.

Maribel accepted the letter and tucked it away with her book, refusing to even look at the handwriting on the outside. Not with this stranger watching her.

"Thank you, Mr. Lopez-Gonzales. I will read this and give it the consideration it deserves."

If her response flustered him, the stranger did not offer any indication of such. "Yes, all right. Might I then let you know that I will be sailing tomorrow on the tide and I wish you to join me? Your family has been most encouraged that I have been able to find you and are very much hopeful that I can bring you home to them as soon as possible."

Your family.

Maribel shook off the strong urge to think the man's search might have culminated with her. Instead, she took a deep breath and allowed the reality of the situation to sink in. This very kind man had mistaken her for someone else. Yes, that was the likely scenario.

And yet he knew her name. Knew Mama's name, though she could not vouch for the string of ancestors he quoted in relation to her.

Along with all of this, he offered hope that the people she had mourned so many years were alive. It was too much.

"Thank you," she managed. "I will give the matter serious consideration, but I do have an allegiance to this orphanage."

"I do understand." He returned his spectacles to his nose. "However, I will need an answer before I sail. And should you decline to accompany me, might I request a letter in response to the one you've tucked away? Your mother and abuelo would then at least have some measure of comfort in knowing you have been found and are alive."

Her heart lurched.

Somehow Maribel managed to keep her dignity intact as she responded in the affirmative and then walked slowly out of the room. She managed to continue to maintain that dignity until she reached the hedge of avocado trees.

There the temptation to run toward the beach and cast herself into the surf almost overpowered the good sense the nuns had taught her. Instead, she straightened her spine and walked past the avocado trees with only the quickest of glances at the sea beyond.

"Gaff-rigged schooner to the northeast," she said almost without realizing the words had escaped her lips.

<hr />

A gaff-rigged schooner was not his vessel of choice, but today it was Jean-Luc Valmont's vessel of convenience. From his post at the wheel of the ship he called the *Lazarus*, Jean-Luc spotted the old convent and orphanage, a landmark he had used many times before to navigate his way into port.

Not the port where ships of the line rested anchor. That was Port Royal over on the island of Jamaica. Rather, he pointed the schooner toward the inlet he preferred that kept all but those he trusted from knowing where he was.

Though Isla de Santa Maria sat within view of Port Royal, the presence of the nuns had discouraged any of the undesirable element of the city to relocate there. Whether it was the prayers of the nuns or the fiercely protective Mother Superior that struck fear in otherwise fearless ruffians, the end result was that the little island—easily walked around in a few hours—was a haven for the orphans in their care and off-limits to just about anyone else.

They sailed past the orphanage with its line of avocado trees and center courtyard marked with a cluster of guango trees rising above the center spire of the chapel. A small boy played in the stream that ran past the chapel, likely hiding from the classroom where the other children would be at this time of day. Beyond the orphanage, a forest of mahogany trees hid an inlet and a small sandy beach.

He called out the order to prepare for docking then turned the wheel over to his second-in-command. "Take us in, Israel," he said with a smile.

If anyone thought it odd that a former slave held such a position of honor on a vessel that was reportedly engaged in the slave trade, no one dared say it. For in his world, the name Valmont opened doors and closed mouths.

It always had.

As was their habit, Israel guided the *Lazarus* past the intended spot for docking. He would order the schooner to circle back around once the man in the watch post indicated he had not spotted anything—or anyone—problematic awaiting them onshore.

Jean-Luc looked up at the forward mast to watch for the signal to land. After all these years, this still brought back memories of a wisp of a girl with flaming hair who was better at spotting and naming vessels than any man with whom he'd sailed then or now.

"All clear," the man on watch called, drawing him back to the task at hand. Two other men on lookout shouted their agreement.

"All clear, Mr. Bennett," he said. "Take her in and let's get on with it."

CHAPTER 14

Maribel tucked her feet up under her damp skirt and tried to make herself as inconspicuous as possible. From her perch in the mahogany tree, she'd hoped to evade Mother Superior—or whichever of the children might be sent to fetch her—while she read her grandfather's letter yet again.

She hadn't planned on evading pirates too.

Past memories that she generally kept in check arose as Maribel heard the slap of sails and the sound of men shouting commands. When the craft bypassed the inlet and continued on, she let out the breath she did not realize she had been holding and retrieved Abuelo's letter from between the pages of *Robinson Crusoe*.

Age showed in the spidery handwriting, but enough of her grandfather's unique script and signature remained for Maribel to know that Mr. Lopez-Gonzales had spoken the truth. According to Abuelo, Mama was very much alive and distraught that she was not allowed to travel with their representative to Isla de Santa Maria to greet Maribel herself.

Your mother and I came to this city we now call our home in hopes of being closer to the place where you were last seen. It was our hope, a hope we never once gave up on, that our precious Maribel would somehow return to us. No expense has been spared in our search for you, my sweet granddaughter. And now at last you have been located.

*We give thanks to God that what we believed to be
forever lost has now been found. Please come home to us,
sweet child. Make an old man happy in his last days.
I am your adoring Abuelo.*

Maribel traced her grandfather's signature with her forefinger, noting the swirl of the oversize *C* that she always tried to imitate in her own handwriting, and wondered about Abuelo's statement regarding his last days.

She sighed. Of course she would go. There was no doubt. But why had Papa told her something that was not true?

Her grandfather had not broached this topic in his letter, but it was a question that would someday need an answer. Had her father truly sought to separate her from Mama and Abuelo? Obviously he had, and yet it made no sense that a man who barely paid her any heed would somehow fabricate a situation that would require him to become her caregiver.

But those were questions for another day.

Maribel folded the letter and tucked it back into *Robinson Crusoe* and then held the book against her heart. From somewhere deep inside her, a gut-wrenching sob arose.

She had a home. And a family. She was no longer an orphan.

An answer to a prayer Maribel had never possessed faith enough to pray.

Thank You, Lord. Oh, thank You.

Her expressions of gratitude continued until the tears that went along with them finally dried. Resting her head against the rough bark, Maribel closed her eyes. In her dreams she saw the sea all around her, heard the splash of a wooden hull through waves and the slap of sails in the breeze.

The sounds engulfed her, growing louder until she opened her eyes to realize it wasn't a dream at all. The gaff-rigged schooner she saw earlier was now sliding into the inlet.

Maribel secured her book and prepared to climb down. If she

failed to get away, she would be stuck in this tree until the vessel lifted anchor and sailed away.

The alternative was to reveal herself to be hiding in a mahogany tree on an island populated with only nuns and children to protect her. Maribel sighed. While Mother Superior might very well take on an entire ship of pirates, it was best she did not.

She moved down lower in the tree, but the schooner was too fast. Scampering back into place, she resolved to hide as best she could.

Moments later, another ship of similar design docked slightly behind the vessel that was already there. Though leaves obstructed her view, it appeared a skiff was being lowered from the first ship.

Leaning forward, Maribel was able to see that skiff when it came into view between the vessels. She gasped. "Slave traders."

While she watched, the boatload of humanity was brought up against the other vessel, and the men, women, and children were hauled aboard. The process was repeated multiple times until finally the skiff no longer emerged from behind the schooner.

After a while, the vessel that was now loaded with slaves lifted anchor and sailed away. However, the other vessel seemed to be making no move to leave.

When Maribel could no longer feel her legs, she had to act. Stretching slowly to bring feeling back to her limbs, she made her plans to escape.

She gave thanks that she'd chosen a dress of drab brown today, for it did help to keep her from being visible to the slave traders. However, her hair would most definitely be a problem should anyone glance in her direction.

Improvising, Maribel removed the scarf from her waist and tucked her all-too-noticeable curls underneath just as the novitiates did. Should the slave traders spy her, perhaps they would think her a member of the convent.

Placing the tree trunk between her and the ship, Maribel began to climb down. Just when she expected her feet to touch solid ground, she felt hands on either side of her waist. A moment later, those same hands swung her about and set her down on the sand.

Maribel whirled around, her fists raised and her heart thudding. Instincts from long ago kicked in, and she swung her fist to connect with a dark-haired stranger's jaw.

The man stumbled backward, and Maribel seized the opportunity to run as fast as she could back to the convent walls. Only when she reached the garden did she realize she had dropped her copy of *Robinson Crusoe*.

Going back was not a consideration, but telling Mother Superior was. Maribel hurried toward the office but found the door closed. She knocked, but her way was blocked when Mother Superior came to the door.

"Not now, Miss Cordoba," she said, as she slammed the door shut once again.

"But Mother Superior," she called. "I really must speak to you. It is of the utmost importance."

"Upmost," a small voice corrected.

She turned around to see Stephan grinning up at her. "That's what I said."

Maribel returned his grin and then affected her most serious expression. This child certainly should not be running freely with slave traders on the island.

"You should be in the classroom."

He made a face. "I would rather not."

Maribel knelt down to speak to the little boy. "I want you to listen carefully and do exactly as I say. You must go into the classroom very quietly and stay there. If you do not, I will see to it that you are not allowed to swim in the creek ever again. Do you understand?"

His eyes began to tear up. "Ever again?"

Maribel shrugged. "Well, for a very long time anyway. You see, if I cannot trust you to do what I ask you to do, then I cannot trust you to have the privilege of swimming in the creek. Do you understand?"

Stephan maintained his stubborn look. Maribel rose.

"All right, then. I am very sorry you have chosen not to be allowed to swim. Now I will have to march you into the classroom without your cooperation." She reached for his hand, but Stephan took a step backward.

"I'll go, but I was just trying to tell Mother Superior about the bad men in the harbor."

"You saw bad men?" She looked around and then knelt again. "Tell me what you saw."

He related a story similar to what Maribel had seen unfold. "And then the man with the scar on his face saw you in the tree and I told him to leave you alone because you were a teacher and you were a nice lady and he said he didn't want to hurt you."

Maribel gasped. "It was very dangerous of you to speak to him, Stephan. You have no idea who he was. He might have been a criminal."

"Oh no," he said. "I've seen him here before."

So slave traders had been using Isla de Santa Maria as their base of operations for a while then. Maribel frowned.

Certainly Mother Superior would have an opinion on this. And a remedy for it.

"All right, Stephan, off to class with you. And promise me you will not speak to any strangers you see on this island unless I or one of the nuns give you permission."

"I promise," he said. "Does that mean I can go swim in the creek again?"

"Not today, and not as long as the strangers are sailing into that inlet. It is too dangerous."

Stephan stuck out his lip but remained stoic as he trudged off to the classroom. Maribel waited until the boy had safely gone into the building before she turned away, her heart racing.

Until she knew whether St. Mary of the Island Orphanage was

safe, how could she leave tomorrow on the tide?

The answer was she could not. Much as she wished to be reunited with her mother and the grandfather she had not seen in eleven years, her current allegiance was to the second family that had raised her. Once she knew this second family was safe, then she could go home to her first family.

And if that meant standing at Mother Superior's door until first tide tomorrow, then she would.

Maribel marched back over to the office and lifted her hand to knock. "Come in, Miss Cordoba," Mother Superior said in that uncanny way she had. She was seated behind her desk, her expression slightly exasperated. "And how may I help you this afternoon?"

She shut the door and returned to the chair she had vacated earlier in the day. "I must warn you about something terrible going on here on our island."

"Oh?"

"I chanced to learn that there are slave traders using our island for their nefarious deeds. If Stephan is to be believed, and I think he is, then this dreadful behavior has been going on for a while."

"I see." Mother Superior paused as if choosing her response. "And other than the testimony of a small child with a penchant for escaping the classroom to lounge about in whatever body of water is available, exactly what proof do you have of such an accusation?"

"I saw it with my own eyes, Mother Superior. There were two schooners, and a man rowed slaves from one to the other and then the vessel with the slaves aboard sailed away. It was absolutely horrific."

"Ah," she said. "And exactly where were you when you witnessed this alleged slave trading?"

Oh. Maribel studied her skirt as she worked out a proper response. There was no way to answer without giving away the fact that she had defied the older woman's edict to cease reading in trees.

"Miss Cordoba," Mother Superior said. "Where exactly is your scarf?"

Maribel touched the edge of the scarf that now was wrapped around her hair. "Well, I covered my head with it."

"And it is usually at your waist." She paused. "You are fond of toying with the ends when you are nervous. For what purpose did you decide to cover your head?"

"Mother Superior, please forgive me for my impertinence, but I don't understand why you are asking questions about my scarf when we have a serious threat to the orphanage happening at this very moment. I absolutely cannot think of leaving Isla de Santa Maria for New Orleans until I am certain you, the nuns, and the children are safe from these awful ruffians."

The old nun sat very still, and Maribel knew for sure she had said far more than she should have. Finally, Mother Superior rose.

"I sincerely thank you for your loyalty, Miss Cordoba, and I applaud your dedication to our safety. You will be greatly missed here at St. Mary of the Island, but you must go with Mr. Lopez-Gonzales tomorrow."

"I simply cannot until I am certain—"

"That an old blind nun and a handful of nuns and novitiates can fend off slave traders bent on harming us?" She chuckled. "Miss Cordoba, do you really think that will happen?"

Maribel perched on the edge of her chair, her nerves taut and her passion for this topic rising. "I really think that men who are willing to trade in the sale of humans would not care if they harmed other humans, be they nuns or children, who might interfere with their commerce. I cannot allow that to happen."

"Admirable, but the Lord has kept this island safe from all threats for some time now. I am merely His steward, but I do like to think that my reputation among the criminal element is such that they do not bother us. Have you noticed that?"

"Until now, yes."

Mother Superior sighed. "I insist you are on that ship to New

Orleans tomorrow. I have given my assurances that you will be."

"But, Mother Superior, I cannot possibly—"

"Miss Cordoba, you have no choice. Leave the handling of these men you call slave traders to me. Go and pack your things and prepare for your journey tomorrow." She rose. "That is my last word on the subject."

Defying Mother Superior was something she never thought she would do, but if it took defiance to be heard, then so be it. "I simply cannot," she said as she stood with shaking knees.

"I am sorry you feel that way." She paused, her expression solemn but without any hint of anger. "Then I must make a correction to what I previously told you. That was not my last word on the subject. These are: Miss Cordoba, you are fired."

CHAPTER 15

Jean-Luc slipped out of his meeting with the Mother Superior—where she once again asked him to thank Israel for whatever was in the package he had sent to her—in the same way he always did. He climbed out the window.

Skirting the edge of the beach, he kept a brisk pace until he reached the inlet where the *Lazarus* waited at anchor. Only when he reached that spot did he look back to be sure he had not been followed.

Given the behavior of the young nun, Jean-Luc preferred to take all precautions.

Mother Superior assured him the novitiate he'd interacted with in the mahogany forest would not pose a threat. However, a woman who wished to become a nun should never be that good at causing a man pain.

Out of curiosity, and possibly to warn the old nun that one of her charges was a danger to others, Jean-Luc retraced his steps to find the tree where the woman had been spying on them. He assumed she had been spying, although Mother Superior indicated this particular female had a past history of hiding herself in trees in order to read her books without being interrupted by the children.

"And you are certain there is no danger because she has seen us?"

He watched the old nun's wrinkled face for any evidence of what she might be thinking. As always, hers was a face that was unreadable.

"I am certain. As I said, she is harmless. Just a girl who grew to a woman who has not yet forgotten childish things on occasion." She paused. "Had I any concern that you and Mr. Bennett's enterprise would be endangered, do you think I would not warn you? I stand to lose much should any of you be caught."

It was a plausible answer, although in his business, plausible answers were not good enough. He would not risk his men's lives over a supposition. And if the girl were to tell anyone what she saw, many lives would be at stake.

He walked down the narrow path, pushing back the foliage as he went. Just around a bend in the path, he tripped on a thick mass of exposed tree roots and went sprawling forward.

As he climbed to his feet, Jean-Luc spied a rectangular object—a brown leather-bound book—wedged into the sand at the base of the tree. He retrieved the book and dusted off the sand to read the title.

And then he laughed.

"Of all the lost books in the world, I would find *Robinson Crusoe* abandoned on a tropical island." He glanced up at the sky through the filter of mahogany leaves and smiled. "Thank You, Lord. I needed some good humor today."

After going in search of the girl who had obviously lost this book, he encountered Mother Superior hurrying down the path. Somehow the blind woman managed to step right over the tangle of roots that had caused him—a man with completely good eyesight—to stumble.

"I must insist that your ship depart immediately," she said as she turned him around and set out down the path toward the inlet beside him.

"Have we overstayed our welcome, Mother Superior?" he asked in jest.

"In a way, you have," she responded with her characteristic lack of humor.

"I was on my way back when I found an item I believe one of your novitiates dropped." He offered her the book.

If the old nun realized he had offered the book to her, she gave no indication of it. "Did the book or she happen to fall out of a tree? Perhaps both?"

"The book might have," he said. "She did not, but only because I caught her first. However, I'm sure she would like her book back. I found it on the path back there."

For the first time since Israel introduced him to the nun, Jean-Luc found something akin to shock in her normally placid expression. He studied her a moment, trying to figure out just what he had said that upset her.

"Please accept the book as a gift from St. Mary of the Island Orphanage and go," she told him, urgency in her voice.

"Are you certain? I don't mind doing a search to find the book's owner, although I do not relish repeating the sort of greeting she offered the last time."

"I am certain," she said. "And make haste. I wish you no offense, but you truly have stayed too long."

"Then in that case, I will accept your gift and take my leave." Tucking the book under his arm, Jean-Luc made his way back to the *Lazarus* with that same smile still in place.

"What's got into you?" Israel asked when he arrived on deck.

"Cast off for home, my friend," he said. "I'm going to go see a man about an island." At Israel's confused look, he gestured to the book under his arm. "*Robinson Crusoe*," he said. "I found it. Can you believe that?"

Apparently the humor was lost on his second-in-command. Israel just shook his head. "How many times have you read that book, Captain?"

"I've lost count," he said. "But when I do get a tally, I'll add one to it. I've needed something to think about other than the mission that brought us here, and now I have it."

"You wound me, Captain," Israel said with a broad grin. "I had hoped to challenge you to finally read Homer's *Odyssey* in the original Greek."

Jean-Luc shook his head. "You, sir, are the expert in the scholarly languages. I keep to English, French, and Spanish."

"A pity," Israel said. "There's just something about reading the philosophers' words exactly as they wrote them. No translation measures up."

"And I would counter with the statement that there is something about reading a book about a man who finds peace alone on a deserted island." Jean-Luc used the book to gesture to the bow. "We've completed this endeavor successfully and our hold is empty. Order the anchor raised, and let's go home, Mr. Bennett."

Once in his cabin, he placed the book on the corner of his desk and then went to work updating the log. Just as he was reaching for the novel, a warning bell rang. In his surprise, Jean-Luc knocked the book onto the floor.

He reached for it and banged his head on the edge of the desk as the schooner tilted. Leaving the book where it landed, he went up to the deck in search of the reason behind the warning bell and found a squall churning ahead of them.

Setting to work alongside his men, they fought the weather. By the time the crew had steered the ship through the storm, exhaustion sent him to his bunk for much-needed sleep.

He awoke during the night as wide awake as if he'd slept until daybreak. Swinging his legs out of the bunk, Jean-Luc retrieved the sandy copy of *Robinson Crusoe* with the intention of reading. The light was not sufficient to see the pages, so he placed the book on the bunk beside him and lay there until sleep finally overtook him.

The next morning he awakened to the book on the floor and a letter with the seal of the Cordoba family beside him on the bunk. Jean-Luc snatched up the letter and then looked around the cabin to see if perhaps it was some kind of joke.

Only one man aboard this vessel knew of his connection to a certain red-haired girl. Surely Israel felt that loss as keenly and would never make sport of anything in relation to her.

Still, what else could be the explanation?

"Come out and show yourself, Israel Bennett," he called to the man he hoped would have a guard posted outside to report back to him. "Your pitiful attempt at a joke at my expense has failed."

Silence.

He called out again but met with the same reaction.

"Truly, your joke has gone too far," he added as his temper rose. "You and I both know what the girl meant to us. To make this sort of jest is not like you, my friend."

Once again, there was no answer. This time his curiosity got the better of his temper. The letter looked real enough, the wax on the seal certainly giving it an official appearance.

And though the seal had been broken, indicating someone had already read it, the letter was intact and appeared to have been recently written. He turned the letter over and then set it beside him on the bunk.

Finally, with shaking hands, Jean-Luc opened the letter. When his eyes reached these words, his heart felt as though it had stopped:

> *Your mother and I came to this city we now call our home in hopes of being closer to the place where you were last seen. It was our hope, a hope we never once gave up on, that our precious Maribel would somehow return to us. No expense has been spared in our search for you, my sweet granddaughter. And now at last you have been located.*

Located.

He let the letter fall to the floor and then picked it up to read it all over again. Located where?

Jean-Luc's eyes went to the book. Surely this letter hadn't been inside.

He breathed in. Breathed out. Forced himself to calm his thoughts.

A man in his position did not allow speculation to rule him. He took action.

"Israel," he shouted as he stormed out of the cabin. "Israel Bennett, where are you?"

He emerged onto the deck and called to the first crewman he saw. "You there. Have this ship turned around. We are headed back to Isla de Santa Maria, and see that we get there as swiftly as possible."

"Aye, Captain," he said, hurrying away.

Jean-Luc found Israel at the wheel, standing in the same place where he had left him last night. "Did you not sleep?" he asked.

His old friend smiled. "I sleep enough when I need it. So what is this I'm hearing about turning the *Lazarus* around?"

Rather than respond, he handed Israel the letter. After reading it, Israel looked up at him. "Where did you get this?"

"It was on my bunk this morning."

He thrust the letter back in Jean-Luc's direction. "An odd place to find a letter from Don Pablo Cordoba, don't you think? I say ignore it. It cannot be authentic."

"I did wonder for a passing moment if you might be playing a joke on me."

Israel's expression showed he took great offense at the suggestion. "Surely you're not serious. Why would you think I would joke about the girl?"

"I wouldn't," he said, tucking the letter away, "but that was my first thought."

Israel, too, bore some measure of guilt over the loss of their youngest crew member those many years ago. But then he also bore guilt that he had not been aboard the ship when the French took them down.

In all these years, Jean-Luc had not managed to make Israel realize none of these things were his fault.

"And your second thought is what?" he asked, his expression now tender. "That somehow returning to the island we just left will answer the question of what happened to Maribel Cordoba?"

"Yes," Jean-Luc said with a smile. "Remember the book I brought back with me to the ship?" At Israel's nod, he continued. "I found that book at the base of a tree. Earlier a young novitiate had been climbing down that very same tree, so I assumed it might belong to her. When I attempted to return the book, Mother Superior insisted I take it as her gift and go quickly because we had overstayed our time."

"All right," Israel said slowly. "So how does all of that relate to the letter from Cordoba?"

"I don't exactly know except that I believe the letter was inside that book."

Something in his old friend's expression changed. "And the owner of the book is on Isla de Santa Maria? I see no reason to believe this, Captain."

He gave Israel an even look. "I don't want to get my hopes up, but possibly. The only way to know is to go back and see if she is there."

Israel nodded to the crewman nearest them and indicated the man should take the wheel. "Stay the course for now," he told the man, and then he ushered Jean-Luc to a spot away from any crewmen. "Think carefully about this, my friend. Do you really want Maribel Cordoba found?"

"Of course I do. Don't you?"

"For my own sake, perhaps. I do miss the girl." He paused and looked past Jean-Luc toward the horizon. "But for your sake? No. I do not." Israel swung his attention back to him. "Think, Captain. Everything you worked for, your reputation and perhaps even your father's could be gone if that girl tells anyone who you were. The Valmonts could lose everything."

"You're assuming she remembers any of it, or that she would connect Jean-Luc Valmont to a privateer working under an assumed name."

"Maribel is a smart girl. I say it because I do know she is out there alive. Just like the Lord spared me and those other three, I have no doubt He spared our Red."

Jean-Luc leaned against the rail. "I know I have hoped He did."

"However, the four on those skiffs who were spared slaughter at the hands of those French dogs, we took an oath."

Not only did they take an oath, but also those four men had made guarding him and his reputation from anything and anyone that might tarnish it their sole mission. To these men he owed his life and everything he had in this world.

Them and Evan Connor.

"I am forever in your debt," Jean-Luc said.

"Between us we have no debts that have gone unpaid, Captain," Israel said. "If you go after that girl, you just may find her. Then you'll have to deal with what happens next. We will not be able to protect you."

Israel was right, of course.

Jean-Luc shook his head. "There's nothing in what you've said that I can find disagreement with."

"And yet you will not rest until you have found her."

He shook his head. "She found me, Israel. That letter did not come to me by accident of fate. There is a purpose behind me knowing our Maribel is alive, and yes, I will not rest, but you are wrong about one thing."

"And what is that?"

"I don't have to find her, but I do have to find out what happened to her."

"Then let me do this. I will go ashore and inquire," Israel said.

He looked up into the concerned eyes of his best friend. "I must do this myself. You will not change my mind, but I do respect your concern. I wish to do this together, though."

Israel stuck out his hand to grasp Jean-Luc's, though the reluctance was still showing on his face. "Then we do this together, my friend."

"Together it is." Jean-Luc caught the attention of the crewman at the helm. "Turn back for Isla de Santa Maria, and make haste about it."

"We'll be weathering the storm once more," Israel reminded him.

"Then so be it," he said. "I doubt it will be our last."

"Of this, I have no doubt," Israel said as he turned to his work, his shoulders noticeably slumped as if in defeat.

"Take heart, my friend," Jean-Luc said as he clasped his hand on the bigger man's shoulder. "You cannot protect me from everything."

Israel turned around to face him. "I wear the scar of a flintlock's wound that proves this point. You wear more scars than that."

Only his friend knew how he hated the fact that first the Spaniard and then the French had marked his body. Every time he looked at the lines etched in his skin—some so deep he'd been told the physician could see bone—he was forced to remember the hands that put them there.

And every time he remembered those hands, he had to release them to the Lord for His revenge. Because Jean-Luc had learned the hard way that seeking one's own revenge was often the true source of those scars.

Israel reached out to place his palm over Jean-Luc's heart. "So when you ask me to take you down a path where you will very likely add more scars to the ones you've collected? I follow your lead because you are my friend and my captain, but I do not follow that lead willingly."

Jean-Luc nodded. "I often say the same thing to my heavenly Father, and yet I do follow Him all the same."

Maribel paced the deck of the *Paloma*, not caring that rain threatened. Half the day was now gone and the vessel had not left port. If it was going to rain, then get on with it. If not, then get on with that as well.

She shook her head. Never had she allowed her nerves—or

perhaps it was fear—to control her. At least not in a very long time. Nor had she thought herself an impatient person until this very moment.

Had Mother Superior not chosen her path, Maribel might still be back at the orphanage trying to decide what to do. Now, with that decision made for her, there was nothing left to do but somehow manage to pass the time until she arrived in New Orleans.

"Fired indeed," she muttered as her fingers toyed with the ends of Mama's scarf.

Of course they both knew why Mother Superior did what she did, but that did not remove the sting of having her choices limited to only one. She had packed her few meager belongings with tears in her eyes.

All the books she read had come from the little library that seemed to grow by a book or two almost monthly. And though the volumes that appeared were often classics such as the works of Homer or other philosophers, Maribel found it curious that the occasional volume of seafaring adventures found its way onto the shelves despite Mother Superior's edict that the books were not fit for young ladies and gentlemen.

Stepping onto a sailing ship after all those years on land had been exhilarating, despite how her last trip at sea ended. Her cabin offered a level of comfort she hadn't expected, but then her comparison was to the hammock she'd had slung between two posts in a tiny space no bigger than a prison cell.

But that prison cell had been a special courtesy to her privacy and a labor of love from Mr. Rao, who fashioned the space in a far corner of the hold, and Mr. Piper, who fashioned a hammock from sailcloth.

Maribel turned her back on the horizon and its ominous black clouds to take another long look at the home that had sheltered her these last eleven years. All the children had come to the dock this morning to see her off, accompanied by the sisters and Mother

Superior. It had been a tearful farewell, made all the more so by Stephan's declaration that he would always have the upmost respect for her.

She had been crying too hard to correct him.

Then, when Mother Superior had tucked the package into her hand, the crying paused only for a moment. "A book?" she said as she looked into the old nun's eyes.

"Two," she said with tears shimmering. "A book of the Psalms and another I've been told is a favorite of yours. I thought perhaps you might make some time to further your education while you are en route to your new home."

Now as she allowed her gaze to drift across the buildings that made up St. Mary of the Island Orphanage, across the avocado trees that lined the beach side and the copse of guangos that filled the center of the structures, she was struck by how small it all looked. Her gaze lifted to the cross decorating the chapel as her mind returned to the first time she arrived here.

Surely the Lord brought her to Isla de Santa Maria. There was no other explanation. And where He took her, she would go.

Even if that meant leaving her home to find another in a strange land.

Oh, but Mama would be there, so all else was of no consequence. Her heart soared even as she felt tears fill her eyes. And Abuelo too. Soon she would see them both and they would be a family again. How terribly had she missed them.

Maribel let out a long breath and said a prayer of thanks for all God had done for her. And then she said one more for the safety of the people who lived in this wonderful place.

The warning bell rang and crewmen took their stations. The man assigned to lifting the anchor began the process. Up at the wheel, the captain stood at the ready, his second-in-command at his side.

But it was not her captain—not the terse but oh-so-kind Captain Beaumont—who would be guiding this vessel. Nor would the gentle African giant Mr. Bennett be assisting him.

Another tear fell, this one for friends lost. And though the light was still quite good, Maribel could bear looking at her island home no longer.

To the north, the black cloud bore down on them. Over on the deck, the sails were being adjusted to turn the vessel out into open water at an angle designed to sail around the coming storm. Overhead the lookout was doing his job, likely wondering when the captain would warn of lightning and send him back down onto the deck.

She smiled. On those few occasions when Captain Beaumont had called her down to a place of safety from the storm, she had not gone willingly. Unlike the others on the captain's ship, she loved to watch the lightning zigzag across the sky.

This much she did remember.

Maribel's heart thudded as an image rose. Sails. Yes. Black night and sails that were only revealed when lightning danced across the clouds.

A memory buried so deep that she wondered whether she had imagined it. She willed her heart to slow its rapid beating. Imagination, that's what it was.

After all the books she read, of course she would begin to see things she hadn't seen at all. Hadn't Mother Superior said as much every time a thought such as this occurred?

She'd told the old nun all about how she got to the island. About the planks of wood that had become her floating home for an interminable amount of time. About the explosion of light that led to her landing on those planks, and ultimately about awakening from a deep sleep on a soft cot in the back corner of the chapel. Somewhere in between were voices and strong hands. Embraces and promises too, but nothing that she could recollect with any assurance.

Mother Superior had listened patiently, her unseeing eyes never leaving Maribel's face. And then, at the end of it all, the old nun patted Maribel on the head and told her it was likely that it had all been a dream.

It wasn't, of course.

She knew very well that Captain Beaumont, Mr. Bennett, Mr. Rao, and Mr. Piper were all very real. But the rest of her memories? Those she'd been unable to sort into real and imagined, so eventually she had ceased to try.

But the lightning? That was a new memory, one she could not recall reading about in any of her novels.

As if on cue, fat raindrops began to plop around her. Maribel gathered the ends of her scarf tight in her hands, gave a cursory glance toward the horizon, and then made her way to the passageway leading to her cabin.

"Sloop to the northeast," she said out of habit just as she disappeared inside.

CHAPTER 16

Maribel froze.

Sloop to the northeast?

She raced back onto the deck. There it was, a gaff-rigged schooner.

Taking a calming breath, Maribel watched the vessel continue its approach. Surely this was not the same vessel she had seen in the inlet. Also, there was no proof that this ship was headed for Isla de Santa Maria. More likely, the schooner would tack around to lay anchor at Port Royal to the west. Most of the ships in this part of the Caribbean Sea were headed there.

Very few ever made a stop on the tiny island where orphans and nuns awaited.

"Yes, of course," she whispered as the rain pelted her. There was nothing of concern in a gaff-rigged schooner sailing toward Port Royal. "It will tack soon."

But the schooner did not tack, nor did it veer off a course that would take it directly to Isla de Santa Maria. That just would not do.

And yet there was nothing she could do to stop it.

She could, however, get a good look at the ship and its crew so that she could report them to authorities. Which authorities she would work out later.

Ignoring the rain that pelted her, Maribel raced to the rail and remained there as the schooner drew nearer. The seas roiled, and the deck heaved beneath her feet. Still she kept her attention focused on the gaff-rigged schooner.

"Excuse me, miss." A crewman came to stand beside her. "The captain has asked all passengers to please return to their cabins until the weather improves."

She spared him a quick glance. "I'm sure I'll be fine here. I've had experience sailing, and you may tell the captain this."

"I do appreciate that you've sailed before, but I am afraid the captain's request applies to everyone and not just those who do not have as much experience sailing as you do."

His sarcasm was evident, but she ignored it—and him—to return her attention to the white sails silhouetted against the black clouds. The vessel still had not made the adjustments to its course that would take it to Port Royal.

"Miss, forgive me, but I must insist," he said as he reached for her arm. "I am only following orders."

She shrugged out of his grasp. "I do see the predicament, but I am in the process of attempting to identify a vessel that is suspected of criminal activity on Isla de Santa Maria. Thus, I am certain your captain will understand if I decline his request that I return to my cabin."

The young man gave her a frustrated look and then nodded. "Be that as it may, you will have to explain this to the captain. I will just go and fetch him."

The schooner tacked and seemed to be changing course. Maribel smiled. Perhaps she was wrong about the vessel's destination.

Still, she wanted to be certain.

"Do as you must," she said as she squinted against the impending darkness. "And I will do the same."

Yes, the vessel was tacking. Then, abruptly, the vessel veered off in the opposite direction and made a straight line for Isla de Santa Maria.

Now the schooner was close enough to see the men running about on deck, the spot where the watch would be, and the wheel where the captain or one of his crewmen would be steering the ship.

There. Now she could almost make out the looks of the man behind the wheel. He was tall but not as tall as the man beside him. That man was dark, possibly African.

Something in how the dark man stood as he weathered the storm sparked a memory. Something buried deep. Not a dream but a memory.

Mr. Bennett. Yes, although surely not. He was long ago lost to the sea.

Yes, this man surely just resembled him.

Turning her attention to the captain, if that was the captain of the schooner, she could make out less of his looks because he had his back to her. They were almost side by side now, separated by a distance no farther than the avocado trees on the beach to the mahogany trees at the inlet.

Slowly, the captain turned toward her. Now they were almost close enough to see facial features. Maribel spied dark hair, broad shoulders, and an expression of surprise on his face.

She leaned closer, her perch precarious as the waves buffeted the ship. But there was something in that face. . .something that she remembered. Surely that was not the captain.

Her captain.

The world upended and tilted. A moment later, Maribel realized she'd been hauled up into someone's arms.

"Begging your pardon, miss, but the man with whom you're traveling, Mr. Lopez-Gonzales? He gave the captain permission to carry you down to your cabin if you would not go peaceably. He says he is charged with delivering you safely to your family, and I do see his dilemma what with you hanging over the side of the ship like that. Common in those who haven't traveled by sea much, though."

"Of all the nerve," she said. "I will have you know I sailed with the best of the best during my time at sea. My job was as lookout up high on the mast, and I only fell off once, but that was not my fault. You see, we were being shot at by the French."

"Shot at by the French," he said in a tone that clearly conveyed the fact he did not believe her. "That does make for a troublesome voyage. I, myself, have not had that experience, so I would not know for sure."

"You're patronizing me," she said as she squirmed against his grip.

"I am stating facts, Miss Cordoba. Never have I been shot at aboard a ship, be it French, Spanish, or any other."

The young man avoided any eye contact as he walked toward the passageway. Only when they reached the corridor heading down to the cabins did the crewman realize he would need Maribel's co-operation to traverse the remainder of the distance to her lodgings.

Though she considered putting up a fight, Maribel knew the vessel had passed behind them by now. Besides, to think the man at the wheel of the schooner could possibly have been the captain she knew eleven years ago was ludicrous.

"I can find my way from here," she told him.

Looking skeptical, he lowered her to her feet. "I'll just watch until you've gone into your cabin then," he said, and he did just that.

Reluctantly, Maribel returned to the tiny room that served as her bedchamber for this voyage. The accommodations, consisting of a bunk, a pitcher and bowl for washing, and a hook to hang her clothes, were much more comfortable than Mr. Rao's makeshift space.

Given the choice, however, Maribel would once again pass the time during this sea voyage in that sailmaker's hammock with the sound of Israel Bennett and Captain Beaumont bellowing orders overhead.

Her gift from the nuns and children was still where she left it atop the traveling trunk Mother Superior had provided. She retrieved the package and then went over to the bunk to open it.

When the wrapping fell away, her breath caught. Beneath a beautifully bound copy of the Psalms was *The Notorious Seafaring Pyrates and Their Exploits* by Captain Ulysses Jones.

Maribel traced the edges of the book and then ran her hand over the words of the title, embossed onto the cover in gold script. "Oh," was all she could manage as she cradled the book to her chest. "Oh," she said again and swiped at the tears shimmering in her eyes.

When she could finally see the pages without the words swimming in tears, Maribel turned to the first page and smiled. It had been a very long time since she'd read this story, since she had traveled the world of pirates and privateers through these tales.

Eleven years, to be exact.

Once she discovered the treasure that was her copy of *The Notorious Seafaring Pyrates and Their Exploits* and the lovely poems that were the Psalms, Maribel was content to do nothing but remain in her cabin and read these two books.

Then one evening as she arrived at the page containing the Eighth Psalm, Maribel felt the words come alive in her heart.

> *When I consider thy heavens, the work of thy fingers,*
> *the moon and the stars, which thou hast ordained;*
> *what is man, that thou art mindful of him? and the*
> *son of man, that thou visitest him? For thou hast*
> *made him a little lower than the angels, and hast*
> *crowned him with glory and honour. Thou madest him*
> *to have dominion over the works of thy hands; thou*
> *hast put all things under his feet: all sheep and oxen,*
> *yea, and the beasts of the field; the fowl of the air, and*
> *the fish of the sea, and whatsoever passeth through the*
> *paths of the seas. O LORD our Lord, how excellent is*
> *thy name in all the earth!*

"The fish of the sea, and whatsoever passeth through the paths of the seas," she read aloud as she heard the gentle sound of waves hitting the ship as the sails slapped above. "Thank You, Lord, for that reminder."

For as the day drew near for their arrival in New Orleans, Maribel had begun to worry about something that until now she hadn't considered. What would Mama and Abuelo think of her now?

When she last saw them she was a girl of twelve years, a child really. And now here she was a grown woman of three and twenty. Educated by nuns and kept from all but the simplest of pleasures, she would be nothing like the girl they knew.

Would they still want her?

More important, would they still love her?

Maribel carried these worries in her heart until the morning the ship's lookout called out that land had been spotted. Unable to sleep, she had long ago prepared for their arrival by packing her belongings into the trunk, including her books. If Mother Superior was correct, a bookish girl was one thing, but a bookish woman was altogether a different sort of creature.

She wished for a mirror so that she might smooth her unruly hair yet again. The next moment, Maribel gave thanks she did not have one, for she would not be treated to the sight she had become after all this time at sea.

A soft tap at the door indicated the time had come. She allowed Mr. Lopez-Gonzales into the cabin but remained standing at the door.

"What will happen next?" she asked as she toyed with the frayed edges of Mama's scarf.

The older man offered a kind smile. "You are nervous," he said. "Do not be. Your family is most anxious to be reunited, so there is absolutely no need for concern."

"All right," she said. "So once we dock, then what? Will my mother and grandfather be there to greet us?"

"Probably not," he said. "The city is young, and its riverfront is a place where proper ladies and gentlemen do not belong. I expect a representative of your grandfather's household will meet us, and you will be taken to the Cordoba home. It is quite nice, by the way. A beautiful new residence within view of the river."

"You said that I would be taken," she said. "Won't you be coming with me?"

"Oh no," he said gently. "I was retained to find you and bring you back to your family. Now that my job is done, I will bid you good-bye."

"I see."

Though Maribel had not developed any feelings of friendship to the older man, she certainly had not expected to continue on to the final destination of her journey without him. Indeed, he was the only person who had the benefit of knowing both her family and her.

"I do wish you would accompany me," she said, "but I do understand. Perhaps you would consider escorting me to their door?"

"Yes, I believe that would be appropriate."

"Thank you," she said. "And just one thing more. Would you be willing to tell me more about my grandfather and mother? There is so much that must have happened in the eleven years since I've seen them. I would like very much to hear whatever you might be able to say in that regard."

He seemed to consider her request for a moment, and then he nodded. "Yes, all right. I don't suppose it would hurt to tell you a few things, but keep in mind if I do not share something it is because that is a tale that your family must tell. Agreed?"

"Yes, of course."

Mr. Lopez-Gonzales smiled. "All right, then. I first came to know your grandfather in Spain when he had been searching for his missing granddaughter some two years, perhaps three. I was recommended to him as someone who might be able to assist him in his search. We determined it would be best for him to move to New Orleans to be closer to the places where we believed you might be living. When I suggested this, he immediately put the plan into action."

Maribel nodded. "My grandfather always was a man of action."

"Any man who leaves all he has in the way of power and influence and moves to a foreign land. . ." He shook his head. "Your grandfather is a very good man, Miss Cordoba. He is fair but honest, and for that reason he and I have worked well together over the years."

She returned his smile. "Then that much has not changed. And my mother?"

"A great beauty, your mother, well liked and highly sought after." He paused. "Beyond that, I will allow her to tell the story."

Above them the warning bell rang, and a moment later, Maribel felt the familiar tugging motion of the anchor catching hold.

"We'll be off soon," he said. "I will send a man down for your trunk."

"A moment more and I will join you," she said. Reaching once more for the book she'd left inside the trunk, Maribel turned to the page that had caught her attention previously. *When I consider thy heavens, the work of thy fingers, the moon and the stars, which thou hast ordained; what is man, that thou art mindful of him?* She took a deep breath and let it out as she returned the book of Psalms to her trunk. "What am I that You are mindful of me, Lord?" she whispered. "What indeed? Oh, but thank You all the same."

CHAPTER 17

Maribel's first impression of New Orleans was not a flattering one. Though the town had been established as the capital of the French territory, the condition of the city left much to be desired.

Water and waste ran from the street into the river, and persons of questionable intent loitered about as if waiting to snatch her or her belongings at any moment. One moved too close and was met with her elbow in his midsection.

As the ruffian went tumbling, Mr. Lopez-Gonzales looked back at her. From his calm expression, he had obviously not noticed the impending attack and its swift resolution.

"Miss Cordoba, the carriage is just up there. I hope all of this is not too much for a lady's delicate constitution."

Maribel stifled a smile as she glanced over her shoulder. "No, nothing I cannot handle, Mr. Lopez-Gonzales, but thank you for asking," she said, straightening her gloves.

Behind her the man groaned but remained on the ground. Maribel returned her attention to the older man's straight back and followed him all the way to where her grandfather's carriage awaited.

Though Maribel had not been used to such fineries while at St. Mary of the Island, she certainly recalled the conveyances her grandfather used back in Spain. In comparison to those carriages with their plush interiors and the Cordoba crest on the doors, this one was certainly no match.

Either Abuelo's fortunes were no longer what they once were, or the luxuries he enjoyed back in the old country were not available here. In either case, Maribel gave thanks that she had any means of transportation at all.

For as much as she disliked trudging through the filth on the docks, the mud that filled the streets of the city was even worse. Between the droppings left behind by the animals that pulled the carts and carriages and the heat of the Louisiana sun, the smell was abhorrent.

How could Mama and Abuelo possibly be happy here?

Then it came to her. They were only here for her. And they had endured this for years in anticipation of her arrival.

Mr. Lopez-Gonzales helped her into the carriage and then joined her. "Would you like me to tell you about the buildings we will see along the way?"

"Yes, please," she said, as much to learn about this city as to have something to discuss that would keep the silence from falling between them.

Silence gave her time to think, but discussion about buildings such as the Place d'Armes, the Director's House, and the Ursuline convent kept her occupied until the moment the carriage lurched to a stop in front of an elegant home built of brick and plaster with a broad porch across the front and four gables across the second-floor roof.

The older man leaned forward to nod toward a rather large building with a two-story towerlike structure next to it. "As you can see, your grandfather's home is just across Dumaine Street from the observatory and the governor's house."

"The observatory is the tall building?"

"It is, yes," he said. "Its owner, Mr. Baron, designed those terraces on the second floor so as to be able to make scientific observations with his telescope. You see, he is a scientist of some renown who—"

The imposing front door opened, interrupting the older man's speech. Expecting a dour servant to step outside and greet them, Maribel was stunned when a lovely woman of middle age and great beauty appeared in the doorway.

"Mama!"

Maribel couldn't get out of the carriage fast enough. When she reached her mother, time fell away as they embraced. The years had been kind to Mama, adding only the slightest touch of silver at her temples and lines at the corners of her eyes.

But those lines meant she had smiled. At least that is what Mother Superior always said.

"My baby," Mama repeated over and over until Maribel knew she would never tire of hearing the words. Their tears fell, and laughter sounded.

The reunion she dreaded had become one she did not want to end.

Gradually Maribel became aware of someone else nearby. She looked up to see her grandfather standing in the doorway.

The years had been less kind to Abuelo than they had to Mama, but he still wore that same smile and had the same gleam in his eyes when he looked at her. He still had the posture of a soldier and the presence of a man used to getting his way.

Mama released her and offered Abuelo a smile as she swiped at her tears. "Look, Don Pablo," she said. "You have succeeded in bringing our girl home."

"My Maribel," he said, his voice quivering with the same emotion that caused a tear to slide down his wrinkled cheek. "Is it really you?"

"It is me, Abuelo," she said as she fell into his arms. "And I am home."

"Come inside," he said when she would allow him out of her embrace. "We have much to discuss."

"Don Pablo," Mama said. "Don't you think you need to rest first? Normally at this time you are—"

He waved away the remainder of Mama's statement with a

sweep of his hand. "Nonsense," he said. "Normally at this time I am wondering where my precious grandchild is and asking the Lord to bring her home. He has answered my prayers, so I have no need of praying them again." He winked at Maribel. "You only thought I was taking my morning nap."

Maribel giggled and followed her grandfather through a beautifully decorated foyer and into a parlor that faced the front of the home. Here and there were pieces that must have been brought from the family home in Spain, but they had been mixed with other furnishings that Maribel did not recognize.

Abuelo took a seat in a chair nearest the window and then indicated that she should join him. Choosing the settee for its proximity to her grandfather, Maribel settled on one end and waited for her mother to seat herself on the other.

A uniformed servant hurried in with refreshments, but Abuelo waved them away. "Nothing for me," he said. "But my granddaughter will likely not feel the same. She's been on an ocean voyage, you know."

"Several of them," Mama said softly as she reached across the distance on the settee to grasp Maribel's hand. "My sweetheart, I cannot believe you are actually sitting here. So many years I hoped and prayed and waited. . . ." She shook her head. "And so many times I wished I hadn't allowed Antonio to make a fool of me."

Her grandfather leaned forward and rested his elbows on his knees. "What did your father tell you about us?"

Recalling the conversation as if it had happened just yesterday, Maribel took a deep breath and let it out slowly before responding. "That you were dead," she managed. "He said you and Mama had been in an accident and neither of you survived."

Silence fell. Outside on the street, a wagon rolled by with two plodding horses pulling it.

"This is my fault," Abuelo finally said. "If only I had not decided my son would be better off sent to Cuba. He was given a nice placement in the colonial office, you know. I thought I had done well by him."

"You had, Don Pablo," Mama said. "But he did not do well by us."

"No, he did not." Her grandfather turned to Maribel. "I do not wish to stir up unpleasantness, but some say my son drowned. Others claim he was murdered. I hope you did not see him meet his demise, but if you have knowledge of this matter, I wish to hear it."

"I do have knowledge," she said. "And those who tell you he drowned are correct. There was a fight. My father shot a man in the back."

Abuelo winced but said nothing further. Maribel continued. "He fought a man on the deck. Their battle sent them over the railing and into the sea. The other man lived, but my father did not."

She let out a long breath and waited for the tears to come. Not since she was a child had she relived that moment at sea. Other moments, yes, but not that one.

"So the question is answered, then," he said as he leaned back in the chair. "I am very sorry you saw this, my dear. I would give anything to have spared you of it all."

Maribel managed a smile. "You know, Abuelo, it was not the childhood any of us expected, but it was a good childhood. I missed you both terribly, but not knowing you were alive and looking for me made the situation easier to bear."

Mama's hand fluttered. "When you are ready, I would love to celebrate your return with a proper party. So many of my friends here are aware of your impending return, and they will be asking for introductions. My dear friend Abigail is begging to host a small gathering."

"Oh, I don't know, Mama. Will they think it odd that I was rescued by privateers and lived among them for nearly two months before spending eleven years at an orphanage in the Caribbean?"

Neither Mama nor her grandfather spoke for a moment. Finally, Mama shook her head. "Maribel, I don't understand. Mr.

Lopez-Gonzales said he found you at an orphanage. He did not indicate anything other than that. Your grandfather and I assumed. . ." She sat back seemingly unable to continue.

"What your mother is saying, my dear, is if any of that did happen, then we are only just hearing of it. Please tell me about this privateer who rescued you. Is he someone I might know?"

The thought of her very proper Spanish grandfather knowing someone like Captain Beaumont made her smile. "No, I doubt you know him. He was a kind man, young for the profession he chose, and loyal to his crew. For the time I was on board, I was treated with kindness."

"I see," he said. "And his name?"

"Captain Beaumont," she said.

Her grandfather looked over at Mama, who shook her head. "I wondered if he might be an enemy of Antonio."

"If he was, I was not told of it," she said.

"Tell me about the orphanage and how you came to live there," Mama said. "I want to hear every detail."

Maribel smiled. This was a topic she could easily discuss at length. And discuss they did until it appeared Abuelo's eyes were fighting to remain open.

"You see, you stubborn man," Mama said to him. "You've missed your morning rest and now you can barely stay awake to entertain our granddaughter."

He chuckled but did not disagree. Instead, he looked over at Maribel and smiled. "I will sleep well knowing you are under my roof, child." He paused. "Although you are no longer a child, are you?"

"I fear not," she said. "But I am not so old that you should despair of me. I taught the children at the convent for several years now, and if it is possible, I wish to continue teaching. Perhaps the Ursulines are in need of someone with my abilities."

"Are you considering joining the convent?" Mama asked, concern etching her voice.

"Oh no," Maribel said with a giggle. "I tried that at St. Mary of the Island and was deemed most unsuitable. Apparently reading adventure novels and climbing trees is not appropriate behavior for a novitiate."

From the look on her mother's face, it apparently was not appropriate behavior for a young lady in the Cordoba household either.

"Yes, well," Mama said. "I can see there have been some lessons on proper social behavior that might have been missed during your time with the nuns." Her expression brightened. "No need to worry. I am here to see to your continued education, Maribel. And once you are ready for society, then I will allow dear Abigail to throw the grandest welcome-home party this city has ever seen."

"Wonderful." Maribel stifled a groan. Gone were the days when she would be allowed to run barefoot across the courtyard or slip off to swim in the ocean. The return of her family had certainly been more wonderful than she expected. It also brought with it a few concerns she had not considered.

"You know, Mary," Abuelo said as he rose, "I think we could all benefit from some rest. Perhaps a siesta and then later we can discuss evening plans?"

Mama rose and nodded in agreement. "I will have refreshments brought to your room, Maribel. Come, it is right this way."

Maribel followed her mother down a corridor that led to two rooms. Ushering Maribel into the room on the right, Mama paused in the door to smile.

"I still cannot believe you are home with us," she said. "I thought you were. . ."

Tears fell, and Maribel caught them with her handkerchief. "Oh, Mama," she said when she could manage words. "I was afraid you wouldn't want me."

"Wouldn't want you?" She held Maribel at arm's length. "After all we did to find you, why in the world would you think we wouldn't want you?"

She shrugged. "I'm not like you. My life, it was different. I thought perhaps that would make me unsuitable."

"My precious child," she said softly. "You could never be unsuitable in my eyes."

"Even if I have climbed a mainmast and acted as lookout for ships on the horizon?"

Mama grinned. "Especially if you have done those things, and do you know why?"

"Why?" she said through happy tears that had Mama dabbing Maribel's cheeks with her own handkerchief.

"Because now I am extremely jealous and want to know every detail of what that was like." She pressed her forefinger to Maribel's lips. "But not now. Rest and have something to eat and drink. Later I will send in a tub for your bath and fresh clothing." Mama's gaze swept the length of her. "Tomorrow we will see to a new wardrobe and perhaps pay some calls, but today?" She paused. "Today I am keeping you all to myself."

Maribel surprised herself by doing as she was told and actually resting rather than reading her book or slipping out to explore her new home. When the maid and her helpers came to prepare her bath, she happily gave over her soiled traveling clothes in exchange for warm, clean water and fragrant soap she remembered from her childhood in Spain.

The dress that appeared in her bedchamber was breathtaking. Like nothing she had ever owned—or seen—during her time at the orphanage, the gown was constructed of a soft floral material and fit Maribel as if it had been made specifically with her in mind.

When she finished dressing, Maribel took up her book and settled onto the chair nearest the window to make the most of the afternoon light. It was there she found herself the next morning, having fallen asleep right where she'd been sitting.

Mama despaired of the wrinkled gown the moment she saw Maribel. "You were exhausted from your voyage. I could not bear to awaken you, even if it meant that your dress would be ruined."

She smiled. "Don't worry, though. I've had the maid prepare another dress for you to wear. Now just go on and let her dress you, and then we will get started on the day's events."

"But, Mama, I haven't had breakfast yet."

"No time," she said. "Perhaps later. After our visit to the dressmaker."

Maribel complied and somehow ended up in the carriage dressed in a floral gown and feeling as though she hadn't eaten in a week. As the carriage turned down Chartres Street, Mama gasped.

"Do put a smile on your face, Maribel," she said as she nodded toward a carriage coming toward them from the opposite direction. "That is Bienville approaching. He's the governor of all of the territory of Louisiana and a representative of the king and Versailles here, you know."

She did not know, but he sounded very important. Maribel did as she was told and offered the older man a smile when his carriage slowed to a stop beside them. The man Mama called Bienville appeared to be a fellow almost as old as Abuelo.

And quite distracted.

"Lovely day, Governor," Mama said with the languid tone of a woman who hadn't just indicated her excitement at receiving the governor's attention.

"It appears your daughter has arrived, Mrs. Cordoba," he said, moving his attention from Mama to Maribel. "Welcome to New Orleans, young lady. We have prayed for your safe return."

"Thank you, sir," she obediently responded.

The governor's attention had already returned to Mama. In truth, he seemed quite interested in her. "Have you called on my nephew yet? He returns to the city as of today, and I do believe he might be able to help you with that bit of trouble you're having."

Mama cut her eyes at Maribel, but her broad smile never wavered. "I have not yet paid him a visit," she said. "Perhaps next week I will find the time to set an appointment. Do you truly think he can help?"

The older man matched Mama's smile. "At my word, of course he can." He made a great show of retrieving his pocket watch and checking the time, and then he returned his attention to Mama. "Please forgive me, but I'm to send my carriage to the docks shortly. I'll let him know you will be paying him a call next week."

"Do think of me fondly, Governor, and know my father-in-law always does enjoy your friendly conversation."

"Then please convey a message to Don Pablo that I wish to engage him in friendly conversation very soon."

"He will be pleased," she said as she lifted her fan and instructed the driver to proceed.

"Mama," Maribel said when the carriage was in motion again. "Do you have a romance or a marriage planned with that man?"

"Oh, dear," Mama said. "That is not how a woman goes about marriage, nor do we plan romance. The proper question is whether I have plans to convince that man he ought to marry me. And the answer to that question is maybe I do and maybe I do not."

Maribel shook her head. "Because you do not want to admit which it is?"

She shrugged. "Because I do not yet know which it is. Bienville is a busy man and a confirmed bachelor. I'm not certain I wish to be wed to such a man, even one as nice as he."

"Then perhaps you can tell me what this trouble is that the governor mentioned." She gave her mother a sideways look. "Is there something wrong?"

Mama waved away the question with a sweep of her hand. "Nothing is wrong, sweet daughter. Just a little wrinkle that needs to be ironed out next week."

CHAPTER 18

As it turned out, there were other wrinkles to be ironed out. Wrinkles in the silk gown that Mama insisted was properly fitted for the celebration of her homecoming. And wrinkles that appeared at the corners of Mama's eyes when she grinned at the seamstress and asked her to send the bill to Don Pablo's home.

Then came the wrinkle of getting from the seamstress's shop to the carriage without getting wet from the rain that had begun falling during the grueling fitting session. Back on Isla de Santa Maria, Maribel would have ignored the rain to allow her gown a soaking.

Not if she had to teach, of course, but during her own time it was nothing to take a stroll in the rain. But here in New Orleans, it was quickly apparent that a proper lady did not do such things.

Nor did a proper lady complain about paying visits or taking tea. She did not complain about the heat in stiff gowns or the sore feet that came from wearing what Mama called proper lady's shoes.

And she did not complain when her mother planned the event of the year in her honor.

Even if the last thing she wished to do was to be paraded among the ladies and gentlemen of her adopted city so they could watch closely to be certain she behaved like a proper lady. Because, apparently, being a proper lady was Maribel's new role.

This last fact Maribel learned as Mama was chattering about

the party that her friend Abigail intended to give. They were to pay this woman a visit, and all Maribel could think of was the faint hope that Mama's friend might offer some sort of sustenance to keep her from evaporating into nothing.

Even as she held out hope, she knew it was unlikely. Apparently ladies did not eat in this city. So she decided to make one last attempt to avoid the visit altogether.

"Mama, I know you wish me to meet your friends but perhaps another day?" she said as her stomach complained loudly. "It has been a busy morning, and I am quite exhausted."

"You slept enough for two days, Maribel," she said as she adjusted the lace on her sleeve. "Abigail has been my dearest friend ever since Don Pablo and I arrived in the city. If you were to visit anyone else before you visit her, she would be heartbroken."

"Then I will take a vow not to visit anyone else," Maribel said. "And tomorrow she can be the first on our list."

"Don't be ridiculous." Mama shook her head. "We are practically on her doorstep. You will behave like a proper lady and enjoy this visit. Do you understand?"

"Yes, Mama," she said, although the events of the morning had been a fair indicator that she did not yet completely understand how to behave like a proper lady. But if that sort of thing was important to Mama—and it appeared that it was—then she simply would have to learn.

"Mama," she said as an idea occurred that just might buy her some time before she was required to be paraded about in public. "Perhaps I need a tutor."

"Tutor? Whatever for?"

"Well," Maribel said as she slowed her speech to allow the idea to properly unfold in her mind, "if I am to navigate the perilous waters of society, perhaps someone of my own age could be of service in showing me exactly how to accomplish this. Of course I do understand you are fully capable of repairing my social deficits, but wouldn't someone of my age group be more likely to give advice that would be relevant? Also, she might know others with whom I could become friends."

At that statement, Maribel almost visibly cringed. The last thing she wished was to join a social circle of proper ladies. Not when Abuelo's home had a library full of books just waiting to be read.

Mama seemed ready to speak and then closed her mouth. Apparently something in what Maribel just said had made sense to her.

"Yes," her mother finally said. "Yes, I do believe you came up with a wonderful idea, Maribel. Much as I would love to tutor you in the ways of a proper lady, a girl of your own age would be much more appropriate." She smiled. "And besides, you know no one in the city."

"Other than you and Abuelo," she reminded her, still wishing she hadn't gone down the path of making Mama believe she wanted to gain a circle of friends.

"Yes, of course," Mama said. "But no one of your age and social standing. Yes, I know exactly the girl who can help you."

"You do?"

The carriage pulled to a stop in front of a large house that stood two stories high and spread out quite a distance in both directions. Before Mama could emerge from the carriage, a footman was there to assist her. Another footman in matching attire aided Maribel.

"But, Mama," she said. "I thought perhaps we would begin my training before I was subjected to any visits."

"Nonsense," Mama said as she allowed a maid to usher them inside. "Abigail doesn't care about any of that. She just wants to meet you after all these years of praying you would come home. And, of course, I will want to discuss your idea with her."

"Whatever for?" Maribel asked as she took in the elegantly carved furniture and crimson silk drapes that filled the expansive parlor.

"Because the young lady I have in mind for tutoring you is

Abigail's daughter, Gabrielle. What better time to ask this favor of her than now? For if there is to be a welcome-home celebration, it makes no sense to wait a lengthy amount of time before holding the party."

"While I do agree," Maribel said as she perched on the edge of a settee covered in navy-striped silk, "wouldn't it make more sense to just let me learn how to conduct myself in public first?"

"My dear daughter," Mama said, her tone soft but firm. "When you were very young, I realized how intelligent you were. There was not a skill presented to you that you failed to master. I despaired of keeping you occupied until your tutor taught you to read." She slid Maribel a knowing glance. "You were not yet four years old."

A horse plodded past, its rider oblivious to the spirited conversation going on inside on the other side of the window. She watched the hooves kick up muddy tracks in the road until she finally could manage a response. Because unfortunately she knew where this conversation was leading.

"Yes, well, while I will agree, I don't follow how this has anything to do with my ability to adapt socially to this new city."

"You do follow," she said. "You are the same now as you were eleven years ago. Anything you put your mind to you can master, and, my darling, you require very little time to master it. Just as now when you believe you have mastered me, but you have not. For you see, I have no doubt that if allowed, you would put off these lessons or fail miserably at them so as not to have to be introduced socially at all."

Of course, Mama still knew her quite well. Thus there was no need to protest. Just to make another plan.

"Mama," she said softly as she gave her a sideways look. "Why did that seamstress seem upset when you did not offer payment? Is it customary here to do such a thing? Back in Spain proper ladies did not handle money. Are things different here?"

Mama's smile went south and was replaced by the neutral

expression Maribel recognized from her childhood. The expression that would let her know just how displeased she was with the question.

"Mary, dear," came a voice from just outside the parlor.

"That will be our hostess, Abigail," Mama said, her voice now taut with irritation. "There will be no more discussion on this topic, either here or once we are back home. Should you make the attempt, you will regret that you did not heed my warning. Do you understand?"

Before Maribel could respond, a voluptuous dark-haired woman a full decade younger than Maribel expected burst into the room. "Please forgive the delay. I was upstairs supervising the opening of Jean-Luc's chambers and up to my elbows in...oh!"

Her hands went to her cheeks, revealing sparkling jewels on several fingers and a clattering collection of bracelets dotted in pearls and diamonds. Matching pearl-and-diamond earrings sparkled beneath inky-black hair that had been swept away from her face with jeweled combs.

The effect was both stunning and intimidating. Then she smiled, and her deep brown eyes lit with joy.

"You must be Maribel," she said as she approached her in the same way one would approach a delicate vase or fragile flower. "You are everything your mother said you would be and more." She looked toward Mama, and her smile rose higher. "She's home, Mary. Can you believe it? She is home."

And then this lovely creature—this proper lady—began to weep.

"Abigail, my dearest friend, meet Maribel Cordoba," Mama said with a tremble in her voice. "Maribel, this is Mrs. Abigail Valmont."

The lady of the house shook her head and swiped at her eyes with a lace-edged handkerchief. "I am so sorry for these silly tears," she said. "I am just so overcome with how very good our Lord can be to us on occasion. When I see the efforts of our prayers standing before us, well, it is just all too much."

"It is indeed," Mama said. "Her grandfather and I are beyond grateful that she has been found. And we are, of course, indebted to you and Marcel for your generosity as well."

She shook her head. "It is nothing. Oh, but, Maribel, you are quite something. Look at you." Her attention went back to Mama. "For a girl who grew up outside of a city with modern conveniences, she seems remarkably well settled here and quite sophisticated."

"She is still learning our ways, but I believe she is happy to be home, are you not, Maribel?"

"I am," she said, even as she knew that happiness came with an equal amount of regret at what she had left behind on Isla de Santa Maria. "And I am thankful for the prayers that kept me safe while I was lost and then brought me here."

"But as to learning our ways," Mama said, sliding a warning glance toward Maribel before facing their hostess once more. "There is much yet to be taught, I'm afraid. You see, Maribel was still but a child when we lost her, and eleven years have passed."

"Eleven years," Mrs. Valmont said as if that number held some significance. She paused a moment, her expression hinting that her thoughts were far away. Then the smile returned and she turned her focus to Mama. "Yes, that is a long time to wait for a child to return."

"I have had the most interesting conversation with my daughter, and I would like your opinion, Abigail."

"Of course," she said with an expectant look as she settled onto the chair nearest Mama.

Mama shifted positions and gave their hostess her full attention, leaving Maribel to take in her surroundings. Although this was a fine home, it was very much a family home as witnessed by the gilt-framed painting over the fireplace.

The artist had captured the family of six seated in this very room. A man easily as old as Abuelo sat next to a younger Abigail on the settee, his expression that of a proud father and happy husband. Positioned on either side of them were a boy and a girl barely old enough to sit alone—who must be twins. Standing behind the couple were two young men in their teen years, one slightly taller and possibly a little older than the other.

While the elder Valmont looked straight ahead, Abigail had her attention focused on her husband, their hands entwined. Maribel's gaze went from the little girl beside her mother to the little boy next to his papa. Then she studied the young men behind them. Very much alike in their facial features, the younger-looking of the two wore a broad smile. The elder one, though he. . .

Maribel leaned forward. There was something familiar about the elder son. Something in the way he looked directly at her as though he could jump out of the painting and stand right in front of her. Something in those eyes, beautifully silver, and that insolent expression—not unhappy but not completely happy either—that struck a memory.

Or perhaps her imagination.

She sat back and let out a long breath. Mother Superior was right. Her imagination made her think things were real when they were, in truth, imaginary. How could a stranger in a painting on some woman's wall in New Orleans possibly be someone who was part of her memories?

And yet she could not look away from that painting. Could not relieve herself of the notion that she had looked into those eyes before.

"Maribel?"

Mama nudged her, and Maribel tore herself from the painting to return to whatever reality awaited in Abigail Valmont's parlor. She found both Mama and their hostess staring at her.

"Yes, Mama. I'm sorry. I was distracted by that painting." She looked past Mama to Mrs. Valmont. "It is lovely."

"Thank you, Maribel," Mrs. Valmont said. "My husband would like another painted, but I do like this one. The children were all so much younger then. Such an innocent time for all of them. And for us as their parents. But as they grow, well. . ." She shrugged.

"My mother used to say little children, little problems. But as they age, it becomes big children, big problems. I suppose that truth has been borne out more times than I wish."

"Isn't that the truth?" Mama said. "Oh, but what blessings your children are all the same."

"Depending on the day, yes," she said with a grin.

"So, Maribel, you likely missed our conversation regarding the subject you and I discussed in the carriage."

"I did, and I am terribly sorry for my inattentive rudeness."

Even Mama looked suitably impressed at her apology. So much so, she actually smiled.

"Oh, darling, I know there are so many new things here that you are unused to. Being inattentive is understandable in the short term." Her smile evaporated. "However, my darling, I must insist that you do pay attention now. Abigail and I have come up with the most brilliant plan, haven't we, dear?"

"Oh, we have," Abigail said, her hands pressed together as if she might soon begin applauding the two of them and their strategies. "While your mother despaired of a way to help you learn our ways here, I did think perhaps I had a solution. You see, my daughter, Gabrielle, is in dire need of a new friend. Suffice it to say, she has not spent her time as wisely as I wish and needs to be redirected to a cause that is worthy."

"And I am that cause."

Soon as she said the words, Maribel wished to take them back. The very tone of them sounded rude at worst and ungrateful at best. Before she could speak to remedy the situation, her hostess laughed.

"Oh, Mary. She is so quick-witted. She and Gabrielle will get along famously, and I will make the introduction right now." Mrs. Valmont rose. "You two just wait right here, will you?"

"Of course," Mama said sweetly. As soon as the parlor door closed behind Mrs. Valmont, Mama's expression changed. "What am I going to do with you, Maribel Cordoba? The moment I think

I have finally gotten through to you regarding the behavior of a proper lady, you prove me wrong."

"I'm sorry, Mama. Truly I meant no offense," Maribel said as she rose to walk toward the painting, now mesmerized by the young man with the fearless look and the memorable eyes.

"You're doing it again," she said. "What is so important about that painting that you have to lose all ability to respond to anyone else in the room?"

"I don't know," she told her. "There's just something about. . ."

Maribel paused. Had Mother Superior's warning about her imagination not been echoing, she might have admitted to Mama that there was something about that one fellow in the painting that seemed familiar. Instead, she chose to keep that to herself.

Mama came to stand beside her, grasping Maribel's hand. She turned away from the painting to face her mother. "I owe you an apology," Mama said gently.

Not at all what she expected to hear from her mother. "Why?"

Her expression softened. "Because I have expected far too much from you. My darling, you have barely been in the city for one day. How in the world would you know how to conduct yourself after so short a time?"

"Yes, well, I was taught manners by the nuns, so I will not allow them to accept the blame for behavior they did not cause," she said, suddenly feeling the need to defend Mother Superior and the others who toiled at the orphanage.

"Of course," she said. "I am a complete fool. Will you forgive me?"

Maribel shook her head. "Again, why?"

"I lived through eleven years' worth of days spent wondering where you were. Eleven years of nights when I fell asleep praying or crying—sometimes both—because my daughter had vanished. I refused to believe you died when the *Venganza* was sunk by those horrible pirates and—"

"Privateers, Mama. There is a difference. And those privateers did not sink the *Venganza*. The idiocy of those in charge of that vessel is what sunk it. The crew had Letters of Marque from the king of France, and they did not seek anything other than the treasure in the *Venganza's* hold. No violence was spent against the Spanish vessel and yet they fired against us."

Mama's eyes widened. "Daughter, tell me exactly who is *us*?"

She had said too much, this Maribel could easily tell. Though the truth of her life was there for her family to know if they wished, it was becoming quite clear that Mama did not wish to know it.

"*Us* would be the crew aboard the *Ghost Ship*, although Captain Beaumont did not prefer that name for the vessel," she said. "I tried to tell you of how I arrived at the orphanage. Did you not believe I spent time aboard a privateer's vessel?"

Mama released her hand and walked away only to return. "There will be an appropriate time to continue this conversation," she said, her voice barely above a whisper. "But that time is not now."

"I tried," she said again.

"Perhaps you did, but there will be questions regarding at what point this *Ghost Ship* became *us* to you, and you have not yet tried to tell me this. This captain, he had a bounty on his head, and not just from the Spaniards who did not take kindly to him accosting their vessel."

"I was on that vessel, Mama," she said, her temper rising. "I can tell you exactly what happened."

Mama's eyes narrowed. "There is no need, Maribel. You can be sure that the father and widow of the late Antonio Cordoba were told the facts surrounding these supposed Letters of Marque and how the *Venganza* came to land at the bottom of the Caribbean Sea. The one fact they got wrong, however, was that you were very much alive and not dead like your father."

"Well, Mama, it appears you will believe strangers over your daughter," she snapped as she heard a conversation out in the foyer, "but I was there, and I can tell you that the facts you were told are absolutely and positively wrong."

CHAPTER 19

Jean-Luc walked into the foyer of his family home and then stepped into his sister's open arms. "You are finally home!" Gabrielle exclaimed. "You promised you would be back days ago. More than a week, actually, and you had us all very worried."

He grinned and spun the spirited girl around then set her back on her feet, slipping a small package into her hand as she tried to find her balance. "There," he said with a grin, "am I forgiven?"

Gaby hurried to open the package. "I am not a child that you can distract with pretty things. I was worried about you. And worse than that, I have been given the most vile of punishments, and all because I dared sneak out of the house to pay a call on a friend. Can you feature it?"

She retrieved a strand of pearls from the package and tossed the wrapping behind her. "Oh, Jean-Luc, they are exquisite."

"As are you," he said. "Turn around and let me see how they look on you."

"Mama will not be pleased if she sees me wearing pearls during the daylight hours." Her grin rose, making her look so much like her mother. "But I am already in trouble, so what can it hurt?"

Jean-Luc held the pearls away from her and frowned. "Oh, I don't know then. I have seen your mother when she's displeased with one of her children. I do not want to be in the line of fire." He pretended to slide the pearls back into his pocket. "I'll just give these to her so that I will be the favored child and you can stay in trouble."

"No," she said as she snatched them out of his hand. "You will do no such thing. Put these on me now so I can see how they look."

He did as she told, but then most everyone gave in to the brown-eyed charmer's demands. It had been that way since her birth, the only daughter in a house full of brothers, and likely would always continue.

"So this friend you went to visit?" he said as he held both ends of the strand and began the process of closing the clasp. "What was his name?"

She whirled around, eyes blazing. He nearly dropped the pearls. Thankfully, the clasp held, or else she would have been throwing the tantrum he knew was coming amid several dozen exactly matched pearls from the Orient rolling around on the marble floor.

"If I didn't adore you so much," she said evenly, "I would be insulted that you would assume such a thing of me."

"I will rephrase the question then," he said.

"Thank you." Her smile returned, just as he knew it would. *Brat.*

"What was his name?"

"Jean-Luc," she exclaimed as she shook her head. "Oh all right. He's a very nice fellow, but Mama and Papa are being ridiculous about the whole thing. It's Mama, I know it, because Papa trusts me."

"Papa trusts Mama to keep you in line," he said with a laugh. "Because if it is left to Papa, he will tell you yes no matter what you ask."

"This time he actually agrees with her." She leaned against his shoulder in mock horror. When she looked up at him, her expression was pitiful. "It is a fate worse than death. I am to be a tutor."

"A tutor?" Jean-Luc laughed. "That is your fate worse than death? Oh, my darling Gaby, you really should tell Papa you're running away to join the theater. I'm sure he would let you, because as we have established, he does tend to do that, and of course, I will vouch for your flair for the dramatic."

"Flair for the dramatic? I will have you know that—"

"Gaby, is that you I hear out in the foyer?" Abigail called from somewhere upstairs. "Where have you gotten off to?"

Gabrielle's eyes widened, and then her gaze darted about the room as if searching for the best place to escape her mother. Jean-Luc nodded toward the closed parlor door.

"I generally hide in there." He shrugged. "The curtains are quite handy if you stand behind them. Or at least they were when I was seven."

"Stop teasing me," she said. "I am not a child playing hide-and-seek. This is serious. And besides, the person I am to tutor is in the parlor with her mother, so that will not work at all."

He nodded toward the room on their left. "Then I would try Father's library. If you climb under the desk and gather up your skirts, she may not find you. Although beware, when she does find you, you'll have to answer to her."

"I'm just trying to buy some time until she changes her mind. I absolutely cannot be stuck teaching some girl from the outer banks of nowhere how to fit in here in the city."

Jean-Luc shook his head. "The outer banks of nowhere? You and Michel were born in this city, true, but I was born in Paris, as was Quinton. Compared to us, *you* are from the outer banks of nowhere, so be careful when casting stones."

"I heard you talking, Gabrielle Valmont, and I will not be ignored," Abigail called. "Where are you?"

Gaby made for the open door to the library, but Jean-Luc grasped her wrist. "What is his name?"

She struggled against his hold on her even as her mother's footsteps echoed above their heads. "Let me go," she demanded. "You truly do not want her to find me right now, and if she does because of you, then I will exact my revenge."

"How?" he said with a laugh. "By forcing me to tutor someone?"

"Perhaps," she said as her expression went penitent. "Please, just let me go."

"Not until I have a name."

Stubborn to the end, Gaby continued her attempt to break free. Finally, as Abigail's tread hit the stairs behind them, she leaned up on her tiptoes and whispered, "Louis Gayarre."

Jean-Luc let her go just in time for Gaby's skirts to disappear inside the office. As Abigail reached the bottom of the stairs, he saw his sister scurry under the desk.

"Jean-Luc, you're home!" Abigail enveloped him in a hug, temporarily distracted from her search by his arrival. She smelled like lavender and hugged him like he'd been gone for months and not weeks.

She released him to hold him at arm's length. "I will never get used to the trips you take, my son. I always worry, and then you come home and all is well again."

"And I am always glad to be home." He cut his eyes toward the library where Gaby had done a poor job of gathering her skirts out of sight. "I understand all is not well, however. What is this about my sister and a young man?"

Abigail let out a long breath and shook her head. "I am at my wit's end, Jean-Luc. She has been sneaking out to go and meet this fellow, and your father and I are plenty worried about this. I've told her if he wishes to court her, he must first discuss his prospects with her papa. She claims courting is not what they're doing, but if that's not it, then I cannot imagine what it is. I am worried sick about her. And now she's gone and disappeared."

Jean-Luc winked and then nodded toward the library. Abigail followed his gaze. She must have spied the skirts showing beneath the desk, for she shook her head.

He kept his voice just low enough to prevent his sister from overhearing. "Tell me about this tutoring punishment that has been inflicted on her. Is it as awful as she claims?"

Abigail laughed. "Not at all. She's a completely lovely girl and the daughter of a dear friend. She's recently arrived in New Orleans and is lacking in some of the social graces needed to establish friends and make a good match. I merely offered Gabrielle as someone who would be willing to assist the young lady in making the transition. If she indicated it was anything more than this, she is being overdramatic."

"Is that even possible?" he asked as he stifled a smile.

The daughter's penchant for these types of antics had definitely come from her mother. Not that he would ever tell Abigail that. Or Gaby for that matter.

"Who is this young lady? Perhaps a rival for her male friend's affections?"

"I am not at liberty to give the young lady's name, nor would I if I were. I do not wish to cause any embarrassment to her mother. It is not my friend's fault that her daughter's education is lacking in certain areas. As to a love rival? No, that's not possible. She's only just arrived here, as I said. She knows no one."

Abigail watched as Gaby gathered up her skirts so they no longer could be seen from the foyer. Shaking her head, she leaned close to Jean-Luc.

"Honestly, I am hoping your sister learns as much from this young woman as the young woman learns from Gaby. Our daughter is a good girl, but there is a level of maturity that I wish was a bit higher than it currently is. She is eighteen years old, for goodness' sake. When I was her age, she and Michel were already on the way."

"Given the fact Gaby is currently playing hide-and-seek with you by climbing under Father's desk, I tend to agree." He paused. "How can I help?"

Abigail tapped her foot on the marble floor as she considered his question. "I suppose something needs to be done about this young man of hers. We've tried for weeks to get the name from her, but she refuses to tell us."

"Louis Gayarre." At Abigail's look of surprise, he shrugged. "I am more convincing than you are, I suppose."

"I don't even want to know how you managed it," she said. "Unless you think I can replicate the process the next time I try and get information out of her."

"I don't know, Abigail." He gave her a sideways look. "How strong is your grip?"

She gave him a playful swat. "Stop teasing me and go tell your sister her father is on his way downstairs and has need of his desk. She will have to find another piece of furniture to hide under."

"Yes, ma'am," he said.

Abigail gave him a grateful look. "Thank you. Some days I truly despair of what I would do without you, Jean-Luc, and not just in the management of your siblings." She nodded toward the closed door of the parlor. "I am being a terrible hostess, so I must go and apologize. Will you be staying with us tonight?"

"For a few days, yes." He had an obligation that would take him out of the house later tonight, but the family would be long abed by then.

"Good." She clasped his shoulder and smiled. "I am very glad you are home, Jean-Luc Valmont. Very glad, indeed. You are good for all of us in this family," she said over her shoulder as her hand touched the knob of the parlor door.

He offered her a broad smile. "And my family is good for me."

The parlor door opened, revealing the backs of two women who stood in front of the fireplace. Both were dressed in gowns that looked very much like the clothing Abigail and Gaby wore, thus he assumed these two were not another of Abigail's charity projects.

From time to time, the woman who raised him would cause Father much concern with the projects she took on. Sometimes these projects were as ordinary as a food drive for the hungry or a knitting circle that donated scarves and mittens for the nuns at the Ursuline convent to distribute.

Then there were the other times when Abigail's good intentions overruled her good judgment. Such as the day she brought home an opera singer from Bavaria who mistakenly thought he had been signed to perform at the New Orleans Opera House. Only after he arrived did the poor man discover there was neither an opera house in the city nor a ship that would accept him as a passenger without payment.

Father had complained for days about the noise emanating from the room at the end of the hallway. Terms like "strangling a wild goose" and "murdering a squealing pig" were tossed about as the men of the family plotted to remove their houseguest from beneath the Valmont roof.

The consensus was that the Valmont family should buy the singer a ticket back to Bavaria, but Father refused. If word got out that the Valmonts would pay for this, there would likely be no end to the itinerant musicians who might darken their doorstep. Not only that, but Abigail would welcome them.

While the men were making their plans, Abigail took action. She organized a week of performances and took donations. After the first show, there was enough to send the man home to Bavaria that evening.

When asked how Abigail managed it, she admitted that before the performance she allowed her friends to compete for places on the list of homes that would host the illustrious singer each night of the performance series. The largest donors to the fund were the ones who had won the right to have him as their houseguest.

Jean-Luc chuckled as the parlor door closed. Since he hadn't heard any inappropriate yodeling or music coming from the parlor, he had to hope that these two ladies might be a project that would require no intervention from him beyond seeing that Gaby understood she would be required to participate.

He found his sister still hiding beneath the desk and reached down to pull her to her feet. "Is she gone?" Gaby asked as she straightened her skirts.

"If you mean your mother, she is no longer in the foyer. If you mean the young lady you will be tutoring, she is in the parlor." He paused to give her a stern look. "Now stop playing at the game of behaving like a child at home and then demanding we all treat you like an adult."

Gaby opened her mouth, likely to complain. Jean-Luc shook his head.

"If you cannot do as your mother asked, then you will not see the Gayarre fellow."

"You cannot stop me," she said as he walked away.

"No, you're right," he said when he stopped to turn around and face her. "But I will stop the Gayarre fellow. In fact, he will be so afraid to be anywhere near you that he will likely find another girl." Jean-Luc nodded. "Perhaps the new girl in the parlor."

"You are cruel, Jean-Luc," she said.

"I am nothing of the sort and you know it," he told her. "Now go do the right thing before I change my mind about allowing that Gayarre fellow access to my sister and do the wrong thing."

He watched Gaby skitter inside the parlor. As the door closed, he still wasn't certain this fellow would be allowed even five minutes' time with his sister. He would never tell Gaby that, though.

Jean-Luc was still contemplating this when he spied Father coming down the stairs. "You're home. Excellent. A moment of your time, if you have it, son," he said.

"I do." He followed his father into the library and took a seat on the opposite side of the desk.

Father sat and then opened a desk drawer to retrieve a stack of documents. Placing them on the table, he glanced over at the open door. From there, women's laughter floated toward them.

"Would you like me to close the door?"

He shook his head. "As long as those two are occupied, I have no further need of privacy." Sliding the topmost document across the desk, he nodded for Jean-Luc to read it.

Jean-Luc scanned the document, a letter from Versailles regarding losses sustained in attacks against vessels flying the

French flag. He handed it back to his father.

"A pity this is happening, but I fail to see why this would be addressed to you."

His father leaned back in his chair, his expression unreadable. "It is addressed to me because I own the trading privileges in the territory. With this privilege comes the responsibility for what happens to the French vessels that come into our port on my behalf. If vessels are being stolen from, then it is my job to investigate and determine who is doing the stealing."

"The letter says nothing of the kind," he protested.

"No, it does not. Nor does it say anything of the kind in any of the other letters that came from Versailles." Father leaned forward and rested his forearms on the desk. "But your uncle has recently returned from Paris. He brought the message back personally. It seems as though rumors of pirates have reached the king."

At the word *pirate*, Jean-Luc looked away. "Again, why is this your concern? Do the French not have a navy to handle this anymore?"

He flexed the knee that still plagued him on occasion, the same leg that had been laid open by a French fleet's weaponry. "How can I help with this?"

"I need names, Jean-Luc. The crown wants men who have come up against the French, be it as pirates, privateers, or simply common thieves. I know we swore an oath to never speak of a time when you were more connected to this sort of trade, but forgive me. We must speak of it. The alternative is to provide no answers to the king and risk losing our trading privileges. If that happens, it will ruin us."

Letting out a long breath, Jean-Luc returned his attention to his father. "What do you want me to do?"

"As I said, give me names. However, I have a plan. I believe I can offer a compromise. If there are enemies of the king doing business in his territories, I believe we are within our rights to go after anything of value that enemy might have. Would you agree?"

"I would," he said. "It has certainly been done before."

Father nodded. "To that end, I have made inquiries into a resident of our city who may have profited from a family member's illegal activities. For reasons I cannot go into at this moment, I cannot tell you that name." He slid a look at the closed parlor door. "Perhaps later once our guests have gone home. However, if the facts are as I suspect, I will have a name to give to the king along with a substantial amount of money for his coffers."

"That should fix the problem," he said. "Or at least buy some time to get the issue of theft under control."

"About that," Father said. "I would like your thoughts on what can be done."

"I have told you," he said with a lift of one shoulder. "Arm the merchantmen well enough and the problem goes away."

"I want you to handle that."

Jean-Luc shook his head. "Give that responsibility to Quinton, please."

Unused to hearing no from anyone, Father frowned. "I assume you will add an explanation to that request."

"If I add an explanation, then you will be party to information you may be required to surrender to the authorities. Do you still want me to add that explanation to my request?"

Once again feminine laughter drifted across the foyer and into the library. "No," Father finally said. "I don't believe I need to have an explanation. I do have a question I would like answered. This thing you are not telling me, does it involve something I would advise you not to do?"

Jean-Luc thought for a moment. "It does involve something that you would likely advise me not to do. However, it is something that you would do without caring what you were told."

His father smiled. "Exactly the answer I expected."

CHAPTER 20

At the sound of raised voices, Maribel crept down the hall to find out the cause. Mama and Abuelo were in the library, and their argument seemed to be over money.

"I must present her as a young lady of the proper social set, Don Pablo," Mama said. "And to do that she must be properly outfitted."

"You must stop," Abuelo said. "These inquiries have progressed to the point where I expect we will soon be paid an official visit to answer questions."

"Do you think so?" Mama asked, her voice suddenly much quieter.

"I cannot imagine that we will not. Our credit is being questioned, and men who were my friends suddenly cross the street to get away from me. What other reason would there be?"

"After all these years," Mama said. "How is it that Antonio can still bring us harm?"

"This time the charges against him are false," Abuelo said. "I cannot imagine anyone would have such proof as the law requires. And you know why this is happening, don't you? Your friend's husband is in trouble and looking for someone to blame."

"You cannot lay the fault on Abigail. She and Marcel have been very kind to us. Nor can you blame the French. Abigail and the governor have both suggested I make an appointment with the younger Valmont to plead our cause. He does much of his father's work for him."

"It matters not who does what work, Mary. Of course, when a Frenchman is looking to make trouble, he picks his fight with a Spaniard. Your friends may treat you well now, but at the first sign of trouble, they will disappear and leave you—leave all of the Cordoba family—alone. Isn't that always how it—"

Her grandfather began coughing and seemed unable to stop. Maribel ran to fetch something for him to drink and then hurried into the library.

"Here, Abuelo," she said as she handed him the glass. "Drink this."

She watched her grandfather take small sips until the cough subsided. "Thank you, sweet girl," he told her. "You have always been a great help to me."

"If I am of help to you in this little thing, perhaps I can also help elsewhere." She paused to look at Mama before returning her attention to Abuelo. "I heard what you and Mama were saying. If someone is making trouble here because you are a Spaniard, then why not just leave? Go back to Spain. Your letter said you moved closer to the search for me. Now that I am found, should we not just all go home?"

"It is not so simple," Mama said. "It took a fortune to move here and settle in. There are debts here we cannot pay." She looked past Maribel to Abuelo. "And your grandfather, he is not as young and healthy as he was all those years ago when we traveled to New Orleans. If we were to attempt a journey back to Spain, I fear it might be too much for him."

"Bah," he said. "If I am to die, better it is on Spanish soil, Mary. And if I die on the way, then at least my bones will reach Spain. I say the girl is right. We should consider this."

"But, Don Pablo, there are obligations. . ."

He waved away her statement with a sweep of his hand. "I am a man of honor, so I will agree that debts are owed." He paused to take another sip from the glass. "However, we must consider the possibility that repayment of certain portions of our debts might need to be delayed."

Mama looked away. Clearly she did not agree, but there was no disagreeing with Don Pablo Cordoba. Not under his roof anyway.

"Then it is settled. We make arrangements to return to Spain. I will speak to those men who have been most generous and execute a document promising I will repay our debts at a time in the future."

"Are you certain that is wise?" Mama asked.

"I am certain this is the only chance we have to leave this city." He set the glass aside and rose. "Mary, I would like you to decide which of our things we will need to bring with us. Perhaps what is left can be sold to settle some of the monies owed."

"Yes, of course." Mama looked troubled. Finally she rose to follow Abuelo out into the hall. "A word with you, please," she said to him before turning to Maribel. "Just your grandfather and me, please."

Maribel complied as the door closed with her still in the library. Of course, she tried to remain close enough to the door to listen to the conversation going on in the hallway.

"You'll find the safe empty," Mama said. "I know I told you that Marcel Valmont did not require any repayment, but do you recall when you awakened from your siesta and I was hosting Mr. Valmont in the parlor?"

"I do," he said. "And I found it strange then, just as I find it strange now."

"Well," she said slowly, "he was here in his official position as a representative of the king. He explained there had been an inquiry and there was a need for us to make good on some portion of the repayment."

"I do not follow," he said. "What did you do?"

"Marcel is a friend, Don Pablo. He wished to help us."

"He wished to help himself," he snapped. "Likely there is something in this for him. A threat to his exclusive trading privileges, perhaps? How much did you give him?"

"Everything," she said. "But do not let this upset you. You know what the physician said about getting overwrought."

"Everything? The coins and the jewels?"

"Yes, but I have an appointment to speak with his son regarding the matter in the coming week. The governor believes at his word the issue may be dropped and the coins and jewels will be returned. I am quite hopeful of this."

Before any more words could be spoken between them, Mama called out. Maribel came running and then froze when she reached the door to the library.

Her grandfather lay prone on the floor.

Jean-Luc left his home that night under cover of darkness, making his way down Dumaine Street without being detected. Though the meeting place was isolated, nevertheless, he took the usual precautions. By the time he reached the bend in the river, the moon was high overhead, but a cloud obscured its glow.

"Is that you?" a decidedly male voice called out. "It seems like I've been waiting for hours."

Circling around with the tangle of brush and trees as his cover, Jean-Luc easily came up behind the fellow and wrapped one arm around his throat. Though the man fought, he quickly gave up.

"I have money in my pocket but not much," he said. "Please, don't kill me. I have a rich fiancée who will pay you whatever you ask for my safety."

"Do you now?" Jean-Luc turned Louis Gayarre around to face him. "Tell me about this fiancée of yours? Is it my sister and you have not told the family yet, or is it someone else and you have not told my sister yet?"

Silence.

"Do not answer yet," Jean-Luc said. "I have a more important question. Why is it you are not paying proper visits to my sister in her home under the supervision of her parents? Is there a particular reason for that?"

Once again, the lad said nothing.

"Well, now," he continued. "Is it because you don't like the supervision of her parents? Because if that's so, then that would also indicate that you do not care about my sister's reputation and what might be said about her if anyone caught the two of you out here together. Is that possible? I hope not, because no man would dare think so little of my sister and then stand in my presence and not expect to be greatly harmed."

The cloud moved away, revealing the terrified face of a man who knew there was nothing he could say to get himself out of the trouble he'd gotten himself into. So he ran.

"Gayarre," Jean-Luc called to the fellow's quickly disappearing back. "I require an answer."

The Gayarre fellow kept running. Jean-Luc shook his head.

"Truly you vex me," he said. "I do not want to chase you down, nor have I brought any weapon that could touch you from this distance. Stop and face me like a man and tell me whether you plan to stop seeing my sister voluntarily or because I have told you to."

Gayarre paused to turn around. "Does it matter? You'll never see me near her again."

Jean-Luc grinned. "If you have met my sister, then you know it matters whether I am guilty in ruining her romance with you or not. So which is it, am I to blame or not?"

"You are not to blame," he said.

"Thank you, now please do continue running. I was so enjoying it."

He heard a noise and smiled. "How long have you been watching, Israel?"

"Long enough to know I don't want to be caught anywhere near your sister."

Jean-Luc laughed. "What report do you have?"

"There is not much notice, but I am told of a vessel making port tonight. Very quietly and without the knowledge of the authorities." Israel paused. "There is time to intercept this ship, my friend. But there will not be time to make the usual preparations."

He thought only a moment. "I will need to make arrangements."

"There is no time." He gestured toward the river. "Your ship is there, as is your crew. What say you?"

Abigail would be frantic and Father would be furious once they learned he had sailed off again. Then there were the issues with the crown that his father should not have to handle alone. None of those issues, however, were as important as the men and women aboard that vessel.

Jean-Luc looked up at Israel, his decision made. "Let's go."

Maribel walked into the offices of Marcel Valmont & Sons and demanded to see the man in charge. The three Monsieurs Valmont were unavailable, she was told by the aide who ushered her back outside.

Of course, she followed the aide right back in and took a seat at his desk. "Then I will wait," she told him.

"Monsieur Marcel is not expected in today, and Monsieur Quinton has sailed to Paris on business that will keep him occupied until the end of the month." He regarded her with lifted brows. "And thus, that leaves only Monsieur Jean-Luc, who is obviously not here."

She shrugged. "Then I will await Monsieur Jean-Luc's return."

"I'm sorry, Miss Cordoba, but I cannot say when that might be. His hours are often irregular." He gave her one last long look and then returned to his work, obviously dismissing her.

Maribel remained seated as long as she could stand it and then rose and began to pace. Eventually someone from the Valmont family would have to come through the doors and speak to her.

She hadn't counted on that someone being Gabrielle Valmont.

"I know he is here, Mr. Landry. Do not cover for him." Gabrielle stormed past Maribel without taking notice of her and threw open the doors to what Maribel soon realized was an office. "Where are you, Jean-Luc Valmont? I know you're here. You do not just leave for nearly a week without telling anyone, so you cannot fool me into believing you aren't here." Doors opened and closed and then opened again. Maribel watched Gabrielle pace back and forth, her anger evident.

"Miss Valmont," the aide called. "I must object. You'll need to leave now."

"I am ignoring you, Mr. Landry, because I know my brother is paying you to keep me from bothering him. I know you're here, Jean-Luc. Don't you dare try to hide from me."

Mr. Landry looked over at Maribel and shrugged. Though he returned his attention to Gabrielle, he did nothing to make her cease her search.

"I know what you did to my Louis," Gabrielle continued. "How dare you try and frighten the love of my life away? Why, he will not even give me the time of day now. I was walking down the street with William Spencer on our way to his shift at the charity hospital, and Louis actually crossed over to the other side of the road. Do you know why? I am certain I do."

She continued to search, even looking beneath the massive desk that decorated the center of the room. Finally she gave up and sat on the corner of the desk, her face crestfallen.

Maribel stepped into the room and waited for Gabrielle to notice her. Such was the younger woman's upset, that she had managed to make a fine mess of an office that once appeared to be quite nice.

"Oh," the Valmont girl finally said as she kicked a pillow out of her way. "It's you. I didn't know we had a lesson today."

"We don't," Maribel said as she looked around at the destruction. "I'm looking for your brother. I assume you haven't seen him."

"Obviously no. If I had, I would have punched him by now." She reached over and another stack of papers went flying off the corner of the desk. "I wouldn't have, actually, but I do want to. He's such a pest and a bother. He's run off another fellow who might have been the one."

"Why would he do that?" she asked as Gabrielle pushed away a stack of papers to make room for her on the desk.

"Jean-Luc will tell you it is because he loves me, but secretly I think he just doesn't want me to be happy." She shrugged. "Oh, who am I kidding? He wants me happy but thinks he knows exactly what that takes." She slid Maribel a sideways look. "Why are you trying to find him?"

"I am keeping an appointment my mother made." She avoided Gabrielle's intent gaze. "Mama was unable to attend the meeting, so I am here on her behalf. Something in regard to a business matter between the Valmonts and the Cordobas."

"That sounds quite official. You are young to be handling family business, aren't you?"

"Not so young as you," Maribel said. "But it isn't what I wish I was doing."

"What do you wish you were doing?"

She offered a half smile. "The truth? I would like very much to find a place to read a book undisturbed and without worrying what a proper lady would do or about whether a dressmaker needs to be paid or whether a reputation is about to be lost. That is what I most wish for today. What about you, Gabrielle? What do you wish you were doing?"

"Please call me Gaby. And what I wish I was doing is. . ." She seemed to be considering a response. Finally she shook her head. "Truly I do not know. I have been told what to do for so long that I have forgotten what it is like to do whatever I wish."

"Oh, Gaby," Maribel said. "I can tell you what that is like. It is the most glorious feeling. I have climbed trees, read books under the stars with just an oil lamp for light, and even managed a swim once or twice in this little inlet where no one else goes."

"It sounds heavenly." She linked arms with Maribel and then leaned back on the desk so that they both were staring at the cherubs painted on the ceiling above. "Tell me more."

"What in the world has happened to my office?"

Gaby looked over at Maribel, a smile on her face. "Jean-Luc," she said with no small measure of glee. "Your appointment is here."

CHAPTER 21

This time Gaby had gone too far.

My appointment, indeed. Jean-Luc stood in the doorway of his office and surveyed the damage. She and her friend were currently lying on their backs on his desk, apparently enjoying themselves by giggling rather than feeling remorse at the mess they made.

Important documents, many of which carried the seal of the crown on them, were scattered like confetti across the floor. He picked up several and then his temper got the better of him.

"Even for you, Gabrielle, this is juvenile. The man was beneath you and not worth the trouble you've gotten yourself into."

She raised up on her elbows and regarded him imperiously. "Truly you are no fun at all."

"Truly you have no concept of the trouble you have caused. Someone will be here for days making order out of this mess, and it will not be me." His attention went to his sister's friend. "Who is she?"

The girl sat bolt upright and regarded him with wide green eyes as a lock of red hair escaped her braid.

"She is your appointment, Jean-Luc." Gaby lowered herself off the desk and then straightened her sleeves. "Truly develop a sense of humor. It will aid you in your old age."

"Go home, Gaby," he said through clenched jaw as he turned to his sister's friend. "I advise you to go too."

"No," she said. "I have business with you."

Something in her haughty demeanor caught his attention. That upturned nose, the way she looked at him as if she and not he was in charge. She shifted positions and another stack of papers fell.

"Truly, just go," he said. "If you do have an appointment, it will have to be rescheduled."

"No," she said as her feet landed on the floor and she straightened. "It cannot be rescheduled. I do see your point about the office, and I am sorry your sister decided to take her anger out on your papers." She looked up at him, her expression somewhere between fearless and fierce. "But my issue cannot be put off."

"I see," he said as something deep inside him began to sound a warning.

He knew her.

Knew of her.

Had been bested, perhaps, in an argument with her.

Something was familiar. Something was. . .

Jean-Luc shook his head. The memory was there just beyond his reach. But what was it?

"Mr. Valmont?" She indicated that he should take a seat behind his desk, and he did.

"Thank you," she said. "Now, it has come to my attention that a sum of money has been put on account for the benefit of my family. I do believe it was in the form of coins and jewels, although my mother is quite distraught and cannot be counted upon for any sort of reliable facts in her current state."

She gave him an expectant look. Somewhere in all the words she just said were facts he should have understood. Or perhaps not. Either way, all he could manage as she began talking again was to look at her and try to think of where he might have seen her before.

Indeed, she resembled his late wife, although only slightly. Kitty had never been this animated or this passionate about a topic. If only he knew what in the world she was talking about.

"Miss," he finally said, holding his hand up to slow her incessant conversation to a halt. "I am having trouble following you. Thus far I have determined that your mother claims something that requires my assistance in regard to a sum of money, that you may or may not have participated in the destruction of my office, and that I have no idea who you are."

She regarded him with a patient look. She even appeared to roll her eyes, although he could not reconcile that sort of behavior with the perfectly proper woman seated on the opposite side of the desk.

"All right, then," she said. "I will clarify."

"Thank you." He sat back and reached for a pen and paper. Thankfully, they had been hidden in his desk drawer and were still within reach. "All right, please do clarify," he said as he prepared to listen to another lengthy diatribe, and this time he would take notes.

She smiled. Then she gave him a curt nod.

"Yes, no, and Maribel Cordoba."

The breath went out of him. Spots appeared before his eyes. The pen fell from his hand and landed somewhere. The blank page in front of him remained pristine. No notes were needed.

"Repeat, please," he managed.

"Yes, no, and Maribel Cordoba," she said, and this time he saw it.

Saw the tilt to her nose and the gleam in her eye when she gave him an answer that she found to be quite clever. Saw the red color of her curls and the emerald color of her eyes.

"Maribel Cordoba."

He hadn't said those words in years. Eleven years. Saying them now felt wrong, as did seeing a grown woman in the place where a child had been.

"Yes," she said. "And to be precise, I also am here in regard to my mother's claim, and I did not participate in what has happened to your office. However, a word of warning. Your sister does have quite a temper, so you might think twice before you interfere with her romance. Was the fellow really not the right sort for her?"

"He seduced her into meeting in an open field near the river rather than courting her properly at her home, and when cornered he offered her up as someone who would pay his ransom. So I would say yes, he is not the right sort. But truly, you are Maribel Cordoba. The Maribel Cordoba from Spain?"

She gave him a sideways look. "Yes, but then you know that because my mother brought you money some two weeks ago, and she definitely would have mentioned that this was regarding an issue between the French and a citizen of Spain. Are you trying to hedge on this? Because I have brought a receipt."

She handed him the paper, and he read it then pushed it back across the table toward her. "Look at the signature. That was signed by my brother Quinton. I was away two weeks ago." He shook his head. "You are here, aren't you? I never thought I would see you again, but here you are."

Color rose in Maribel's cheeks. She was lovely when she was angry, much more so than when she was a girl aboard his ship. How old must she be now? Two and twenty perhaps, possibly older.

"If this was not an urgent matter, I would leave and return with my grandfather. However, he is ill and cannot come himself. As I said, my mother is distraught and cannot be relied upon for her facts or, quite frankly, for her behavior. Thus, I am the only remaining member of the family with whom you can discuss this matter." She viewed him primly. "You have seen the receipt. I wish a refund at once."

"You don't know who I am, do you?"

Her gaze swept the length of him and then returned to his face. "I know you are a Valmont and you are apparently not Quinton. Your sister calls you Jean-Luc, so I will answer by saying I believe you are Jean-Luc Valmont."

"Yes, I am," he said slowly as he decided how to proceed.

It was apparent Maribel did not recognize him. He knew all the arguments against revealing his identity, and he could not disagree.

Gradually he became aware that she was speaking again. "So," he heard her say as his focus returned to the woman seated before him, "I will expect to have the items listed on that receipt returned to me immediately."

"I, well. . ." He shook his head in hopes that he could dislodge something appropriate to say. "Since my brother signed the receipt, he is the one who would have to verify what has been left with us, and he would be the one who would return it. Unfortunately, he is in Paris and not expected back until the end of the month."

Yes. That ought to buy some time.

"That is unacceptable," she said as she rose. "Your father is the man in charge of this endeavor. It says so on the sign beside the door. Marcel Valmont & Sons is what I read. So, since the son who took my grandfather's money is unavailable, Marcel Valmont himself should easily be able to stand in his stead and handle the transaction."

Jean-Luc stood and stuffed his shaking hands in the pockets of his coat. "Under normal circumstances I would agree. However, since I know nothing about this case, I will have to investigate further and—"

"Sir, excuse me." Mr. Landry stood at the door. "Your next appointment has arrived. I put him in Mr. Quinton's office. Shall I tell him you'll be right in?"

Jean-Luc managed a nod before he turned his attention back to Maribel Cordoba. "I'm sorry. My next appointment is here."

An appointment that certainly hadn't been on his calendar this morning. But then, neither had meeting Maribel Cordoba again.

She gave him another of those looks he remembered from their time at sea. "I am leaving reluctantly, and only because you have made a decent case for rescheduling this appointment. I can see that you will need time to look over the transaction documents."

"Thank you," he said, hoping his relief did not sound so obvious in his voice.

"I will see you tomorrow, then. Same time." She cast a glance around the room and then turned her attention back to him. "Although I would suggest we meet in your brother's office. You seem extremely distracted, and I wonder if it is because of this mess. Do consider it, won't you?"

Jean-Luc left the question unanswered, holding his breath until the redhead was safely outside the building. He was still staring at the closed door when Landry stuck his head into the office.

"Your next appointment, sir?"

"Oh," he said, "I thought you were just trying to help me get rid of Miss Cordoba." He straightened his jacket and walked over to Quinton's office, throwing the door open as he stepped inside.

"Good morning, Mr. Valmont."

❧

Maribel was nearly home when a carriage caught up with her. Gaby Valmont climbed out and hurried to fall into step beside her.

"I am so sorry for all the trouble I am sure I have caused you." She stepped in front of Maribel. "Please let me make it up to you."

"Don't be silly," Maribel said as she stopped to keep from running into her. "What makes you think you've caused me any trouble?"

She shrugged. "Maybe because I listened to the conversation and I know you didn't get what you came for."

"Oh. That." She stepped around the Valmont girl and kept walking. "It was a simple matter of scheduling a meeting with the wrong Valmont. I'm sure he will read the documents and have my money for me tomorrow."

"Yes, I hope so." They walked in silence until Maribel reached her doorstep. "Would you like to come in?"

"Thank you," she said, "but I don't think your family would like to have a Valmont pay a visit right now."

"Your mother and mine are close friends," Maribel protested. "I see no trouble in it."

"Perhaps, but I will decline all the same." She paused. "I'm sorry your grandfather is ill. Has he been seen by a physician?"

"My mother is attending him," she said. "But perhaps a physician would be a good idea." She shook her head. "No, forget I said that. Until your brother refunds my mother's payment, we have nothing with which to pay a physician."

Gaby grinned. "What if I were to tell you that I know a physician who would come and see your grandfather at no cost? He's a very nice man and often practices at the charity hospital so that he can be of help to those who cannot pay."

"Who is he?"

"Well," Gaby said, "he is sort of my brother, only not. We grew up as siblings from when I was very young. My parents adopted him." She paused. "Sort of, but not."

Maribel gave the matter a moment's consideration. "Yes, then, please do send for him."

She smiled. "I can do better than that. I was on my way to fetch him home for lunch. Come with me. As long as you've got something to feed him, I'm certain he will allow the detour to examine your grandfather."

"I would be forever in his debt. And yours." Maribel paused. "However, I have been away all morning and I'm sure my mother will be concerned by now as to what is taking me so long to return."

Gaby smiled. "Of course. You go and see to your family, and I will bring him to you."

"Thank you." She lingered a moment and then gave her new friend a direct look. "Your brother," she said, "can I expect him to be fair with me?"

She laughed. "Oh, Maribel, he is so fair it is ridiculous. In fact, my brother believes there isn't a rule in existence that is worthy of being broken. If your business affairs require Jean-Luc to administer them fairly, then you have nothing to concern yourself with. Truly, I have never met a more exasperating and boring man."

"Thank you," she said as she made her good-byes and watched the Valmont carriage drive away.

Exasperating and boring.

Maribel let out a long breath. Funny, because in her imagination Jean-Luc Valmont was a pirate standing at the wheel of a gaff-rigged schooner, his hair tossed like the sea-green waves beneath the vessel and his giant of an African friend by his side.

He was a man who slid beneath the rules in a vessel that could escape even the fastest enemy. And he was absolutely anything other than boring.

Exasperating? That she could agree on, however.

Certainly Gaby's version would be much easier to deal with. Why, then, could she not get her version—the imagined man that came from the same creative mind that Mother Superior warned against—out of her head?

"Is that you?" Mama called when Maribel closed the door behind her.

"It is," she said, following her mother's voice to find her in Abuelo's library. The room looked to be in much the same condition as the office she had just left.

"What happened in here?" She reached down to gather up a pile of papers that had been carelessly strewn across the carpet. "Have we been robbed?"

"We have," she said, "but not by thieves outside the family."

Maribel set the documents on the desk and bent down to reach for more. "These are Abuelo's, Mama. You shouldn't be looking through them, and you certainly should not be tossing them about as if they have no meaning."

"Well, they don't have much meaning," she said, clutching a paper with a seal that looked important. "Not to me, anyway. I despair of this, but I cannot make sense of why our family has all of this and yet we are destitute."

"Destitute?" Maribel released the pages she held and watched them flutter to the ground then sat down behind the desk. "That is impossible, Mama. I will get the valuables you've put on deposit with the Valmonts for you. Then we will be fine."

Mama sank onto a chair without bothering to clear off the papers that it held. "So you succeeded, then? What a relief." Her smile rose quickly and then became laughter. "What a mess I have made and all for nothing. Here, help me pick all of this up before your grandfather surprises us by recuperating enough to walk down here and see this."

Maribel opened her mouth to correct her mother. To tell her that while she had not yet had assurances from the Valmonts that the valuables would be returned, she certainly would get those assurances tomorrow.

Perhaps not certainly, but likely.

Instead, she closed her mouth, rested her palms on the desk, and watched her mother transform from frantic and distraught to practically dancing around the library as she set the room to rights again.

And she said nothing. She could not. Tomorrow she would keep that appointment with Jean-Luc Valmont. She would get all the things back that had been taken from the family, and then the Cordobas would no longer be destitute.

What she could not do was explain why Mama thought that the threat to their financial security came from within the family. Surely Abuelo had nothing but their best interests in mind.

It made no sense.

Neither did the ledger beneath her hand. Ignoring Mama altogether now, she allowed her gaze to slide down the list of entries, some with dates going back more than ten years.

Each entry was written in her grandfather's familiar hand-writing. The same handwriting that had been on the letter that brought her home to New Orleans. It was the name in the other column that stopped her cold.

"Is Abuelo awake?"

She shook her head. "He has not awakened since he fell. Is

there something there that needs his attention?"

"Nothing that cannot wait until he is able to provide answers," she said as she gathered up the ledger and stuffed it into Grandfather's leather valise. "I must go out. Gabrielle Valmont is bringing a physician to look in on Abuelo. Would you make my apologies for not being here?" She took three steps toward the door and then turned around. "And the doctor will expect lunch. I promised Gaby," she said. "Is that a problem?"

"Of course not," Mama said, her smile still in place. "I will see to everything. You just go on and handle whatever it is. Nothing urgent, I hope."

"As do I," Maribel said just after the door closed behind her.

CHAPTER 22

Antonio Cordoba sat behind the desk and looked up at Jean-Luc as if he owned the place. "Sit down, won't you? I believe you and I have some business to discuss."

Age had not been kind to the Spaniard, but he would have known the man anywhere. "So you lived after all," he said through clenched jaw. "I suppose it's true that you cannot drown the devil."

The Spaniard laughed. "Well, not this one," he said as he picked up Quinton's jeweled letter opener, fashioned in the style of a small cutlass, and studied it. "Truly though, sit. Your refusal to accept my hospitality is most annoying."

"Why are you here?"

"I am a man of business now, as are you." He shrugged. "I find we have business in common. Namely, my father's estate."

"Your father is very much alive," he said evenly as his mind struggled to reconcile what he now knew of this man with the death he thought he caused. "If I have business with any Cordoba, it is he and not you."

"Oh, but it is me," he said, pointing at Jean-Luc with the letter opener. "My father is an old man. He believed he was protecting my wife and child from me, so he made certain decisions on my behalf. Unfortunately, he has met with reduced circumstances of late. Most unfortunate."

Protecting his wife and child.

Maribel.

Jean-Luc let out a long breath as he tamed the temper that was rising. Anger would never work against a man who thrived on that very emotion. Rather, he must be smart. Calm. The better man.

Help me, Lord.

"What do you want from me, Cordoba?" he managed.

"Much less than you want from me." He dropped the letter opener and threaded his fingers together, resting them on the desktop. "I merely want what is in your vault. Had my wife not been so stupid as to bring the coins and jewels to you instead of keeping them at home as I instructed, none of this would have been necessary."

"You are assuming I have possession of these things."

"I know you do." He shrugged. "I have seen the receipt."

The same receipt Maribel had in her hands this morning. "Who else knows you are alive?"

He laughed. "Are you worried about my daughter? Trust me, Valmont, she is oblivious to my existence. My father insisted that be part of the terms of our agreement. So far I have seen no reason to break that agreement. And my wife? She has known all along, but Mary always did know how to look after herself. The old man had the money, so she joined him here in New Orleans and played the part of the grieving widow and hostess to the old man. Perhaps you've met her. She's quite stunning."

Had he met anyone named Cordoba, Jean-Luc would have remembered. As he avoided any social circle to which his parents might belong—by his own preference and against theirs—it was possible he had not seen her, although he might have, owing to the size of this city. Impossible, though, that they would have been introduced and he not recall.

"Make your point or leave," he told the Spaniard.

"My point is you have items in your possession that were not meant to be here. They are mine, and my wife had no ownership in them or any right to distribute them elsewhere. You and I are both men of business. I say we complete this transaction and then go our separate ways."

"You're right, Cordoba," he said. "We are men of business, but I conduct my business in a very different way than you do. I will look into your claim and speak with my father to make a decision on the ownership of anything that might be in our vaults."

"I see." He rose. "You know, the last time I saw you I tried to put a bullet through your heart."

"I remember it well."

Cordoba smiled. "I did not miss."

"No," Jean-Luc said slowly, "you did not. Nor were you successful."

"I am older now, and wiser," he said as he came around the desk to stand in front of Jean-Luc. "And I have eluded you and everyone else for eleven years," he said as he walked to the door.

"Only because I was not looking for you," Jean-Luc said to his retreating back.

❋

Maribel set off walking with no idea exactly where she was going. Returning to the Valmont offices was one option, but so was going off by herself to look over what she had found and make a plan. She certainly hadn't been able to think with Mama around, and it was unlikely she would fare better in Gaby's brother's presence.

So she set off toward the river and the stand of live oaks that had intrigued her since she arrived in the city. Thus far she had been practicing the art of being a proper lady and had not fallen back into her old ways.

Today, however, she would make an exception. For where better to be alone and read something as important as this ledger?

After looking around to be certain she had not been followed, Maribel tucked the strap of the valise over her shoulder and hiked up her skirt just enough to allow her to climb into a welcoming spot out of sight of anyone who might be passing by.

How long she remained in the tree, Maribel could not say.

However, when the light began to fail her and her stomach pleaded for her to eat something, she folded the ledger back into the valise and rested her head against the oak tree's gnarled trunk.

She had long ago given up wearing Mama's scarf at her waist. In fact, Mama had taken it from her and declared it unfit for a proper lady to wear. But as she sat here quietly mulling over what she had read, Maribel wished for the gentle comfort of the scarf that tied her to a home she thought she knew.

Though she preferred to remain exactly where she was rather than return to what she'd left in her grandfather's home, Maribel nonetheless stretched her legs and then reached for the branch that would aid her in climbing down.

A loud crack split the air and the world tilted. The valise slid from her shoulder and landed with a thud on the ground.

She, however, did not.

Rather, she landed in the arms of a man with silver eyes and a broad smile. "Reading in the dark will damage your eyes, you know."

The same thing the captain said almost every night when he came to check on her. "Yes, sir," she responded out of habit.

The captain. Maribel's heart soared. The captain!

"Captain," she finally managed to say aloud. "When I saw you in the office this morning, I knew it was you," she said. "Well, not exactly *you*, but someone *like* you. You see, Mother Superior told me that what I thought were memories was just my imagination, but I never was certain if she was correct. I mean, she is a nun and I am sure she would never tell me anything but the truth, but it always seemed as though I was reliving something that had happened and not making something up. Anyway, I knew you would turn out to be a nice man. I prayed for that, you know, and I have been for all these years, and now—"

"Maribel. Stop. Talking."

She clamped her lips shut against the torrent of words still demanding escape. Still, she could not look away from those eyes. From that smile.

"I just should have known it was you," she said. "I sat in that office and made all sorts of demands on behalf of my family and all the time I was in front of the one person I had always wished I would find again. I never really stopped hoping you were alive, you know."

"I looked for you," he told her. "Looked everywhere. We sent out boats and search parties and scoured every inch of any place we thought you might be. When you walked into my office, I couldn't believe it was you. I thought you had died out there on that ocean. The cannonball took out the entire lookout post and part of the mainmast. How could you have survived?"

"Captain. Stop. Talking," she said as she nestled her head against his chest and felt, for the first time since she left the island, as if she was once again in a familiar place.

"You can't call me Captain here in New Orleans," he finally said as he set her on her feet.

She looked up at him. Really looked this time instead of ignoring the fine details of the once-familiar face that had aged very little. "Why not?"

"It would compromise certain things and complicate others," he said, apparently reluctant to go into any further detail.

"Are you still a privateer?"

The captain ducked his head and then lifted it again. "When the French set a bounty on my head and then nearly killed me, I decided it was time to leave that part of my life behind, so no, I am not."

Her face must have registered surprise, because he shook his head. "No, I don't suppose you would have known any of that."

"You were working for the French," she said. "Why would they want you dead?"

"It all comes down to politics, I suppose. Or maybe it was just God's way of letting me know that it was time to stop and follow Him instead of trying to do things my way," he said as he reached down to retrieve the valise. "This is heavy."

She nodded, but when her gaze collided with his, she found words nearly impossible. "Important papers."

"That's what you were reading in the tree? So have you given up your adventure books?"

"Of course not." Maribel shook her head, as much in response to his question as to dislodge the fog that was surrounding her now.

The captain lived, and he was standing right here in front of her. All those prayers, all those times she wondered if he lived, wondered if it had all been something her imagination conjured up, and now here he stood.

"Is there something wrong?" he asked.

"No," Maribel said, tears now shimmering as the realization hit her with full force. "It's just that. . ." Again she shook her head. "You're real and you're alive and you're not just someone I imagined."

His chuckle was exactly as she recalled. "Yes, I am very real."

She fell into his arms again, and this time she held on tight, until he stepped back to drop the valise. "I don't want to let you go," she said, reaching for him again. "I am just so very happy you're alive."

After a while, the captain held her at arm's length. "You're not a little girl anymore, Red."

"It has been eleven years since we parted, so I would hope not," she said. "You, however, look exactly the same."

"And that, Miss Cordoba, is your imagination speaking. I am eleven years older and many decades wiser." Jean-Luc retrieved the valise. "Walk with me. I would prefer to escort you somewhere that is more secure so we can speak without being seen. I have a few things to tell you that I prefer not be overheard."

She shook her head. "There is nowhere more secure than up in that tree."

"You're joking."

"I am serious." She nodded toward the valise. "Would you like me to take it up with me, or do you think you can manage it? What with your advanced age and all."

"Pick the limb," he said as he threw the valise over his shoulder.

CHAPTER 23

When Jean-Luc managed to settle himself on the limb beside Maribel without doing anything more than minor damage to himself, he made a solemn vow. He would never climb a tree again.

Yet here he sat quite a distance from the ground with a leather valise in his lap and a beautiful redhead beside him. So, overall, he could not complain.

Much.

Though he would likely pay for his exertion with sore muscles later.

"All right," she said. "Which of us is to go first?"

"You," he said, not because he had any particular interest in hearing all the details of the past eleven years but because he did enjoy looking at her when she talked.

The girl had become a woman in their time apart. And though she still rattled on incessantly at times, he found he rather enjoyed listening to her now.

"And so when I arrived at the orphanage on Isla de Santa Maria, Mother Superior despaired of convincing me that the things I recalled were not real. She said they were just products of my imagination and that a girl like me couldn't have possibly been on a privateer's ship or watched for approaching vessels in the top of the mast or even—"

"Wait," he said as he shifted the valise off his lap and hung the strap over a sturdy limb. "Are you telling me you were at St. Mary of the Island Orphanage this whole time?"

"Until recently, yes," she said. "Why?"

All the warnings he'd been given by Israel, Rao, and the others rose up in his mind. Every time he brought a ship into the inlet he had risked Maribel Cordoba recognizing him. And to recognize him was to jeopardize everything.

Jean-Luc shook his head. "No reason. I'm just surprised."

"Yes, well, apparently my grandfather was not surprised at all." She nodded toward the valise. "I found his ledger. He has been paying my maintenance since the second year I was at the orphanage."

"Who paid the first year?"

She gave him a strange look. "I never thought of that. I don't know. But still, don't you find it strange that my grandfather would know where I was, pay for my upkeep, but only send for me recently? When I arrived, he behaved as if I were his long-lost granddaughter returned. Yet he knew where I was all along."

"Not so strange when all the facts are known," he said. "I wonder if your grandfather might have been protecting you from something. Or someone."

"You mean my father?"

Maribel asked the question in such a matter-of-fact manner that it took him aback. "Yes," he said. "I assume there are payments in the ledger to him as well."

"You assume correctly." She looked away. "Apparently my father is very much alive and has been draining my grandfather dry." Her gaze returned to him. "It is not what I had hoped when my mother told me Abuelo was destitute."

"What did you hope?" he said gently.

"Oh I don't know. That he had spent all his fortune searching for me, maybe, although that would bring its own guilt too. Or perhaps he was just a man who did not have as much as I remembered, and he had outlived his funds." She shrugged. "Anything but what I saw there."

Jean-Luc let out a long breath and then chose his words carefully. "Never judge a person's heart by what you see on a balance ledger. And never assume you know the motivation behind someone's actions by that measure either."

She nodded. "I understand. But the truth is there."

"The truth is, you cannot go back to your grandfather's home. It is too dangerous."

"I must warn my mother," she protested.

"She knows, Maribel. She has known from the beginning."

The breath seemed to go out of her. Finally she shook her head. "Yes, I believe you. Mama is capable of many things, but being unaware of what is going on around her is not one of them. She has always been a strong and intelligent woman. I assume my father has either charmed her or frightened her."

"Have you sensed that your mother is frightened lately?"

"Only of not being able to retrieve the valuables placed in your care."

Jean-Luc gave the statement a moment's thought. "But she does not fear for her safety?"

"Her comfort, yes," Maribel said, "but her safety? I would say no."

"That answers your question in regard to how your mother feels about your father. You will not go back to that house," he said. "I won't allow it."

She shook her head. "I have nowhere else to go."

He reached to take her hand in his. "Not as long as I am here to protect you. It is my job as your captain."

"I do remember you saying that a time or two, oh, about eleven years ago." She smiled even as tears shimmered in her eyes. "I am never supposed to call you that, remember?"

"That doesn't mean it isn't true," he said. "As long as I draw a breath, you will be under my protection. For eleven years I have believed I failed you when I lost you to French cannon fire. I will not fail you again."

Maribel smiled and then she leaned toward him. "While I am

perfectly capable of taking care of myself, I do very much thank you," she said as she briefly touched her lips to his cheek.

The action, obviously spontaneous, seemed to surprise her. Then a beautiful pink color rose in her checks.

"I'm sorry. That was terribly presumptuous of me."

"No, Maribel," he said as he gathered her closer. "It was wonderfully presumptuous. I wonder if you would mind doing it again."

She leaned in, and Jean-Luc was ready. As soon as she got close enough, that kiss on the cheek would be a kiss on the lips.

"Wait a minute." Maribel leaned back, her eyes wide. "If my grandfather knew where I was, then who in the world is Mr. Lopez-Gonzales, and why did he pretend to be the person who found me and brought me home to my family?"

"I don't know," he said as he struggled to change his focus. "Who did he say he was?"

"When he came to the island, he told Mother Superior that he had been employed at great expense by my grandfather to find me. He said he was the one who encouraged my family to move to New Orleans so they would be closer to the place where I had last been seen."

She shook her head and gave Jean-Luc a look that said she was still mulling over the facts in her mind. Silence fell between them as he allowed her to continue thinking this through.

"Only here is what I do not understand. How could anyone know where I was last seen other than my father? Was there ever a location given for where the *Venganza* went down?"

"I am sure dispatches were sent from Cuba once the news arrived that the ship was lost," he said.

"Yes, likely," she said, warming to her topic. "But the ship was headed from Spain to Havana. Why relocate to New Orleans, which is a French territory, not a Spanish one, when there are a number of other cities in the Caribbean that would have been much closer and friendlier to a Spaniard?"

"Perhaps the answer to that question will provide the clue as to who this man Lopez-Gonzales is," he offered.

"And for that matter," she continued, "why not Havana itself? Abuelo obviously had friends there if he was able to secure a position for my father in the city."

"Perhaps he had friends here too."

A thought occurred, but he would not be sharing it with Maribel. There was a connection to this city that might explain it all, especially in light of Father's complaints of pirates operating in the region.

"You need to be taken to safety," he told her. "Once I know you cannot be harmed, then I will solve this mystery."

"*We* will solve this mystery," she told him. "You have a poor memory if you think I am going to run and hide when I am confronted by something unpleasant. I did not do that when I was twelve, and I will not do that now."

Jean-Luc ignored her attempt at argument in regard to who would do the solving. "Never did I use the word *run*. I am simply stating that we need a place of safety for you so that a plan of action can be developed."

"I am a grown woman, and as such, I will take complete responsibility for figuring out just what has happened and remedying it."

He chuckled. "And yet we are having this conversation while sitting in a tree."

She offered him the beginnings of a smile. "You do have a point."

"I do," he said, "and so does this branch where I have been sitting. If I am still able, I would very much like to climb down to solid ground. You and I have work to do, and we cannot do it up here."

"What kind of work? It is obvious what these entries are."

"Is it?" He shrugged. "Often there are patterns in these things. Entries that repeat and others that are possibly encrypted so that their true purpose or recipient is not evident. I would like to take a look at the ledger to see if any of those things might be true."

"Yes," she said. "There were a few things that made no sense. I think that's a brilliant idea."

Much more brilliant than allowing himself to be convinced to climb a tree. Although if he examined his actions closely, Jean-Luc had to admit that it had not taken much in the way of convincing to get him to follow the redhead up into the branches of the old live oak.

Somehow he managed not to make a fool of himself as he climbed down. His only explanation for this miracle was that the Lord had taken pity on him, because his knees were aching and his legs had very little feeling at all.

He was, indeed, an old man.

Twelve years older than the beauty who easily slid down the tree trunk to land nimbly on her feet. Apparently his thirty-five years to her twenty-three made a huge difference in how well a person might scale a tree.

However, with no plans to repeat that performance, he felt decently secure in offering her his arm and taking the heavy valise with the other. "Surely all of this weight cannot be the valise and ledger."

She shrugged. "I put nothing else in."

He adjusted the leather strap and continued on, glad to finally set the thing down on his father's desk. Abigail and Gaby were thankfully absent as he shooed away the servants and closed the library door.

If Father was around, he would soon find them. If not, they would manage nicely without him.

Setting the valise aside, they opened the ledger on the desk between them and began looking over the entries. At some point, a servant came in and lit the lamps. Awhile later, Cook brought a tray of food. By the time the noise of female voices sounded outside, they had made substantial progress.

"What will I tell them?" Maribel said as the front door opened and the voices of Gaby and Abigail drifted through the closed library door. "If we are to decipher all of this, I need a reason to spend time here."

"I, um. . ." His usual wit failed him, as apparently did his brain.

The door flew open with Gaby leading the way. An instant later, Maribel leaned over the desk and kissed him soundly.

On the lips.

"Oh," Gaby said. Out of the corner of his eye, Jean-Luc saw his sister stop so quickly that Abigail ran into her.

"Oh," Abigail added as she adjusted her hat to peer around Gaby.

"Oh," Maribel said sweetly as she removed her lips from his and smiled at his family. "We didn't expect you home so soon."

"Apparently not," Abigail said, her attention squarely focused on him and not on Maribel. "Might I have a word, Jean-Luc?" She gave Maribel a look that might have been interpreted as sweet and welcoming by anyone who did not know her. "Please excuse us for just a minute, won't you?"

He spied Maribel's expression and couldn't believe what he saw. The redhead actually looked amused. Did she not realize she had practically ruined her reputation in this city if either of these two chatty women decided to speak of their little adventure in falsifying a romance?

Apparently not, for she was still smiling when Abigail led him from the room.

Though he expected she would give him a brief lecture in the parlor, Abigail bypassed the welcoming front room to grasp his elbow and haul him back through the house and out into the courtyard.

Sticky evening heat remaining from the afternoon enveloped them as they stepped out into the evening shadows. There she finally released her grip, but she was only just getting started on showing how she felt about what she had seen. "Your sister's friend? Truly, Jean-Luc, could you have found anyone more unsuitable?"

"Yes," he said. "I could have. I fail to see what the problem is with Maribel."

"The problem is twofold. First, you hardly know her. And second, she is Spanish."

"Abigail," he said, his eyes narrowing. "I will concede the first point, although I do have evidence to the contrary. However, I never figured you for an elitist who would care about a person's country of birth."

"Do not be so judgmental, Jean-Luc. I don't give even a passing interest in where she was born. I don't even care where she lives or of what social class she is. Why, did I say a word when you married Kitty? And she was a poor nurse whose family depended on her to provide for them."

She hadn't mentioned his late wife since the funeral, so to hear the name from her lips surprised him. "I do remember you warned me not to toy with her affections. But, no, I do not recall any objections of that sort."

"That is because Kitty suited you, and you needed each other. She had cared for you, and truly, Jean-Luc, she had fallen in love with you before you were ever aware she existed. That you cared for her in return was something I would never have offered comment on."

"Then what is wrong with Maribel?"

The question was ludicrous because the answer truly did not matter. Still, he felt a responsibility to defend the woman Abigail apparently thought he loved. Or, more likely, thought he was toying with.

"Maribel is a lovely girl. Perfectly lovely," Abigail said as she reached for her fan to chase away the heat. "In fact, were she not Spanish, I would highly recommend her." She paused. "For Michel."

"For Michel?" Outrage rose. "You would recommend her for my brother and not me?"

"Yes," she said. "You are far too old for a vivacious young woman like her. What in the world would the two of you ever have in common? It is ridiculous."

"Not so ridiculous as you think, Abigail," he said, even though he knew the comment strayed into dangerous waters where he ought not go.

"Well, you have offered no reason that I should think otherwise, so I have given you my opinion of the matter."

"Thank you, Abigail, for your opinion," he snapped. "I will concede your point on age only because it is based on observation alone. However, I still fail to see what her Spanish heritage has to do with making a good match for me."

"Oh, darling, are you so blind?" She gave him an appraising look. "Yes, you are. You've had that look ever since I walked into the room. You are so in love with that girl that you absolutely cannot see that it is not her who is unsuitable but rather you."

In love? Hardly, although her kiss did take him off guard and he had found it difficult to breathe when she reached for him. Then there was the strong desire to march right back into the library and repeat the entire event, this time with anyone who cared to watch in attendance.

But love? Hardly.

"Jean-Luc?" Abigail said. "Have I said something that made sense?"

"The opposite, actually. Now I truly do not follow."

Abigail sighed. "Oh, darling," she told him as she touched his sleeve. "I so want to be wrong about this, but should her grandfather and my friend Mary learn that you are pursuing Maribel, I fear there will be much opposition to the match."

He shook his head. "Correct me if I am wrong, but her mother is not a Spaniard. I do not detect any evidence of it."

"True. My understanding is she fled home to marry Antonio. He's deceased, you know. I believe she is originally from somewhere in the colonies. Virginia, perhaps?" She shook her head. "But her grandfather? Don Pablo Cordoba will never agree to a marriage between the two of you."

Marriage. He tried to keep his expression neutral. "And why do you assume that is where my relationship with Maribel is leading?"

"Because if you have moved from calling her Miss Cordoba to Maribel and you feel it appropriate to bring her into our home and kiss her in front of me and your sister—"

"Excuse me, Abigail, but we were not kissing in front of you. You and Gaby walked in on a private conversation."

"Excuse me, Jean-Luc," she said as she returned his neutral look. "But there was absolutely *no* conversation going on when we walked in. Did I miss something?" she added sweetly.

"Nothing that we intended for you to hear," was his impertinent answer. "Truly, Abigail, you worry for nothing."

"I worry because except for the fact I did not actually give you life, I am your mother in all ways and in my heart. So you, my beloved son, worry me terribly."

He leaned over to kiss her forehead. "Stop worrying. I am fine."

"The last time I heard that, a French lieutenant brought you home in bandages and on death's door. You were up to something before you left on that voyage, and you're up to something now. And you know what?"

"What?" he said, half amused and half touched at her fervor.

"I think both times it involved Maribel Cordoba."

"Stop worrying," he told her. "I am fine. Now I'm going to go back into the library to see if Gaby has had any more luck getting information from Maribel than you have had getting it from me."

Abigail hurried to catch up to him. "If she has, she better be prepared to tell me."

Jean-Luc laughed as the coolness of the house enveloped him once more. "If she has, she will be prepared to tell everyone."

CHAPTER 24

Jean-Luc returned to the library to find Maribel alone. "Where is your inquisitor?" he said with a grin.

"Likely off to spread the word of our engagement," she said as she returned her attention to the ledger in front of her.

"You're joking, right?"

She lifted her head to regard him with a look that told him she was not. "I doubt she will go far. She headed out the back door, not the front."

"That is because the back door is nearest the carriages. No doubt she's working her way down the street announcing our betrothal to everyone who is anyone in New Orleans."

"Why bother telling the rest?" she said with obvious sarcasm. Then her expression went serious. "Oh. I'm sorry. I've ruined a courtship you're having with someone, haven't I?" She sat back in her chair and shook her head. "I was raised by nuns. I have no idea how any of this works, but I am fairly certain I have caused you trouble. My thought was to break the engagement once a proper time had passed."

He had to laugh at her serious expression. "There is no courtship other than the one Abigail believes we have been carrying on without her knowledge. And as to being unused to the way courtship works, I promise your lack of knowledge at the feminine airs that are put on during this ridiculous ritual is refreshing."

"I have been learning," she told him. "Your sister has been a great source of knowledge on how to be a proper lady. My mother and Abigail insisted she tutor me."

He groaned. "I do hope you haven't been paying attention."

"Well, I did try, but somewhere between which fork to use at the table and which way to hold a fan to signal an intention, I gave up." She paused. "She has no idea, though, so please do not tell her. Gaby does have such enthusiasm for the topic. I would hate for her to know that I do not."

"Your secret is safe with me." He glanced down at the ledger and back at Maribel. "But neither you nor that ledger are safe here. I have a place I can take you, but you will have to trust me."

"I trust you," she said. "But what about my mother and my grandfather? Won't they be worried if I do not come home? Or suspicious?"

"Let me take care of that." He looked up at the clock over the mantel as the front door opened. "And here is the man for the job."

Jean-Luc stepped out into the hall and motioned for him to come into the library. "Maribel," he told her. "I think you might find this fellow familiar."

She looked up from her study of the ledger to fix her eyes on the young man who had spent the last eleven years as a ward of the Valmonts. "William Spencer?" she said on a soft breath. "My Will Spencer!"

The physician's expression froze. "Red?" He looked over at Jean-Luc. "Is it really?"

"It is," she said before he could respond.

And then Maribel practically launched herself into the young doctor's arms.

Over her head, William gave Jean-Luc a stricken look.

Likely William Spencer could climb a tree, remain there all day, and still climb down without any aches or pains to show for his effort. And he could certainly pass Abigail's test of appropriate age.

"Maribel was raised by nuns," he said, irked that he felt even the slightest amount of jealousy rising up inside him. "She doesn't realize her enthusiasm at seeing you again is inappropriate."

"Then I hope she never figures that out," he said as he returned the embrace. "You look prettier than a picture," he told her when she finally let him go.

"There is nothing inappropriate in letting my friend know I am happy to see him again." She offered William a smile. "I thought you were dead."

"And I thought the same of you."

"And yet you both are obviously very much alive," he snapped before catching himself and changing his tone. "As much as I know you two have to discuss, it must wait. There's a situation brewing, and we need to take evasive action."

Will knew exactly what he meant, for he had used the words they all agreed upon. "Aye," he said. "But first I should bring news of her grandfather." He focused his attention back on Maribel. "He is of decent health as of today," he said. "I prescribed a change in his diet and indicated that he should be taken from his bed to be allowed to walk more. I find that does a body more good than lying there with the fireplace going."

"So he will be fine?"

"These determinations are never exact," he said. "But he is strong and appears he will recover."

"And my mother?"

He shook his head. "Was I supposed to evaluate her too?"

"No," she said, "but I wondered what your impression was of her current state?"

"Oh," he said, "well, she seemed happy that your father was home."

"He was there?" she asked Will.

"Not at the moment, but she did mention that fact at least twice during our conversation. I thought it odd she spoke of him so much." He paused. "Now that I've seen you, is it also true, then, that your father survived the *Venganza*?"

"He did," Maribel said. "Although I have only just learned this."

Jean-Luc looked to Maribel. "What do you think of your mother's mentions of your father to Will?"

"I believe I can answer," Will said. "Perhaps she then would expect me to convey the news to Abigail?"

"She might," he agreed. "Can you think of another reason?" he asked Maribel.

"No," she said. "In looking through this ledger, have you seen any expenses that my mother might have benefited from?"

"Not directly," he said. "Why?"

"It is as much a hope as a theory, but perhaps she and my grandfather are both afraid of what my father will do if they do not cooperate. If she and Abigail are so close, perhaps Mama wanted Abigail to know my father had finally come for her."

He thought a moment. "You may be right."

Jean-Luc addressed Will as he nodded toward Maribel. "I will see to her safety. You alert the others."

"So soon?" Abigail stepped into the room, her smile intact. "Yes, I know. You didn't think I realized what was going on here."

"If you'll excuse me," Will said. "I'm just going to go and wash up for dinner now."

"Stay." A command, not a suggestion. Of course Will obeyed. When Abigail used that tone, generally they did.

"Maribel," she said gently. "Please accept my apology for the way I am about to speak of your father. I understand we are all given our parents and have no choice in the matter, so do not think his behavior reflects on yours or your family."

"Thank you," she said.

She turned to Jean-Luc. "There is a man out there somewhere who has been terrorizing my friend for the better part of ten years. Don Pablo has paid to keep him away from Mary and has paid dearly to keep this girl hidden away and safe. The money has run out." She paused to look at Jean-Luc. "It ran out three years ago, actually."

"Three years ago?" Maribel shook her head and then closed her eyes. "Oh," she said when she opened them again. "You and Mr. Valmont. . ."

"Have been helping," she offered. "Yes, although that would just as well be our secret, thank you very much. Your grandfather is a proud old man and it would kill him if he knew, and I did tell your mother that information would not be disclosed publicly."

"How does he think money has gone into his coffers, then?" Jean-Luc asked.

"It is my understanding that he believes his son has finally come to his senses and contributed his share." She paused as if considering her words carefully. "The ruse worked until Antonio had the audacity to arrive on their doorstep. I cannot prove it, but I believe his presence in that home is what caused that old man's illness."

"It is possible a shock of some sort would contribute," Will said. "But impossible to say for certain."

"Jean-Luc," she said. "I engaged you in a spirited conversation regarding this young lady because I needed to see what your intentions were. And I had to know if she is safe with you." She paused. "Given factors and situations we do not discuss, I have reason to believe she may be in only slightly less danger with you than she would be at home with her mother."

He said nothing, allowing the accusation to hang in the silence between them. Sadly, she was likely speaking the truth.

But then Abigail usually did, even if the truth was not welcomed.

"I will spare you my opinion of this supposed relationship between you and Miss Cordoba. However, I stand by what I said in the garden. And, you," she said to Maribel. "I have no doubt you kissed him first as a diversion so that we would not know why you two were conferring at that desk."

Maribel slid Jean-Luc a glance and added a smile. "I like her."

"Just wait," he told her. "We like her too, but her honesty can be a bit brutal."

Abigail stifled a smile. "However, both of you enjoyed that kiss far too much for my comfort. I suggest once this trouble is behind you, the two of you should have a serious discussion about whether the marriage plans you have tormented Gaby with should in actuality take place."

"See," Jean-Luc said. "Brutal."

"But honest," Abigail said. "Now, I need no knowledge of whatever plans you've made for situations like this, but I have no doubt there are plans. Go on about it all, but do one thing first."

"What is that?" Jean-Luc asked.

"Get that young lady's mother and grandfather out of his house and back here so we can keep them safe."

Jean-Luc glanced over at Will. "Send Rao and Piper. Tell them they'll need at least two extra men, and make sure they know they could be facing danger."

Will hurried away but then stopped just short of the front door. "Maribel," he said. "It's great having you back." And then he was gone, leaving Jean-Luc and Maribel alone with Abigail.

"Now, as for you two," she said. "Something happened between you that has bound you together." She nodded to Jean-Luc. "You spoke of her constantly during your recovery. She has meaning in your life." Then she turned to Maribel. "You were a child and now you are a woman. Do not confuse how you felt about him when you were a child to any feelings that may grow as an adult. They are not the same. Do you understand?"

"Yes," Maribel said. "But there is nothing—"

"There will be." She shook her head and then reached for Jean-Luc's hand. "I have done all I can do here. Please, Jean-Luc, take care of her."

"You have my word," he told her. "Now if there's nothing else you wish to say, then we must go."

Abigail smiled. "Oh, there is plenty more I wish to say, but I best keep my mouth shut."

"Will wonders never cease," he said as he kissed Abigail on the cheek. "Do tell my father I have seen a miracle and will report back on it when I return."

"Watch your manners, son," she told him. "And yourself."

"I promise," he told her then caught Maribel's attention. "We should go now. It'll be best if you don't ask for any details. Just know we're going and your family will be safe."

She nodded as he retrieved the ledger and returned it to the valise. "Thank you," Maribel told Abigail. "The words seem so very inadequate."

Abigail offered an embrace and Maribel accepted. Apparently Abigail whispered something that caused the redhead to lift her head in surprise. A moment later, they stepped apart and Maribel followed him outside.

"What did she tell you?" he asked.

"That when you asked what she told me, I should tell you it is something you already know."

Of course. All Jean-Luc could do was laugh.

❈

Maribel followed the captain's lead as they traveled under cover of darkness toward the river. Bypassing the docks, they climbed into a small skiff that had been tied up not too far from the live oaks where they spent the afternoon.

A man wearing a dark cloak awaited them. He revealed his face only after their journey downriver was under way.

"Mr. Rao," she said softly. "It is you."

"Always was me when you thought it was," he whispered. "Sure wish I could've admitted it sooner, but promises were made, and, well, I was always one to keep my promises."

"I do understand."

"Quiet, both of you," Jean-Luc said.

They were in the skiff so long that Maribel's eyes began to drift shut. When the skiff thudded against something, her eyes opened and she found herself cradled in Jean-Luc's arms. The skiff was now tied to a larger vessel.

"Gaff-rigged schooner," she said out of habit, and both men looked at her oddly.

Maribel shrugged. "A habit I acquired during my youth," she said with a grin. "I just can't seem to break it."

Jean-Luc helped her onto the schooner and then climbed over the rail, the valise slung over his shoulder. "Cast off," he said as Mr. Rao reversed his rowing and pulled away from the vessel without boarding.

"Isn't Mr. Rao coming too?" she asked as she watched the skiff disappear into the night.

"Not this time." He crossed the deck and indicated she should follow. "Your cabin is at the end of the passageway. Take this valise and hide it."

She did as he instructed, following the passageway until it stopped at a door. Opening the door, she saw she was given the captain's cabin. Although luxurious, the room was not exceptionally large.

Given the choices of where the valise might fit, she picked the least obvious and stuffed the leather bag into the hole between the wall and the bunk. Returning the loose plank, Maribel stood back to admire her handiwork.

Her next order of business was to find the captain's library, for surely he had books stored in here somewhere. She opened one cabinet only to find a change of clothes and a pair of boots. The other cabinet held tools and rain gear.

The desk had three drawers. Two were unlocked and void of any reading material. The third, however, was locked tight.

Maribel sat back to examine the lock and then removed a hairpin from her hair. Such was the benefit of teaching a group of children from diverse backgrounds. Occasionally they were taught the most interesting skills. And of course children did love to brag about what they could do that no one else could.

The lock turned with a satisfying click. Like picking the occasional lock.

She tucked the pin back into her hair and opened the drawer carefully.

Inside she spied two books. One was the captain's log.

Her fingers stilled as she reached for the log. Hadn't she chastised her mother for looking through Abuelo's papers? And yet, the information those papers contained had proved of great value. So, too, could whatever had been written on the pages of this log.

Maribel tucked her guilt aside and opened the log and then scanned the entries. Nothing of any interest here.

But the other. She reached for the book, bound in dark leather and edged in gilt.

Footsteps echoed in the corridor, warning her that she might be sharing this book with a visitor if she kept the drawer open. Returning the log to its place above the book, she closed the drawer and hurried to perch innocently on the bed just as the door opened.

"Captain wishes to see you, Miss Cordoba," a crewman said.

"Yes, of course," she said, rising to follow him. Pausing in the door, she cast around at the secrets hidden there and smiled. This room's secrets were safe.

For now.

CHAPTER 25

Closing the door, she hurried to keep up as the man led her to the deck.

"Over there, miss," he said as he indicated two men standing near the bow.

Maribel crossed the deck and then froze. The man standing beside Jean-Luc. . .

"Mr. Bennett!"

She cared not for propriety as she closed the distance between them. "Oh, Mr. Bennett!" she said as she buried her face in his coat. "I am so glad to see you."

"I did notice that," he said with a chuckle. "And I am so glad to see you."

He held her at arm's length and studied her. "Oh my, you did grow up to be a beautiful young lady, didn't you?"

"Oh, I don't know about that, but I did grow up."

"Trust me," Jean-Luc said just loud enough for her to hear. "What my friend says is correct."

Mr. Bennett reached up to slide her hair off her forehead. "Yes," he said with a nod. "No doubt it is you."

"Why did you do that?" Jean-Luc asked him.

"She has a scar," he told him. "Right there." He indicated a spot on her forehead. "Happened aboard the *Venganza*. Connor treated it, but she would only bind it with that infernal scarf of hers. Whatever happened to that scarf, Miss Cordoba?"

"I wore it every day until my mother confiscated it. Said it was ratty and belonged in with the rubbish. Truly she was right, but I do miss it." She paused. "I missed you too, Mr. Bennett. I spent my childhood with the nuns on an island near Port Royal. Did you know that?"

His expression went neutral. "I believe I did hear something about that. Did you enjoy it?"

"Immensely," she said. "The nuns treated me well, and when I got too old for the orphanage, I was hired as a teacher." Maribel smiled. "I even taught the children how to read Homer in the original Greek."

His laughter filled the night air. "Perhaps someday you will teach our captain that."

"Hush now," he told them. "I will learn eventually."

Mr. Bennett shook his head. "I have things to do. You two behave."

And then he was gone, leaving them alone on the deck. A comfortable silence fell between them as the river carried them downstream. Finally Jean-Luc turned to her.

"Did you really have such a good childhood? With the nuns, I mean? It sounds lonely."

"Lonely?" She shrugged. "Hardly. Not when you're on an island filled with children and nuns."

He nodded. "I felt responsible, you know. When I couldn't find you, I didn't want to go on. Abigail is right. I did call out for you. I still do. Or did. I always felt you were out there and I was supposed to find you."

She smiled. "And then you did."

"No, I think it was you who found me. This Lopez-Gonzales fellow was the one who found you." He paused. "Or did he? I've been wondering about that, and I think he and your father were in league with each other."

"Do you?"

"Unless you have another opinion. Did he indicate any association with your grandfather that you were able to prove? Such as seeing them converse?"

"He had a letter from Abuelo when he arrived on the island, but he elected not to go with me inside my grandfather's home when I arrived in New Orleans. In fact, while my mother was greeting me on the front steps, he seemed to just slip away."

"And you never saw him again?"

She thought a moment. "No, but can we change the subject?"

"Of course," he said as he rested his hand on the rail. "What do you want to talk about?"

"You," she said. "Tell me what I missed in your life."

He looked away. "You don't want to hear all that."

She moved her hand over to rest atop his. "I do. Tell me, please."

"Not here. Come with me, then."

Maribel followed him to a quiet spot away from the men who were working. "You're sure?" he said. "Much of my story is not pretty."

His eyes went soft when she nodded. "Tell me, but only what you wish to say."

And then he did. And she cried, especially when he got to the part where he told her about his wife and his son and the awful fever that took them both. About how he, too, had the fever, and although he begged the Lord to take him, He did not.

"And until now I did not know why He saved me," he said.

He held her then, and she went willingly into his arms. "It is late," he finally said, his voice gruff.

"I suppose," she said as she looked up into his eyes.

"No one knows me as you do," he told her. "I haven't told anyone the things I've told you."

"I don't find that odd at all," she said. "What I do find odd is that you haven't kissed me yet."

At his look of surprise, she smiled. "What? Remember I was raised by the nuns and I was not taught the social graces."

He laughed. "And for that I am forever grateful."

And then he kissed her.

"Did you mind that?" he asked after.

"Not at all," she said. "But to be sure, might we try that again?"

Once again Jean-Luc laughed, but he did not argue.

Later when Maribel found her voice again, she asked him, "Why Beaumont?"

"What?" He shook his head. "Oh, that. Well, it was not my idea. In order to have Letters of Marque, I had to make application to the crown. My father was enthusiastic about the endeavor— to tell the truth, it was his idea—but my uncle would have been horrified."

"The governor? Why?"

"Depending on the year, sometimes the month or day, the Spaniards were either friend or foe. Uncle Bienville had friends from both countries. Father was still making his fortune and had not yet secured the exclusive trade agreement, so his idea was for both his sons to set sail, and possibly him too. He never liked the Spaniards ever since my mother and brother were killed."

"By my father," she said. "I am so sorry."

He touched her cheek with his palm and looked into her eyes. "That sin is his to bear, not yours. So when the time came to make application, he chose familial names that were close but not ours. Thus, I was Jean Beaumont after my paternal grandmother's maiden name. I was young, about your age, and I was allowed no opinion. Looking back, I see it was advantageous not to have my name known."

"Because there was a bounty on your head."

"Still could be," he said with a shrug. "I have no idea whether that has been rescinded. Far as I know, Captain Beaumont was reported killed and some French lieutenant claimed the glory." He shrugged. "End of the story."

"That is a story I am glad to see end."

He traced her jawbone with his finger and she shivered. "Cold?"

"No," she said as she snuggled closer. "Are you too old to fall in love with me?"

He chuckled. "According to Abigail, yes and no."

"What do you mean?"

"Yes, apparently I am too old for you. She would prefer for you to be spending your time with Gaby's twin, Michel. However, she feels I have already fallen in love with you."

"What do you think?" Maribel said.

"If I didn't know you grew up with the nuns, I would believe you're flirting with me."

It was her turn to laugh. "How exactly does one flirt?"

"By doing exactly what you're doing, Maribel Cordoba."

And then he kissed her again.

"Captain," Mr. Bennett called. "You're needed up here."

Jean-Luc stretched out his legs and frowned. "Duty calls."

She smiled. "I am tired. It's been quite a day."

"That it has," he said as he helped her to her feet.

"I can see myself to my cabin. You go find out what Mr. Bennett needs."

He walked her down the corridor anyway and stood on the other side of the door until she proved to him that it was locked. When she was certain he'd gone, Maribel went to the drawer and removed the leather book.

An hour later, she stuffed the book into the valise and slammed the drawer shut, anger pounding in her temples. By the time she found Jean-Luc and Mr. Bennett, she was so mad she could barely control her words.

"So," she said to the two men, now standing together at the wheel. "I have a question."

Jean-Luc grinned. "For both of us or just for me?"

"I suppose since you are the captain, I should ask you."

He moved around to stand beside her and then wrapped her in his arms. She looked up into his eyes, her own arms held tight at her sides.

"Exactly when were you going to tell me that you and Mr. Bennett were slave traders?"

When neither man spoke, she had her answer. Maribel turned her back and walked away, tears stinging her eyes. Jean-Luc stepped in front of her just before she reached the corridor.

"It isn't what you think."

"I saw you," she said, angry now that her tears were falling. "You and he were at Isla de Santa Maria. You pulled your boat into the inlet and loaded slaves from your ship to the other. I watched you do it."

"From a tree?" he said, sarcasm touching his voice.

"Actually, yes," she said.

"Then you should not base what actually happened on what you think you saw."

She let out a long breath and looked up into his eyes. "I saw it, Jean-Luc. I saw you and I saw him." She nodded toward the wheel where Mr. Bennett stood. "And I saw the slaves leave a gaff-rigged schooner very much like this one. Are you now telling me that did not happen?"

"Captain," Mr. Bennett called. "We've got a ship coming up behind us."

Maribel moved toward the rail so she could see. "Brigantine to the south," she said.

"Brigantine? You're certain?"

At her nod, he smiled. "Raise the French flag," he told Israel. "It appears my uncle would like a word with me."

Sure enough, the vessel carrying the governor came alongside and greetings were exchanged. When Jean-Luc was invited aboard, Maribel asked if she could go along and was allowed.

Only when Jean-Luc spied her carrying the valise did he seem to realize her voyage with him was over. "Might I have a moment of your time, Governor?" she asked the older man.

Though his brows raised, he did smile and agree to a meeting. When she retrieved the leather book and handed it to him, he seemed confused.

"That is evidence that your nephew is a slave trader," she told him.

The governor shook his head. "I do not understand, young lady. Why give me this?"

"Can you not stop him? This is piracy of the worst kind."

The older man rose and left Maribel alone in the room, the book still on the table where she put it. A short while later, he returned with Jean-Luc and left them together without a word.

"My uncle wished to let us know your father has been captured. Apparently the word of a French spy was good enough to give away his dealings."

"A French spy?" She shook her head. "Who?"

"One Mr. Lopez-Gonzales." He shrugged. "Though your grandfather was not a well man, he was a smart man. He was able to feed information to those who were eager to prove whether the Spaniard who had been stealing from French ships was indeed Antonio Cordoba."

"And it was."

Jean-Luc nodded. "It was. Your mother and grandfather are safely back home, and your grandfather's valuables have been returned to him along with a substantial reward for helping to capture an enemy of the French."

"I see." She thought a moment. "So I can go home now?"

"Aboard this very ship," he told her. "My uncle is returning tonight. He could see you home safely. By the way, he told me you've accused me of piracy."

"Thank you," she said, those stupid tears returning. "And, yes, I have." Why had she thought she cared about this man? She hadn't even known him.

"Maribel," he said gently. "I asked you if you would trust me and you said you would." He pressed his palm over the book that sat on the table between them. "Will you trust me when I tell you this is not what it seems?"

"Why should I?" she demanded. "I see nothing but proof here. Proof that lines up perfectly with what I saw on Isla de Santa

Maria. What possible evidence would you offer to refute it?"

"The word of a nun and more," he said.

She shook her head. "You're making no sense."

He reached beyond the book to take her hand. "Trust me, Maribel. Come with me and I will show you. Look at me." When she did, he continued. "Do you truly believe that Israel Bennett and I would be involved in something as vile as slave trading?"

She sighed. "No," she said. "But the book. . ."

"But the book proves something entirely different." He nodded toward the vessel still tied up beside the brigantine. "Come with us and I will show you."

"All right, although for the life of me I cannot tell you why."

"Because we were always meant to be a team, Red. I just didn't know it when you first tried to join up with my crew." He gave her a broad grin. "I'm older and wiser now. Welcome to my crew, Maribel."

She gave him a frown that she had a hard time maintaining. A short while later, they were back aboard the schooner and headed into open waters. Maribel avoided Jean-Luc during the voyage, preferring to remain in the cabin below.

Thanks to the generous contribution of books from Mr. Bennett's library, the time flew past and soon the lookout was calling for land. Maribel emerged onto the deck to see the familiar beaches and structures of Isla de Santa Maria coming closer.

"Home," she said softly, and for certain she knew it to be.

Though New Orleans was nice and reuniting with her family had been God's own miracle, this sleepy island with the children, the nuns, and the sandy beaches was her home.

By the time the ship neared land, all the children and the nuns were waiting for them. Strangely, they bypassed the docks and continued around the island, only returning to dock at the inlet after a roundabout pass through the open ocean.

Maribel waited on deck for the skiff to be lowered. When Jean-Luc came to stand by her, she froze. There had been nothing in the way of conversation between them for almost a week, and now he stood close enough to touch.

"What you are about to witness is what Israel and I have done for years. More years than I can count. When the Lord spared me after my privateering days, I made a promise I would use the remainder of my life for His purpose. Israel and I believe this is His purpose. His piracy, if you will."

A bell sounded, and then Maribel heard a door open and footsteps heading toward them. Out from the hold came dark-skinned men and women, boys and girls, dozens of them.

"Jean-Luc, no," she said softly as another schooner slid into place behind them. "They were with us all along?"

Without sparing her a glance, the unexpected passengers filed into skiffs that were lowered into the water. She stepped into the line and grasped the arm of a young woman carrying a baby. "You don't have to do this," she said.

The woman gave her a confused look. "She doesn't understand what you've told her," Mr. Bennett said. He said something to her that she understood, and the girl smiled.

"Going home," she managed in broken English. "To Kongo."

"What does she mean?" she asked the men, but no one answered.

The girl returned to the line and disappeared into a skiff. Once they were all gone, another bell sounded and the other schooner departed.

Jean-Luc moved closer and wrapped his arm around her. "I tried to tell you. We are sending them home. That's the sort of pirates we are."

"When we can, we intercept vessels carrying human cargo," Mr. Bennett said. "Just as the captain did for me when he freed me from a vessel like the one we found these people on. Sometimes Rao and Piper come along. Spencer, he's a doctor now, so we bring him when we can, but mostly he's with those who need him at the charity hospital in New Orleans."

"Is he telling the truth?" she asked Jean-Luc.

"He is," he admitted.

"It started out as a search for my wife, Nzuzi," Mr. Bennet said. "We started doing this regularly because after a while of working for the captain, I earned enough to go back and get her. I went back to find out she was gone—captured by traders and sold off, so every ship we stopped for years, I held out hope she was on it."

"Oh," she said and then found herself incapable of saying more.

Tears were flowing and Maribel could barely speak. All she could do was turn around and allow Jean-Luc to wrap her in his arms. "I'm so sorry," she finally managed. "I—"

"Hush," he told her. "If you don't collect yourself, we will be late for the celebration."

"Celebration?" She shook her head. "What do you mean?"

"Your homecoming," he said. "Apparently there is quite a party being held, and we are missing it."

She swiped at her eyes and laughed. "But how did they know?"

"How does Mother Superior ever know?" He nudged her. "By the way, use of the inlet has always been at her discretion. And she has never failed to know when we would be arriving. You may not have noticed, but there is a signal that goes up when we bypass the inlet. Once we are given the signal, we know it is safe to land."

"I would ask what that is, but there's no point, is there?"

"Not really."

He laughed and escorted her off the ship. A few minutes later, she found herself surrounded by laughing children. Standing at the edges of the circle were the more soft-spoken nuns.

Mr. Bennett pressed past them to disappear into the chapel. A moment later, he returned carrying a tiny dark woman. The children giggled as the woman's good-natured complaining drifted toward them.

Finally the pair reached Maribel and Jean-Luc. "Miss Cordoba," he said as he returned the lovely lady to a standing position. "May I present my wife, Nzuzi?"

"You found her," Maribel said as tears welled in her eyes.

"He did," Mr. Bennett said, nodding toward Jean-Luc. "And thanks to him we have two sons now. Named Evan Connor and Jean-Luc." He grinned. "I felt I ought to honor both men."

Evan Connor. The name should have meant something, this much Maribel knew. And yet like so much of her childhood, the memory had been lost. "Do I know this Connor fellow?" she asked.

The men exchanged looks and then Jean-Luc's expression softened. "That is a story for another day, but suffice it to say that Evan Connor is a greater man than I ever could be." Jean-Luc smiled at Nzuzi. "And what will you name the next one?"

Mr. Bennett looked down at his wife, who did appear to be expecting. "She says this one is a girl, so it will be up to her."

"So very pleased to meet you," Nzuzi said in softly accented English. "I have heard much about you."

"Do not believe all of it," Maribel said, and they both laughed.

Off in the distance she spied Mother Superior. As the old nun approached, everyone else parted to allow her to walk through. Even little Stephan gave way as she moved past him.

"Welcome back," she told Maribel. "I knew you would return."

"You did?"

"I did," she said. "In fact, I have taken the liberty of preparing the cottage for you and your husband. And one for your mother and grandfather when they come to visit."

"I have no husband," she said, shaking her head.

"I wish to remedy this," Jean-Luc said as he came to stand beside her. "In the absence of her parents, might I ask you for her hand?"

Mother Superior laughed. "My boy, I think you'd best ask Miss Cordoba. She always was the independent type."

"Maribel?" he said as he took her hand. "Will you marry this pirate and sail the seas with me now that you know what our mission entails? I cannot promise you smooth sailing, but I can always promise you my love."

"And a cottage on Isla de Santa Maria," Mother Superior added.

"And that is of the upmost importance," Stephan called from the crowd.

"Let me think about it," she told him with a grin.

She would marry him, of this she was certain. But for now, she would let him guess whether she would become this pirate's bride.

And then he kissed her.

AUTHOR'S NOTE

and Bent History:
The Rest of the Story

As a writer of historical novels, I love incorporating actual history into my plots. As with most books, the research behind the story generally involves much more information than would ever actually appear in the story. In truth, I could easily spend all my time researching and not get any writing done at all!

Because I am a history nerd, I love sharing some of that mountain of research I collected with my readers. The following are just a few of the facts I uncovered during the writing of *The Pirate Bride*. I hope these tidbits of history will cause you to go searching for the rest of the story:

The opening quote of the novel from Stede Bonnet's sentencing speech by Judge Trot is part of the transcript of a lengthy speech actually given by the judge upon this occasion. Throughout the speech, which spanned a number of manuscript pages in my resource book, the judge liberally refers to scripture and salvation and calls on the name of Christ to save the sentenced pirate's soul.

Maribel's favorite book, *The Notorious Seafaring Pyrates and Their Exploits* by Captain Ulysses Jones, is loosely based on *A General History of the Robberies and Murders of the Most Notorious Pyrates* by Captain Charles Williamson, which was first published in London in 1718.

The position of Consul General is a fictional one. Havana, Cuba, was a Spanish colony ruled by the king of Spain. As such, Spanish noblemen were regularly posted to this and other colonies.

Speaking of the king of Spain, in January of 1724, Louis I of Spain became king upon the abdication of King Philip V. When Louis I died from smallpox just over seven months later, Philip V returned to the throne and reigned until his own death in 1746.

An interesting side note: Philip V was the grandson of Louis XIV of France. Thus, there were times during the tumultuous history of Spain and France when the two countries were allies. For the purposes of my story, it is assumed that during the periods the novel takes place, the two were once again at odds.

Letters of Marque are essentially licenses issued by an entity—usually a country—that allow their holder to capture and claim ships or their cargo, or both, for that country. Holders of these letters are generally referred to as privateers although some might incorrectly call them pirates. Essentially, these privateers had a license to steal from one country's vessels as long as they followed the rules—very specific rules, including appearing before admiralty courts to report and receive shares taken from vessels—and only chose to seek out ships flying the flag of countries covered by their letters. Even when those rules were followed, privateers were still occasionally branded pirates and hung for their "crimes." Letters of Marque have been used throughout history—including by our own American government—and are a fascinating topic for study outside the scope of this novel.

Although Captain Beaumont considers that Maribel may end up at the Ursuline nuns' convent, in truth, the Ursuline nuns did not arrive in New Orleans until 1727, and their convent was not completed until 1734. An interesting fact associated with this building is that although France owned the land upon which the city of New Orleans was built at the time, the designer of the building hailed from Bavaria and held the honor of the King's Master Carpenter.

Upon the death of King Louis XIV of France in 1715, King Louis XV succeeded his grandfather to the throne at the age of five. Because of the new king's young age and due to political struggles among those closest to the crown, the Duke of Orleans—namesake of the city of New Orleans, Louisiana, and closely related to Spanish nobility—acted as regent until the new king came of age in 1723. Because the French and Spanish royal families consisted of marriages between the two royal houses, there were many noblemen from one country who claimed relatives in nobility in the other country.

Though you would think that wars among folks who were related would be less likely, the countries of Spain and France continued to be either friend or foe depending on the day, month, or year. When relations with England is factored in, suffice it to say that at almost any given time for the past few centuries, one or all of these three countries were at war with one another. Because of this, it was easy to imagine a scenario where my poor hero gets in trouble with politicians who previously encouraged him. However, this scenario is completely fictional.

Jean Baptiste Le Moyne, Sieur de Bienville, was a French-Canadian explorer and the founder of New Orleans. Jean and his brother Pierre founded New Orleans on the banks of the Mississippi River on March 3, 1699. As a fun fact, for those of you who know of Louisiana culture, this date coincides with Mardi Gras, which, similar to modern convention, was the day of celebration before Lent in that year. Bienville was governor of Louisiana from 1706 to 1713, 1717 to 1723, and 1733 to 1743. The last period, he returned as the ambassador of the king during French rule. History does not record the names of the children of his siblings (there were more than a dozen children born to his parents), but I promise my hero Jean-Luc is not really one of them. That association is completely fictional.

Isla de Santa Maria is a fictional island I created and plopped down in the Caribbean Sea near the island of Jamaica. It is not to be confused with the actual Isla de Santa Maria in the Azores chain off the country of Portugal. The orphanage and nuns are also a figment of my very active imagination. However, any mention of the city of Port Royal or the island of Jamaica is based on my understanding of the history of the area at the time my story is set. And, yes, there really was a hurricane that hit Jamaica in September of 1734.

The real-life city of Mbanza Kongo, first settled in the 1300s, was a city of substantial size and sophistication during the time of this story. The name was changed by the Portuguese to Sao Salvador in the 1500s. When Angola received independence in 1979, the city's name was changed back to Mbanza Kongo, which means city of Kongo. Kongo is the original spelling of the current version, Congo. The judgment tree I mention in my story is real and can still be seen in downtown Mbanza Kongo. It is the site of a rectangular ground-level structure where local tradition claims the king's body was washed before burial.

The character of Marcel Valmont is loosely based on a real French merchant named Anthony Crozat who, in 1715, was given the exclusive privilege of trading in the Louisiana Territory. Upon signing this contract, Sieur de Bienville was dismissed from office and replaced by Lamothe Cadillac. While Crozat had no luck with the venture, I have allowed my fictional character to be much more successful. I also allowed him to be married to the fictional sister of the real man who lost his job after the contract was signed. As you have read above, however, Sieur de Bienville got several more chances to be governor of the territory, so everything did work out fine for him.

The city of New Orleans is very old. By the 1700s, a number of buildings had been erected, including the ones described by the fictional Mr. Lopez-Gonzales as he escorts Maribel to her grandfather's home. The streets were laid out in 1721, and the Director's House was built on the corner of Levee (now called Decatur) and Toulouse Streets facing the river. Like most of the early buildings in the city, it was built with wood timbers directly touching the soggy ground. To be certain, the house did not last long. The governor's house was built two years later on the corner of St. Ann and Chartres Streets. Governors Perier and

Bienville lived in the home during their administrations. Scientist Pierre Baron built the observatory in 1730 on a lot adjacent to the governor's house, and he did make accommodations to the building that would allow him to study the stars with his telescope.

Bestselling author **Kathleen Y'Barbo** is a multiple Carol Award and RITA nominee of more than eighty novels with almost two million copies in print in the United States and abroad. She has been nominated for a Career Achievement Award as well as a Reader's Choice Award and is the winner of the 2014 Inspirational Romance of the Year by *Romantic Times* magazine. Kathleen is a paralegal, a proud military wife, and a tenth-generation Texan, who recently moved back to cheer on her beloved Texas Aggies. Connect with her through social media at www.kathleenybarbo.com.

Continue Following the Family Tree through History...

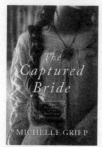

The Captured Bride
by Michelle Griep

A War-Torn Countryside Is No Place for a Lady

Mercy Lytton is a lady like none other. Raised amongst the Mohawks, she straddles two cultures, yet each are united in one cause. . .to defeat the French. Born with a rare gift of unusually keen eyesight, she is chosen as a scout to accompany a team of men on a dangerous mission. Yet it is not her life that is threatened. It is her heart. Condemned as a traitor, Elias Dubois faces the gallows. At the last minute, he is offered his freedom if he consents to accompany a stolen shipment of French gold to a nearby fort—but he is the one they stole it from in the first place. It turns out that the real thief is the beguiling woman, Mercy Lytton, for she steals his every waking thought. Can love survive divided loyalties in a backcountry wilderness?
Paperback / 978-1-68322-474-7 / $12.99

The Patriot Bride
by Kimberley Woodhouse

Spies Work Together for the Patriot Cause

Faith Jackson is a wealthy widow, friend of George Washington, and staunch supporter of the Patriot cause. Matthew Weber is friends with both Ben Franklin and his son William, who increasingly differ in their political views; and Matthew finds himself privy to information on both sides of the conflict. When a message needs to get to a spy among the Loyalists, Faith bravely steps up and in turn meets Matthew Weber. Suddenly she believes she could love again. But someone else has his eye on the Faith she portrays in elite social circles. What will Matthew and Faith have to sacrifice for the sake of their fledgling country?
Paperback / 978-1-68322-606-2 / $12.99

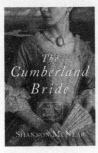

The Cumberland Bride
by Shannon McNear

Love and Adventure Are Discovered on the Wilderness Road

In 1794, when Kate Gruener's father is ready to move the family farther west into the wilderness to farm untouched land, Kate is eager to learn and live out her own story of adventure like he did during the War for Independence. She sets her sights on learning more about their guide, Thomas Bledsoe. Thomas's job is to get settlers safely across the Kentucky Wilderness Road to their destination while keeping an ear open for news of Shawnee unrest. But naïve Kate's inquisitive nature could put them both in the middle of a rising tide of conflict. Is there more to Thomas's Shawnee connections than he is willing to tell? Is there an untapped courage in Kate that can thwart a coming disaster?
Paperback / 978-1-68322-691-8 / $12.99

The Liberty Bride
by MaryLu Tyndall

War Forces a Choice Between Love and Country

A trip home from England to Maryland in 1812 finds Emeline Baratt a captive on a British warship and forced to declare her allegiance between the British and Americans. Remaining somewhat politically neutral on a ship where her nursing skills are desperately needed is fairly easy—until she starts to have feelings for the first lieutenant who becomes her protector. However, when the captain sends her and Lieutenant Owen Masters on land to spy, she must choose between her love for him or her love for her country.
Paperback / 978-1-68322-617-8 / $12.99

JOIN US ONLINE!

Christian Fiction for Women

Christian Fiction for Women is your online home for the latest in Christian fiction.

Check us out online for:

- Giveaways
- Recipes
- Info about Upcoming Releases
- Book Trailers
- News and More!

Find Christian Fiction for Women at Your Favorite Social Media Site:

 Search "Christian Fiction for Women"

 @fictionforwomen